THE VENGEANCE EFFECT

ROGER NEALE

The Vengeance Effect

Published by Wheatmark®
2030 East Speedway Boulevard, Suite 106
Tucson, Arizona 85719 USA
www.wheatmark.com

ISBN: 978-1-62787-573-8 (paperback)
ISBN: 978-1-62787-574-5 (ebook)
LCCN: 2017957280

CHAPTER ONE

"Something's happened," said the woman on the phone. "Can you help us?"

Sam Troshin wrote the sports page for the *North Coast News*. Though he had never covered anything but sports, the editor had asked him to do a story on a parolee book group the district court had created. Sam said he'd give it a shot. He was paid by the story and needed every inch he could get.

The book group met Saturday mornings at the community college. Sam had just returned to the news office after sitting in on a group session and was typing his impressions of the meeting. Compared with the previous sessions he'd attended, this morning's meeting had been weirdly constrained and uncomfortable. One-word responses to the instructor's questions were followed by awkward silences. No one made eye contact with anyone else. The instructor looked at the five participants with a quizzical expression and didn't press for more discussion.

As they filed out of the classroom, Zoey, the older of the two women in the group, caught up to Sam. She asked if he would be free a little later. She might need help with something.

Her call came less than an hour later.

"Just tell me where to be," Sam answered.

"Can you come back to the school?" she asked.

"Sure," said Sam.

"I need a favor. A big favor. Might have consequences."

"Nothing illegal," Sam ventured.

"I'll wait in the parking lot," she said.

Ten days ago this woman had saved his life.

"On my way," he said.

Port Teresa was a town of fifty thousand people on the coast of Washington state. Large enough to have a daily paper and a television station, small enough that finding parking on the streets was never a problem. Some days the spruce and Douglas firs of the Olympic range soaked up the rain driving off the Pacific and kept the town dry and sunny. Other days, weather coming in from Canada and the strait forced residents to pull up hoods and collars to keep the chill, wet wind from blowing down the back of their necks. Today the winds were chill, and the collars were up.

He saw her waiting at the far end of the parking lot.

"I'm sorry, it's ugly," she said. "If you didn't owe me, I wouldn't get you involved. But we need you."

"Just show me what's going on."

Zoey turned without saying anything more. He followed her along the sidewalk that led from the parking lot around the perimeter of the campus. The women's soccer team was running passing drills through a pattern of orange pylons on the soccer field. Sports in the Pacific Northwest, you trained in all weather. He heard the pock of a ball from the tennis courts, good players hitting the ball hard. Only a few classes were scheduled for Saturday afternoons. He didn't see anyone walking between the red brick buildings. Sam followed her to a rustic wood gate at the south end of the campus, leading to a trail through the forest of cedars and towering maples that climbed into the foothills. The day was dark and overcast. There would be no view from the viewpoints gained by climbing the foothills. Not a day for a casual summer walk in the woods above the campus.

What kind of problem could Zoey be having on a forested hillside behind the school? Something, he guessed, that would require his strength.

When they had gone a couple hundred yards, Zoey stepped off the trail onto a barely visible path. Sam ducked his head and pushed aside branches as they followed the path through the trees. Zoey stopped as they approached a clearing. He could see the figure of a girl ahead. Alison, the teenaged parolee from the book group.

There was someone lying in the middle of the clearing.

What the fuck, he said to himself.

Both women turned and looked at him. They were waiting for him to go closer.

"Jesus Christ," he said as he approached the person lying in the brush. Gary, the big guy from the book group. He lay sprawled on his back with an arrow embedded in his chest. One arm was thrown out to the side, the other hand still clutching the shaft.

"What's happened?" said Sam.

"He raped her," Zoey said. "After the meetings."

"Jesus," Sam repeated, trying to get past the initial shock and clear his thoughts.

"Is he …?"

"He's dead."

"Who did this?"

He stared at the girl. "Her?"

Zoey nodded. The Katniss theme, he'd read the book with the group. It was a fantasy. But a man who looked dead was lying in front of him with an arrow in his chest.

"So this is self-defense."

But he knew it wasn't that simple. She had come with a weapon, and the girl apparently knew how to use it. Had they planned this together? Shooting him was self-defense, and it was revenge.

"It won't work," said Zoey. "His dad's a cop. They'll get her. We need to get him away from here."

Sam held up a hand and said, "Give me a minute here."

He was not prepared for this. But he was going to have to decide. He was sure they were telling him the truth, that the man had raped her. And if the woman, Zoey, hadn't intervened a week ago when a group of men tried to beat him to death, he wouldn't be here.

The possible consequences of what he did next bore down like a weight across his back. These two women from the book group had just killed a man. He needed time to think, but he didn't have it.

He couldn't turn away from the debt he owed this woman.

"What do you think we should do?" he asked.

"We need something to carry him in."

Just breathe, he told himself. You need to think. "What if you just left him? Get the arrow out. Does anybody know she can shoot a bow?"

"They'll figure it out. Can't have this connected with the book group. We have to move him."

Sam squinted at the figure lying half-covered in the foliage.

"We need something with wheels," said Zoey.

"Okay," said Sam. He looked at the girl, who was watching Zoey. Apprehensive, taking deep breaths, but he didn't see panic. Had she really shot this man with a bow and arrow?

"Okay," he said. "Okay. I work here at night, you know that?"

"At the college?"

"I'm a custodian. You got a truck, right?"

"In the lot."

"Wait, okay? Give me twenty minutes. Throw brush on him in case somebody comes."

Sam hiked back to the administration building and the custodian's equipment room. He opened his locker, took out his gray coveralls, and slipped them on over his street clothes.

What would happen now? If he was caught, they would find his record easily enough, and he could be in real trouble. He could go back and tell the women there was nothing he could do except promise not to say anything about what he had seen.

Then the thought came to him: what would his daughter have wanted him to do?

He buttoned up the coveralls, threw some gear in one of the canvas carts, and pushed it out the door. He had just committed himself.

He returned across the campus and up the path. The path off the trail wasn't wide enough for the hamper, but he forced it through the brush.

"Can you get the arrow out?" Zoey asked.

Sam sucked in a breath and stood over the body. He didn't want to look at the face but couldn't help it. Luckily the guy's eyes were closed. The mouth drooped open, an expression of momentary surprise. Sam grasped the arrow and pulled.

"Shit," he muttered, and pulled harder with his good arm. Probably had barbs so it wouldn't work loose in a deer's side. The embedded arrow released like a weed giving up its grip in the soil and slid out. He was relieved there wasn't a lot of blood.

How could this girl, fifteen or sixteen, have done this? Use a hunting bow and take an accurate shot at her attacker?

"I got some Visqueen. We can roll him on it and wrap him. Use these."

He handed heavy gardener's gloves to the two women, then laid out a sheet of Visqueen at the side of the body. The three of them rolled the body into several wraps of the glossy black plastic. Then they tried to lift him into the hamper. Sam struggled for leverage with his useful arm. They could barely lift the body off the ground.

"Shit," said Sam.

"Turn the cart on its side," said Zoey.

Right. He should have thought of that. He tipped the cart over. The three of them rolled the body in, and wrestled the cart back upright.

"Throw that brush on it," he said. "We can say we're getting botany samples or something if anyone asks.

"Where's the bow?" Zoey asked.

"Where I hid it," said Alison. Her voice was a little gravelly but steady. Maybe she's in shock, he thought.

"Get it."

Alison went into the woods behind the clearing and came back a minute later with a black case crusted with brush and dirt.

"We need to get rid of it," said Zoey.

"I want the bow," said Alison.

Her expression, a crease between her eyebrows, lips pressed together, was the same as when she was formulating her words in the book group discussions. His daughter had been this age. This girl, already in jail and out on parole, who knows what kind of experiences behind her, raped, killing the man who did it, a big, aggressive man who used violence against her. Someone her age was supposed to have the protection of a secure family life. His daughter ... he needed to focus on what he was doing.

They pushed the cart through the brush out onto the trail, through the gate and across the back of the campus to the parking lot. Zoey had two boards they could use as ramps to push the hamper up into the pickup bed. Sam watched her tie the hamper down with a length of rope, running the line through the truck bed eyelets and tying it off with an efficient knot. She was somebody who got things done. Even though she was asking him to do something that for someone with his history could lead to real trouble, he knew as he walked to his locker he was going to help. She had appeared when he was about to be killed or left braindead, and had known how to handle the situation. Just happened to have a shotgun in her pickup, for Christ's sake. He owed her.

Zoey told Alison to take the bus home. She said she and Sam would do the rest.

"I want the bow," said Alison.

"I'll take it," said Zoey. "We should get rid of it. You can't be connected with having a bow."

"I'll hide it good," said Alison. "I need it."

They saw the determination in the girl's eyes and the set

of her mouth. The bow was her security. In its black case most people would take it for a musical instrument, the kind of thing a girl her age would be expected to carry.

"Okay," said Zoey.

Alison nodded, stared at the hamper in the pickup bed for a moment, and walked to the bus stop. Zoey and Sam sat together in the cab of her truck.

"What do we do now?" he said.

"I know a place," she said. "East of town. We can roll him down a hillside into a culvert."

"Jesus," Sam murmured.

"At dusk, just enough light. We can see any cars coming."

There was tension in her voice, but he could see her thinking it through, no panic. If she'd panicked, he would probably have been right there with her, head still floating in the soft fog of the pain meds he was taking, helpless.

"Can you meet me at nine, here?"

Sam stowed his coveralls and the gloves in his locker in the custodial office and drove back to the newspaper office. Before unlocking the door, he stopped. Some unthinking reflex must have brought him back to the paper; he wasn't going to be writing any more sports stories today. He turned and walked toward the main street. He passed a group of senior citizens having a cheerful conversation in front of the Crystal Café, all of them turning to wave at the person they were waiting for, a hefty gal fluttering her fingers to signal she was coming as fast as she could. At the Shefft Gallery, he saw an older couple looking at pictures and carvings in the window. The woman, dressed in the well-pressed cotton casualness of upscale tourists, said something, and they went in.

What had just happened reawakened his awareness of how different he was from the people on the sidewalk. They were walking alongside a violent, convicted felon. An irony he could never have imagined, being called upon to help avenge a rape. Except this wasn't a case of vengeance, the girl had simply defended herself. Nothing he'd done this day added to his guilt, though it could certainly add to his troubles. He just had to be careful.

At a quarter to nine, he was waiting in the parking lot. Zoey pulled carefully into the space next to him. The hamper was there exactly as it had been, lashed to the pickup bed, a few green boughs visible.

They drove east of town for several miles. "I checked the place out."

She turned onto a road that gradually climbed toward the mountains. It was just dark enough that car lights would be switching on. She pulled to the side of the road.

"Anybody coming, we should have at least thirty seconds."

She didn't need to give Sam instructions. They unlashed the hamper and let it roll down the boards to the asphalt. Zoey had managed to wrap the body with duct tape so the tarp wouldn't unwind as the body rolled.

"Didn't get fingerprints on the tape?" said Sam.

"I used gloves."

Sam grunted with effort as they tipped the body out of the hamper over the rail. It rolled once and stopped. Sam climbed over the rail, braced himself against the rail, and shoved with his foot. The body rolled and bounced down the hillside with the sickening sound of a person falling and unable to use his arms to protect himself. Sam took a long breath to fight down a surge of nausea.

There was no more conversation during the drive back to town. Neither had questions for the other.

Until Zoey pulled into the lot next to Sam's car, shut off the engine, and said, "So what made you want to be a sportswriter?"

Her tone was casual, but he looked at her and saw the need that made her ask. The two of them, who knew only a few superficial facts about one other, were now bound together by their actions this day. They would never, if they were lucky, share what they had done with anyone. He understood her need to know, not more about him necessarily, but simply to know him.

So he told her about how he had become a sportswriter.

CHAPTER TWO

One Month Earlier

A woman in khaki slacks and a casual, collared blouse was waiting in the visitor's room. She introduced herself by her first name as a judge from the Clallam County Superior Court. Her hair was pulled back in a ponytail, and she was smiling. Nothing like the judge at Zoey's hearing, a pasty-faced middle-aged woman who glanced balefully at her the few times they made eye contact.

The judge said she could be released on parole if she would be willing to participate in a weekly book group discussion.

"How come me?" she asked.

"First offense, nonviolent misdemeanor, waste of DOC budget keeping you here. This is a long sentence. You probably made somebody mad. You give any lip?"

"No, ma'am, not at all."

She gave Zoey an appraising look. "You kind of radiate defiance. Actually, the teacher organizing the group asked for you."

"Me?"

"Teaches English at the high school. So the deal is Saturday mornings for an hour, two months. You in?"

"What teacher is that?"

"Leah Mossery. You ever in her class?"

"No, but what do you know," said Zoey. "Sure, I'm in."

A felony charge, she would have hired a good lawyer and fought that. But she was so pissed at herself for selling meds to an unreliable client she decided to accept the situation and see what prison was like. Her curiosity could be an inconvenience to say the least, but she often chose to follow wherever it led her. She began the admitting process with the attitude that any new experience had useful lessons if you paid attention.

In her merchandising business, there was always a risk that a customer could get her into trouble. Some of the products she moved were not strictly legal. She vetted the customers for those transactions with some care. The one who'd given her away was probably not even aware of what she'd done, just a well-intentioned airhead chattering carelessly with the wrong person.

What she noticed the first day: coils of stainless razor wire along the fences glittering under the heavy floods like Christmas tree decorations, almost festive. The only thing the signs in the visiting room forbade was braiding hair. She would have to ask why that was an issue. Maybe that's how narcotics were passed. She wasn't called a prisoner or an inmate; she was an offender. Management's way of saying being here wasn't something done to you. It was something you brought on yourself.

She wondered if it would be a little dicey with the guards. At 135 pounds she wasn't fat, though with a little better portion control, she thought she could get back to 125. She'd been what was called voluptuous since she was fifteen. She had learned how to cool the ardor she saw in the eyes of men and women alike. She'd heard if you looked at certain female guards either a bit too friendly or too defiantly, you could find yourself escorted by two or three of them to a classroom for an unspecified health exam that would involve taking some of your clothes off and seeing what developed. When she was around staff, she wore a sour but nonconfrontational expression, a look that had served her in the past.

There turned out to be no problem. Like most organizations, the jail was understaffed. "What?" one of the female corrections officers said to her. "Do I look like I stand around all day guarding you people? I get a checklist start of every shift. Single-spaced, both sides of the page. End of a shift, I'm wiped out. Ready for that vodka martini."

Prison was less confining than she expected. She didn't think of her room as a cell since most of the day she didn't have to be there. It was the light that made her feel the hand of arbitrary authority. Outside you could switch on lamps or pull down shades. Here you lived on someone else's schedule of light and dark. That, the razor wire, and the lines on the floor marked "boundary."

But by the third week, she was getting bored. In her view boredom was something you really should be able to avoid. So she was ready to listen to the ponytailed judge.

CHAPTER THREE

Before the snitch trouble and her court date, she had called a number written on a card pinned to the Safeway bulletin board. She had a route of stores and community bulletin boards she checked weekly.

A woman answered.

"You got a Honda generator for sale?"

When the woman yelled, "For you!" in a loud and sour voice instead of saying anything more to her, she had an instant picture of the fat, druggie girlfriend of a dipshit petty thief.

The man who took the phone—it was midafternoon, so probably not employed—gave her an address and said come take a look.

The house was off the highway two miles out of town up a road bending through a growth of scrub pines and laurel. Paint was flaking off the siding and window frames. A vegetable garden from a few years back had gone to seed. Old furniture, a sofa and a couple of overstuffed chairs, and a chrome-and-plastic kitchen set rotted under a frayed blue tarp at one side of the house. A dump run was obviously not a priority. The only thing being taken care of was a glitter-blue Harley Sportster with fresh leather saddlebags leaning against its kickstand on the lawn.

The man who answered the door had a patchy beard and hair slicked back with something oily. When he led her through the house to the back, the woman she assumed had answered the phone was doing something in the kitchen, glanced at her, but didn't say anything.

Lowlifes. Her typical customers.

"Can you start it up?"

The generator was almost new and started easily. No way he bought this legit, advertising it on a few bulletin boards instead of Craigslist, where the owner might spot it.

"You got the instruction book, that stuff?"

The man shook his head. "Traded a guy for it."

She squatted next to the generator and pretended to study it.

"Looks okay. Too bad there's no papers with it. Give you two hundred cash."

"Two hundred? That's not what I'm asking. Shit, this is two thousand watts. Goes for a grand new. I'll get five hundred for this easy."

"Yeah. Maybe with proof of purchase. Might find somebody to give you that."

She got the guy's best effort at a sneer.

"You can sell it right now if you want." She pulled four fifties out of her pocket and thumbed them apart like a poker hand.

"Throw in twenty if you lift it into the truck for me."

"Whatta you need a generator for anyway?"

"Same as you. You know, generate."

"Fuck," the man muttered, swinging a kick at the generator. "You're rippin' me off."

"I'm giving you two hundred bucks. Nobody else is."

He spat, reached for the bills, gestured for her to bring the truck around the side of the house.

She drove briskly out of the yard with the seller glowering at her, looking like he might change his mind and take the generator back. Halfway back to the highway, she pulled over so she could lash the generator more securely to the truck bed. As she was getting in the truck, she saw someone flit like a deer across the road ahead in the shady area where the pines were thick—a girl, quick and graceful. As she drove past the shady area, she saw her, a half-hidden figure in the trees, looking at her. She pulled to the side of the road and got out of the truck again.

"Hi there," she called out. "Nice day, huh?" She leaned back against the truck and gave her a smile. Then she opened the door, reached into the jockey box, and pulled out a baggie. She took a cigarette and matchbox from the baggie and lit the cigarette. Leaning back against the truck, she blew a stream of smoke into the air.

"You smoke?"

After several seconds the girl took a step from behind the trees. She appeared to be about fifteen. She had alert blue eyes and nice, well-shaped lips. She'd be an attractive woman someday. Except that there was really only one blue eye. The whole left side of her face was swollen and purple-orange. The left eye was pinched down to a slit by the swelling.

"No," said the girl.

"Good on you. It's a shitty habit." She dropped the cigarette in the gravel and ground it out. Zoey didn't actually smoke. She kept a few cigarettes and matches in the jockey box because there were certain situations where lighting up was a good ice breaker. Kind of signaling that you were a nonthreatening fellow lowlife. It seemed to have worked here, even though the girl didn't smoke.

She crossed the road and picked her way through the brush clumps. She tried not to move quickly and scare the girl.

"What are you reading there?" she asked. The girl had a book in her hand. After staring at Zoey a long moment without moving, she held the book out.

"*My Antonia*. Bet that's for English class, right?"

The girl nodded.

"I'm Zoey. What happened?"

"I fell," said the girl.

"Bad fall. What's your name?"

After another hesitation the girl said, "Alison."

"Nice to meet you, Alison. I saw you run across the road. You're pretty agile. I bet you don't fall that much. I just bought the generator from him back there. That your dad, or just your mom's boyfriend?"

"Boyfriend."

"I don't want to be offensive. Guy struck me as an asshole."

Alison looked at her without blinking.

"He do that?"

The girl pressed her lips together. "Don't get the police," she said. "He'll kill me."

"He try to do, you know, shit to you?"

"I stay out here a lot."

"In the woods, you mean?"

The girl nodded.

"I would too. Must be tough in the winter."

"I got a kind of cave back there." She pointed past the house to where the forest rose into the hills. "It's okay."

"They don't come looking for you?"

"Nah. Most of the time he doesn't want me around. She just wants to keep him happy."

"Your mom doesn't care what you're doing?"

"Sometimes she does. I tell her I'm with friends and staying out of trouble."

Zoey nodded. "So, you like school?"

"Yeah," said the girl.

"Port Teresa High. I went there. You got a favorite teacher?"

She held up the book. "Miss Mossery. My English teacher."

"Must be new, I don't know her. Let me ask you something, Alison. You have many friends?"

"A few."

"You hang out with them much?"

The girl looked away.

"Not really."

"Friends are good. People you can trust. You have anybody you trust?"

After a moment the girl shook her head.

"What do you think about you and me being friends?"

Why did she ask that? She wasn't someone who went around looking for friends. Maybe the kid's age. She was exactly at the age a child's innocence is about to be overwhelmed by the assholes of the world.

Alison looked at her with what seemed to be caution but interest.

"Why?" she asked.

"I like having friends. I can always use another friend."

The girl shrugged.

"That's great," she said, and flashed her best smile. "Let's try it. I'm going to write my phone number. Any time you want to talk or text, just do it. You got a phone?"

"They won't let me," said the girl.

"Huh. No phone. Tell you what I'm going to do. Day after tomorrow? I'm going to come back here and leave a phone behind that pine you're standing next to. It'll be good for forty-five minutes. I'll put my number in it. Zoey."

The girl didn't smile but looked at her with unwavering eye contact and said thank you. Not "thanks," but the two words.

"We're friends. I didn't like that asshole at all."

She went to the truck and came back with a length of twine.

"Here, tie this around that tree so I'll get the right one. Get the phone in two days, and you call me if you ever want to talk. Like if you're not feeling safe. Call."

A gesture of kindness, or shoving a stick into the spokes? She couldn't have imagined that day the consequences of an impulsive conversation with a fifteen-year-old girl.

CHAPTER FOUR

The next day she called the high school and made an appointment to see Miss Mossery.

She'd climbed these linoleum-covered stairs what, five hundred times? They'd built a wheelchair ramp since the last time she was here, which was what, six years since she graduated? The hallway seemed smaller than she remembered, but that's what they say about the places you grew up. She introduced herself in the office and took a seat. Not that many years ago, she'd waited in one of these chairs for a disciplinary meeting. When the bustle of departing students had quieted, a woman only a few years older than her walked hesitantly toward her. Probably expecting a parent, and she was too young.

"I'm Leah Mossery. You wanted to see me."

Zoey introduced herself.

"I don't have an office," she said. "Want to sit outside on a bench?"

Miss Mossery was a nice-looking woman, straight brown hair cut just above the neck, firm nose, a little long, running straight down from her brow, not a soft profile, but she had a comfortable smile that lingered instead of popping on and fading a second later. She would probably be good with kids.

"You have a student named Alison?" Zoey asked.

"You mean Alison Greenleaf."

"I don't know her last name. You know what happened to her?"

"She said she fell."

"You believe that?"

A vertical line formed on Leah's brow. "I'm not sure."

"I was out there yesterday. Bought something from the guy. You know she hides in the woods after school to keep away from him?"

"She hides?"

"I don't think he's fucking her yet. Won't be long. The mother's one of those, pretends there's nothing going on."

"How do you know that?"

"I saw enough. She likes you. She a good student?"

"Alison's actually very bright. She reads a lot on her own."

Miss Mossery had long, arching fingers that gestured actively as she spoke. She tilted her head to one side as she listened. She listened like somebody who wasn't just going to blow Zoey off. She wasn't going to ask what business it was of hers.

"You're maybe the only person she can trust. Do something, Miss Mossery. Do something."

"Tell me again who you are?"

"Zoey. I came to see you instead of the cops. I'm just somebody who hates to see shit like that going on. Nice to meet you." She stood and reached a hand for Miss Mossery to shake. "Sorry to dump this on you. But she believes in you. I don't think there's anyone else who can help her."

She thought she'd given it her best shot. She turned and walked away before the teacher could think of anything else to ask.

CHAPTER FIVE

The book group met in a classroom at the community college. The campus was a cluster of modern glass-and-concrete buildings backed up against a heavily forested slope that rose into the foothills of the Olympics. Zoey had taken accounting and a computer class here.

When she stepped into the room, Miss Mossery smiled at her. "Come on in."

The first thing she saw was the girl, Alison, sitting in one of the chairs that had been placed in a circle. What was this? Alison on parole from the juvie? What had happened?

Miss Mossery had certainly done something. Was it possible Alison was the reason the parolee book group had been formed?

The guy sitting next to Alison was an African American in his twenties, thin and hollow-cheeked. He kept shifting from a slouch to sitting upright in the chair and rubbing a hand back and forth across the back of his neck. Tweaker, she thought, here because he wasn't violent, and somebody thought he had half a chance to kick it.

A minute or two before ten, two males entered the room.

One was in his late thirties and stood tentatively a moment in the doorway.

"Mr. Barrett, come on in," said Miss Mossery. The second male followed Barrett into the room saying, "The jailbirds, right?"

"You're in the right room," said the teacher. He was big and sturdy. His upper lip pulled away from his teeth and made any smile on his face a leer. His jug ears were so low they seemed to grow out of his neck rather than his head.

Miss Mossery introduced herself as Leah. The ground rules, she said, were they'd have about two hours of reading a week. She wouldn't test them; she just wanted to know they'd done the reading. They'd talk about what they thought of the book. She'd give a report each week to the parole officer. She handed out copies of a novel called *The Outsiders* and told them they could probably finish it by the next session. Did anyone have any questions? They didn't.

She said that was it for today, and they could go.

Zoey touched Alison on the arm. "Looks like we'll be reading the same books for a while. How'd you get here?"

"Possession with intent to sell."

"Where'd you hear an expression like that?"

"What the prosecutor said."

"I didn't take you for a user. Are you?"

"I don't do that stuff," said Alison. Her mouth twisted a little with disgust.

Good, Zoey thought. I wondered if you'd be like me.

Where Zoey grew up, unless you were one of the brainy kids taking AP classes and scrambling to get community service projects on your college applications, people expected you to give drugs a shot. Her view now was that it depended on who your friends were when you hit adolescence. It depended on how you defined cool. People tried to shame you into doing shit with them. You were chicken, or worse, still a kid if you said no. What helped was if you knew a few people, maybe older than your buds, who'd been living the drug life and had made the transition from cool to stressed and pathetic. Role models for what not to do with your life.

Given her curiosity she had to try some weed, some coke, but her curiosity balked at meth or heroin. That shit scared her. What really turned her off was getting her trading business started and dealing with meth-head thieves. The quick-eyed, panicky, skating-near-the-edge behavior, she had to work at keeping her face bland when she was dealing with them. The real turnoff was the physical ugliness that worked on the ones she'd known for a while. Like they'd signed up for a fast-spreading cancer of the physical features. Sucking up their calcium. She'd read Faust in English class; she knew the bargain she was seeing.

"So how come you're here?"

The girl shrugged.

"You can tell me; it's okay."

"He can't get me in jail."

"You didn't call."

She looked away and gave another shrug of her shoulders.

"You should have."

"You couldn't do anything."

"Maybe more than you think. Listen to me, kid. We can get you away from that son of a bitch. You safe right now?"

"It's okay. He's afraid I'll say something to the parole people."

Zoey waited until the others had left and went up to Leah.

"Is this because of her?"

"Basically yes," said Leah. "I went out there. It's like you said. Mother says everything's fine. Threatened to pull her out of school if there were any hassles. I decided to have the police check. Next thing I hear Alison's in the juvenile system, some drug charge."

"You pick up on her being a user?"

Leah winced. "I didn't think she was."

"I didn't think so either. She got herself arrested to get away from the place."

"Deliberately?"

She nodded. "This is a good thing you're doing."

"A woman in my yoga class works for the court. We've actually been talking about doing something like this for a while. There's programs like it in the east. I met with a judge and a couple of parole officers who said they were ready to go if I'd do it. Seeing Alison in the juvenile system decided me."

"And me?"

"That was a surprise. We wanted five people. They gave me bios and photos on some candidates, and I recognized you. They said you weren't the best candidate because your sentence wasn't that long, but I said I particularly wanted you."

"Well, thank you for that. Who knew I'd be a good candidate for parole. But that's great. I was getting tired of the place."

CHAPTER SIX

The Outsiders was about juvenile delinquents in the era of Elvis and the Beatles. S. E. Hinton, the author, was a female, a girl, in fact, sixteen, when she wrote the book. Zoey was amazed a sixteen-year-old could do this. The juvenile delinquents had this very sweet relationship with one another. The brothers were orphans. There didn't seem to be any adults around.

Not much like her adolescence. No shortage of adults. Her father died when she was five. She had memories of him that might be based as much on her mother's photos as actually remembering him. She thought she could recall his smile. He probably hadn't smiled that much, but he did in the photos. After a few years, her mother remarried, a long-haul truck driver, a handsome man named Dalquist. He was gone most of the time and flopped on the sofa when he was home, watching TV with his legs stretched out and a beer in his hand. He kept his distance from Zoey and was careful not to be drawn into disciplinary situations. He knew instinctively that stepdaughters are potential trouble. And she probably had a well-developed expression of contempt by the age of nine.

But her mother got bored with Dalquist. She saw her mother standing with her hands on her hips watching him pad around the house in his slippers or doze and guessed that the situation wouldn't continue. He might be an attractive man, but he was passionless, obsessed with running up miles and dollars on the road, though he didn't spend much money on anything, and, yes, boring. When she was fourteen, her mother divorced him.

Then came Bob Potterwine. Bob was not boring. He sold real estate. He was decent looking, bright-blue eyes in a round face, with good teeth and a cheery smile. Her mother was aging and knew it. She was still pretty, but there were creases under her eyes and a fold of skin that appeared beneath her chin when she didn't hold her head up, which she began to make a point of doing. Bob flirted with her and was publicly affectionate. Her mother groused that he paid too much attention to other women. He was just comparing so he could appreciate his best gal, he said.

When Zoey was fifteen, her butt got rounder and her breasts enlarged from average to a size that had the men in the room predictably studying her cleavage if she was showing any. Her mother began scowling at her clothing choices.

"You can't hang around here looking like a slut," she said.

"I dress like everybody else."

"I don't care. On you it looks like you're trying to get guys to squeeze your tits."

"What, you want me to wear pajamas like a Mormon?"

Her mother half-raised a hand to slap her. "Do not be smart with me," she said.

Bob was one of the men who occasionally studied her cleavage. He flirted with her the way he did with others. Sometimes her mother glowered at him when she heard his banter. There was an occasional affectionate hand on the shoulder, but nothing more. That was until one evening when Mother was out.

"You know," he said, "you are really cute. Sexy. I'm just going to say it. It's getting hard to ignore you."

She thanked him and said she was flattered.

"Okay," he said, "thanks is okay. What I'm saying is I could show you a few things. And I would really like to do that. We wouldn't want your mom to know how I feel. It would make her unhappy, wouldn't it? That maybe I like you better than her."

"I guess it would," she said.

"Well, this is an offer. You think about it."

She did. Bob was smart in his way. He understood how appealing it was to a fifteen-year-old girl whose mother treated her like a frivolous child instead of the woman she'd become to prove she was more woman than her mother by stealing her man.

She was tempted. She didn't have a lot of the throbbing hormonal drive that would have her peer group popping out babies in the next couple of years. And she acknowledged to herself she was more drawn to older men than to the clumsy boors her own age. Older men knew things; they knew how to make things happen. Having power, that was sexy.

She realized if she let Bob have his way, there were two ways it could turn out. One, he could become infatuated, addicted to his bit of teenage ass, willing to do anything to continue to have sex. Or he could be stricken with guilt and remorse, resent her for giving in, and tell Mother she had seduced him. She'd be out of the house in an hour. That would be ugly, and she didn't want to be paying rent just yet.

She decided the first was more likely. One evening she put on a skimpy dress and said to Bob it looked like Mother would be out till late. He didn't need to have a picture drawn. He gave her a kiss, big but not sloppy, not bad, actually. He fondled her at a pace that matched her body warming up. He did know what he was doing.

Before she let him place her on all fours on her bed and hike her dress up around her shoulders, she took a good look to be sure he had sheathed his cock with a prophylactic.

She let him have sex with her for the next year. She was tempted a few times, especially when Mother condescendingly accused her of being naïve, to drop a hint or two, but she didn't give in. Bob stayed smart about the relationship, not pushing to be with her too much.

"I could wipe myself out with you," he said with a wry chuckle, "but I gotta be able to keep your mom happy." Apparently he did. He also let her pick his brain about the real-estate business. He was a successful salesman, residential and commercial both, and knew a lot. She listened to his stories and learned how businesspeople think: where exactly the money is, the art of trading information to get more from the other guy than you give him. He said he couldn't introduce her to people, that wouldn't be wise, but he talked about the major players in town in detail. At the end of a year, she could have passed the real-estate license exam.

A year before she graduated from high school, she told Bob and her mother she was leaving home. Bob understood she was ending their relationship. He said she'd been a good student and would make her way. He put ten thousand dollars in a bank account in her name for seed money and said she could get his advice any time she wanted. She kissed him with probably more affection than she'd shown during sex and set out to begin the career of entrepreneurship she'd been preparing for.

CHAPTER SEVEN

At the first discussion meeting, Leah asked what the group thought about *The Outsiders*.

"I don't get it," said Gary, the big guy. "This chick, Cherry. Does she fuck? It doesn't say."

"You're right," said Leah. "It's not clear. What do you think?"

"Bet she does. Those sosh dudes wouldn't hang with a chick that didn't put out."

"Hinton is very discreet about revealing sexual information. Anybody find any clues?"

So the big guy was going to play smartass. "The bedrooms," Zoey said. "She talks about the bedrooms at parties. I think this is before people at parties went into bedrooms to do lines or shoot up. So she's saying there was sexual activity without showing it."

Leah's eyes lit up. Zoey felt sorry for her. The decent teachers strained to make some subject interesting that for most students was just an obstacle to get past. She couldn't imagine the life of a high-school teacher, repeating the same annual arc of disappointing experiences over and over. This one deserved support for stepping into Alison's life. She would do her part to keep the meetings lively.

The old guy, Barrett, didn't add much. She'd seen people like him, fallen into the system and losing hope they could ever get out. Once someone like Barrett gets into trouble, the rules that keep you out of more trouble are too complex to understand. The system is lazy. It always picks the low-hanging fruit, those with records. She guessed he'd worked his way through the book twice to be sure he could answer the questions. Denton, the black guy, waffled when Leah asked what he thought of the book. He didn't seem to have much confidence in his opinions. But he'd read the book and gave an occasional "yeah!" when somebody said something he agreed with.

She found herself nodding encouragement when Alison was talking. The girl was plenty smart, she could see that, though she tended to talk about the characters as real people. Leah cautioned them that novelists create characters for their stories by blending features of people they've known with imaginary histories and thoughts.

When the group was over, she took Alison to the cafeteria for lunch. The kid had a big appetite but didn't go for the junk food. Salads and chicken sandwiches. She probably didn't hang around for long at mealtimes at home. She said she'd wrapped the phone in plastic and kept it in her shelter. She hadn't used it but was glad it was there if she needed it. With her unwavering look, she thanked Zoey for giving it to her. Now that the swelling around her cheek and eye had gone down, she really was a cute girl. No wonder the asshole mom's boyfriend was after her. She had to admire the girl. She didn't act entitled to have people take care of her, but neither did she embarrass somebody with gushing thanks.

The big guy, Gary, turned out to be an asshole. He slouched back in his chair and made snide witticisms and asides. The message in his joking was anyone who took this stuff seriously was either stupid or an ass-kisser. Leah was pretty good at deflecting his comments.

"These books supposed to reform us or something?" he asked at the next meeting, with his mouth slanted in a sneer. She found him repulsive.

"They're just stories you can think about or not. Nobody's going to reform you but you."

"Yeah, good fucking luck with that," he said.

She wanted Leah to chastise him. Maybe that was something the teacher didn't feel comfortable doing. She heard his dad was a cop, a detective. What did a cop think about a son going to jail? Disappointed? Pissed? Was that why Leah cut him some slack? Which she did until the Saturday Gary hadn't done the reading. They were discussing *The Hunger Games*.

"So, Gary, what do you think Katniss would be like if she lived here in town?"

"Ah, she'd just be like any other girl, I guess."

"You read the book, Gary?"

Gary's lip pulled up into his familiar toothy sneer.

"Sorry, teach, I just had a really busy week."

She looked at him levelly. "Each of you gets one pass. You just used yours. The next time you don't do the assigned reading, don't waste my time coming here. Just go to the parole office and tell them you're out. Then maybe you won't have so many really busy weeks for a while."

Zoey had to cover her grin. Way to go, Leah. The comment shut Gary up for the rest of the session. Maybe there was something about being a cop's kid that made it natural for you to be a shit.

When she took her seat at the book group session the following Saturday, there was a man she hadn't seen before waiting with the teacher.

"This is Sam Troshin," said Leah, when they were ready to start. "He's a reporter for the *North Coast News*. He's going to sit in for a few meetings. Everyone okay with that?"

No one said anything.

"Don't worry. If he does write something, he won't use your names."

"So what are you going to say about us?" Gary asked in a wary tone.

"No idea," said the reporter. "I just got here."

He was a solidly built guy, no beer gut, blocky jaw, eyes squinted a little as if the sun was glaring into the room. Hair trimmed down to what Zoey's Vietnamese hairdresser would call a number two. She'd never met a reporter and wasn't sure what she expected one to look like. His face was pleasant enough. And a good answer.

During the session the reporter just listened without taking any notes. "Who had the idea to write about us?" Zoey asked him at the end of the session.

"Somebody must have heard about your group," said the reporter. "The editor said go sit in for a couple sessions and see if there's a story. Actually, I'm a sportswriter." He gave an apologetic shrug. "What about you? What do you think about coming here and talking about books?"

"Beats sitting in jail."

"Cool," said Sam Troshin. "So what kind of work do you do?"

"I buy and sell stuff. Help clients find things cheap. You have anything hard to find you want at a good price?"

"Not really. No, wait a minute." Sam grinned at her. "Okay. How's this? I've been thinking about joining a team in the town softball league. Rawlings Primo, that's the glove to have. Twelve-inch model. No way I could pop for a new one. But a good used one at a good price? Can you do something like that?"

She grinned back. "You might be surprised. Rawlings Primo twelve-inch. Give me a little time. I'll get back to you."

The following Saturday discussion hadn't gotten very far before Zoey knew something was different. Something was wrong. It wasn't just the presence of the reporter. Alison kept her head down and didn't speak. Her responses to Leah's questions were brief and spoken with a flat, expressionless voice. Gary answered the questions he was asked, no insight, but without the sneering efforts at comedy. When they were done, Zoey asked Alison what was going on. The girl didn't look at her.

"Come on, let's get lunch. We're still friends, aren't we?"

She shook her head again and continued looking at the floor. "I can't."

Alison was usually good with eye contact. She didn't watch you out of the corner of an eye. She looked right at you. She was pushing Zoey away. Zoey stayed where she was and watched Alison walk out through the classroom doorway. Instead of heading toward the bus stop in the parking lot, she turned and walked across the campus to a path that wound up the slope behind the college into the forest.

A minute later Gary appeared. He walked up to Alison, gave her a small push in the back, and followed her up the trail into the woods.

What the fuck.

She stood wondering if she should follow them or just wait. Fifteen minutes later the two came back down the path, this time Gary in the lead. He strode with a bounce toward the parking lot, not looking back at the girl, climbed into his Camaro, and drove off with a squirt of acceleration. Alison walked with her head down, dragging herself as if she was hauling a fifty-pound backpack to the bus stop.

Zoey hurried after her. "What's going on?" she said. "You didn't want to go up there with that guy. Why did you?"

"Leave me alone," said Alison.

"I'm your friend, remember?"

The girl's lower lip jutted out, trembling.

"Tell me what's going on."

Alison didn't look up.

"He's an asshole. Has he got some kind of hold on you? What's going on?"

The girl looked up abruptly. Her eyes glistened with tears. But she didn't blink. Her hands were clenched into fists.

"I want a bow and arrow."

"Whoa, a bow and arrow? What are you talking about?"

"I want a bow and arrow. I can learn to use it."

The Hunger Games, that's what she was thinking about. The

heroine, Katniss, a girl Alison could identify with, at home in the forest, defending herself with a deadly bow.

"Tell me. He's got something on you. The fucker, I know he does."

Alison dropped her eyes back to the pavement. Her clenched fists shook.

"Come on. Let me give you a ride out to your place."

They didn't talk. Zoey felt her jaw tighten. One of the signs when she got angry. She forced herself to relax. Not asking any more questions was her best chance to get the girl to talk. When Zoey pulled off the highway at Alison's road, the girl sat before getting out of the truck.

"He'll tell them I tried to sell him dope." Her voice was gravelly with stress. "His dad's a detective. They'll believe him. He said they'd put me in for two years."

"Jesus, the dumb son of a bitch." She reached across and put her hand on the girl's shoulder. Alison didn't respond but didn't pull away. After several seconds Zoey felt a sob, then another, jerk through her body.

"Okay. Let's think about what to do," Zoey said. Even though the asshole was a loser on parole, the dad would probably blow her off if she tried to talk to him. She could talk to the guy himself, tell him she'd tell everybody what he was doing.

"I can get him to stop."

"He won't. I want a bow. I'll practice."

"We can talk to Leah. She's got some connections with the court."

Alison pulled her lip between her teeth and bit down. The lip went white.

"Doesn't matter if he goes to jail. He still did that to me."

Zoey wasn't somebody with a vivid imagination. But she could see it. The ugly bastard getting her pants off, pinning her with his massive weight so she couldn't move, grunting and slobbering and pushing himself between her legs. It horrified her to think about it.

And the horror of it fractured her image of herself as a strong and capable person. These moments happened, when she realized she was a fragile, vulnerable woman who worked to maintain a veneer of toughness. She knew that her belief that she had been in control was a delusion, that she was a victim of sexual abuse, and that Bob Potterwine was just a gentler and more courteous version of Gary McCord. An urge to cry rose in her, and she pushed it away with an angry shake of her head.

Okay, she murmured to herself.

Zoey didn't believe much in women's self-defense classes. They were mostly an illusion. Fights between men were about weight. Bigger guys beat smaller guys, unless the smaller guy was a welterweight martial arts competitor or something. And guys always had fifty pounds on the woman. But the confidence, false or not, a woman got from practicing kicking an instructor in the balls or shoving a pen at his throat was worth something. The classes could strengthen a woman's a sense of sisterhood. The spirit of other women was with you if you were attacked. Would that help you cope with an assault? Maybe.

The girl's desire for a bow might be an expression of some escapist fantasy about an act of self-defense that could never happen. But Alison wasn't a drama queen. There was no teary bluster in her request. The kid had grit. She was somebody who could have a plan and follow it. She would get a bow; she would learn to use the bow. It was unlikely she'd actually shoot an arrow at the asshole. If she got good with the bow, though, maybe she could put an arrow in his leg. Let him think the next one might nail him in the nuts. That should get him to lose interest.

In the meantime, she would learn what she could about Gary McCord. If she could find things about him he didn't want known, she might gain the leverage to make him leave Alison alone. She knew how to learn things about people.

The problem was that Alison wanted more than stopping the abuse. Even finding a way to get Gary back in jail wouldn't make the shame and humiliation go away. She wanted to look him in the face and hurt him back. She wanted vengeance.

Exactly what Zoey would have felt.

She hadn't expected to be so taken with Alison. She'd always thought she would have liked a little sister. When she was a kid she envied friends with siblings, even though they squabbled and griped about the mean behavior of their brothers and sisters. Maybe she wanted Alison to turn to her for help. Maybe that's a selfish thought. But help she was going to get.

"Would you actually try to kill the guy?" she asked.

"He hurts me," Alison said. "I want him to stop. I want to hurt him."

She wondered whether you could actually kill someone with a bow and arrow. Unlikely to come to that. But if Alison could learn to use the bow, the confidence gained by having a defensive skill would help her deal with whatever was going to happen.

"All right," Zoey said. "The bow. Let me work on that."

CHAPTER EIGHT

Zoey was a trader. People who did business with her called her the Craigslist Queen. There are people desperate to sell things, and people looking to buy things, who don't use Craigslist. She bought from the ones desperate to sell and sold to those eager to buy. Long hours scrolling through Craigslist categories had given her a read of where the good markets were. Electronics were tricky. You couldn't hold inventory, things got obsolete in a hurry. Old furniture had become lucrative. She'd developed a clientele of antiquers who could afford things. But the best markets were sporting goods and tools.

The sporting goods and hobby categories were filled with gear offered by people who spent more than they should in a fit of enthusiasm and then lost interest. Hobbies were like love: infatuation undermined by the passing of time and turning to disenchantment and too much work. That's what she hunted for, people who had lost interest in things they owned. And tools. Guys took pride in their tools and bought good stuff when they had work, then sold in desperation when the rent was due, a kid was on the way, and jobs were scarce. There was a lot of that in Port Teresa. Tool styles didn't change much, so you can hold a little inventory. A Snap-on wrench was a Snap-on wrench.

She'd begun with a small but steady supply of oxycodone. People who need painkillers are more desperate than anyone. They would barter whatever they owned, or had recently liberated, for a handful of pills. The things she acquired, golf clubs, portable generators, TVs, outboard motors, went on Craigslist. Every time she bought or sold, she would ask her customers about other things they might be in the market for. Her list of contacts and wanted items was growing all the time. Though more and more of her transactions were direct, bypassing Craigslist, especially if she thought the item might be stolen. She worked now with two associates who trolled certain for-sale and wanted categories online and carried out some of her transactions. One she paid a cut, the other she compensated with meds.

The nest egg Bob gave her had multiplied. When the right investment opportunity came along, she would have the capital.

The past spring she had tried something new. She rented a double booth at the town's first annual Peninsula Days Fair. Port Teresa has a complex about its tourist business. Plenty of tourists passed through the town on their way to the Olympic National Park or to Victoria and Vancouver Island. But they stayed only long enough to top off the tank and have lunch. The commercial interests were acutely aware of the continuing success of Forks. It was an hour down the highway and a tourist attraction thanks to the *Twilight* movie series. Forks, a town a quarter the size of Port Teresa with nothing to offer beyond cloudy weather, trees, and the annual Logging and Mill Tour. But people make pilgrimages from all over the world to see where Bella and the werewolves lived.

They didn't need the world to come to Port Teresa, the chamber of commerce decided, just Seattle. "Think locally" was the theme. There were five wineries in the area that sourced their grapes from the Yakima Valley and two creameries that made marketable cheeses. They could be romanced into a tasting tour. When the chamber got the local TV station on board for a week-long publicity campaign, Zoey decided it was worth a shot. She borrowed a van and drove to Eugene, where she knew about an apparel store selling high-grade vintage dresses going out of business and picked up the cream of the inventory for a song. If the fair was a success, she would consider touring the western Washington fair circuit for the summer.

She needed an assistant and advertised on Craigslist for someone to help with the booth. When the fourth applicant walked into the classroom she'd rented at the college for interviews, she knew she'd hit the jackpot. The girl's name was Kirstin, she was six feet five inches tall, and she was stunning. She said she was a volleyball player who trained on weekdays and was looking for a weekend job. When she smiled, Zoey understood for the first time what an infectious smile was. You can't help smiling back. She offered a higher hourly rate than she intended. She knew this radiant young woman would draw every casual visitor at the Peninsula Days fair to the booth.

She wasn't mistaken. Customers crowded into the booth, chatted with Kirstin, tried things on, and came back later to talk more and buy things. She had never met anyone who could get people smiling and talking as quickly. It was a pleasure to watch her interacting with people. If I had her gift, I'd be rich, she thought. Bob had told her about the best salesman he knew, a man who appeared to be simply giving information, not trying to sell anything. Sales were like a side-effect of the conversations Kirstin had with people.

When they'd secured the booth at the end of the first day, Zoey offered to buy her dinner. She was entranced by her smile. Kirstin said she was a senior and was being recruited by several college volleyball teams. Her ambition after volleyball was to be a journalist.

"There's so much that's wrong that's hidden from the public," she said with some animation. "How can people make things better in the world if they don't know?"

By noon the second day of the fair, most of the inventory was gone. Now that the traffic was slowing down, Zoey noticed a guy hanging around the booth talking to Kirstin. He was what, in his forties at least, gray in the goatee, but he was flirting and being a little persistent. She caught Kirstin's eye. The girl kept smiling but gave her a small helpless shrug. Zoey walked over.

"Hi there," she said to the man. "Looking for something in particular?"

"Yeah," said the man. "She's right here."

"Great," she said, stepping between him and the girl. "Kirstin, maybe you could get the stuff in that last tub on the table. Now then, the person you're shopping for, tell me what she's like and maybe I can suggest something."

"Yeah, right," said the man, giving her a sarcastic smile. "See you around, babe."

When he was gone, Kirstin said, "Thanks. I don't like having to avoid somebody, but he makes me uncomfortable."

"You're too nice," Zoey said. "Be a little rude to the prick, and he'll get it."

At the end of the day, Kirstin helped with several trips to the truck with the display fixtures and leftover merchandise. When Zoey picked up the daypack with the day's receipts, two punks wandered toward her booth. She'd been aware of them watching. One of them, narrow-shouldered and bandy-legged with his hoodie hood pulled in to cover most of his face, stepped up to her and pressed a knife against her stomach.

"Gimme the fuckin' bag," he said.

"Okay, okay, okay," she said. "Take it easy, okay? Here, I'm giving it to you."

She bent over the pack and grabbed a tube from a side pocket, then held out the pack to him. He seized the pack, and the two ran.

She took off after them, yelling "Thief, thief!" as loud as she could. A couple of vendors closing up their booths stared but didn't react. Then Kirstin appeared at her side.

"They took the money," Zoey yelled. "My bag!"

After a second's hesitation, Kirstin sprinted ahead. With her long, athletic strides the volleyball player closed on the fleeing thief and gave him a powerful shove in the back that sent him sprawling. By the time he got to his knees and was reaching for the knife, Zoey was on him. She thrust the canister of bear spray she'd snatched from the daypack in the punk's face and sprayed, hitting him straight in the eyes from two feet away. He yelled and began frantically rubbing his face. She grabbed her daypack.

"Get out of here, asshole," she yelled as he scrambled to his feet and ran toward the parking lot.

"You could have been hurt," said Kirstin. "He had a knife."

"He wasn't going to get the money. Wow. Thanks for running him down. You're fast."

"You okay?"

"Yeah," she said. Her shoulders heaved for a minute while she tried to catch her breath. Then she put her arms around Kirstin, which was a reach up. Kirstin bent forward and made it easy. She must be used to it.

CHAPTER NINE

She had already bought and sold a compound bow, clearing seventy-five dollars on the deal. It was a weird-looking thing, nothing like the bow Robin Hood and the Comanches used. It looked more like some kind of space-age harp. Multiple strings ran through a network of pulleys and oddly shaped parts made from anodized alloy drilled with big holes.

She spent some time on Google and Wikipedia learning about bows and shooting. The virtue of the compound bow was that it took strength to start the pull, but once you had the string and arrow back to your ear, you could hold it easily and take your time to aim.

She called a guy who helped with sporting goods and had him buy a bow she found on Craigslist. It had a forty-pound pull, suitable for what the Wikipedia article called a "fit woman." She called a contact in Spokane and asked her to do a little research. The next day the contact called back with the name of an archery instructor not associated with the local sporting goods stores.

One of the things she had learned selling possibly stolen merchandise was how to leave the faintest of trails. It was conceivable this bow would be used in a way that would result in a police investigation. She made sure that a detective scouring through Port Teresa looking for a connection between herself, Alison, and archery would find nothing.

She tracked down Alison at the city library, a place the girl told her she liked to hang out during the summer.

"Can you be gone a couple days?" she asked her.

"It wouldn't matter," said Alison.

"Tomorrow at eight, at the highway. Bring a toothbrush or whatever."

In the morning Alison was waiting at the roadside with her daypack over her shoulder.

"Had breakfast?"

The girl nodded.

"Great. Get comfortable. We're going to Spokane."

Zoey drove through the peninsula pasturelands toward Poulsbo and the Bainbridge ferry to Seattle. She made a few comments about bicycle tourists on the road and the strong thrusting wingbeats of a heron moving toward the sound.

"They look huge, but they only weigh five pounds."

But she didn't ask questions. Neither did the girl. Zoey liked it that she trusted her without asking.

On the ferry Alison followed her up the steel staircase and through the heavy doors to the passenger deck. Once the ferry was underway, Alison asked, "They let you walk around?"

"Sure." Apparently she had never been on a ferry, never been to Seattle. Maybe she'd never been away from Port Teresa.

Alison roamed the boat, then settled against the front rail, wind in her face, gulls coasting near the railing looking for passengers holding out french fries, and watched the approach to the Seattle waterfront.

Zoey drove off the ferry, around the stadium complex, and onto the freeway that crossed Lake Washington and wound into the Cascades. As they approached the summit at Snoqualmie Pass, Alison looked wide-eyed at the motionless ski lifts and rugged mountains. She said nothing but gazed out the truck window with avid interest.

Zoey asked her about spending nights in a forest shelter. "Can you keep dry?"

She said she was covered from the rain, but dampness was the worst problem. She didn't want soggy, dingy clothes giving away her crap home life when she got to school. She told Zoey about a routine of catching the earliest bus into town and taking her clothes to an all-night laundromat. She worked two days a week after school at the Frosty Freeze, so she had quarters for the dryer, money for lunch, and batteries for the booklight she used for reading in her shelter. She had told the Frosty Freeze manager she was taking a leave when she learned she was going to be arrested so she could have her job back when she was released.

She didn't say anything about how she came to be arrested, and Zoey didn't ask.

In the afternoon they drove out of the rolling farmlands into the scattering of pines and rusty-gray basaltic rock along the approach to Spokane. Zoey took a room at a motel just west of the city. She unlocked the galvanized box in the bed of the pickup and took out a black case.

"It's for you," she said.

In the room Alison opened the clasps and gazed at the bow bedded in gray foam. She looked at Zoey with the alert, unreadable eyes of a cat and said thank you. Then she asked how much she owed.

"On me," said Zoey. "In the morning we go see somebody who'll show you how to use it."

When she turned off the bedside lamp, she listened for the sounds of the girl's breathing. She was somebody who slept rough and had probably never been in a motel. She wondered if the nightmare Alison was living affected her sleep. But there was no movement, no sound of breathing, as if there was no one there.

After a forty-five-minute drive the next morning through the pine forests and farms north of Spokane, following the GPS directions, Zoey pulled into a filling station on the north side of

Loon Lake. A man was seated on the open tailgate of a pickup with a bow between his knees.

"You must be Frank?"

"You must be Jane." He was a lean old man with a gray beard kept trimmed. The gaunt, weathered face would have looked right under a big-brimmed Stetson, but he wore a boonie cap that matched a well-worn camo shirt and pants.

"And you must be the shooter," he said, holding out a hand to Alison. "I'm Frank." Alison took the hand and said hello.

"This is Grace," said Zoey.

"Just follow me," he said, latched the tailgate in place, and got into his truck. Zoey followed him up a dirt road that led to what looked like a shallow gravel pit.

Frank carried a big straw-filled burlap bullseye to a dirt embankment and set it against a stump. Then he took a look at the bow.

"Not a bad model for you," he said. "Take a little effort at first."

He showed her how it worked, then had her assemble, disassemble, and reassemble the bow. Then they began shooting.

Alison followed everything Frank did with unbroken concentration. They both ignored Zoey. After the first few shots, Frank went to his truck and came back with a fistful of arrows.

"We'll use these so we don't have to be runnin' back and forth so much. But it's bad practicing with a lot of arrows. You don't want to be like those cops on TV with their Glocks and shit, waving their gun in the general direction of something and emptying a twenty-round magazine in about four seconds. The bow is all about one shot. You focus, you pick your moment, you make your shot. You're doin' good. Let's keep at it."

At one point the man asked Alison if she wanted a break. She said, "No, we can keep shooting."

"Well, I need one," he said, and opened a cooler with soda and bottled water, oranges, and a package of cookies. He handed Zoey a can of soda.

"Thanks," she said. "I didn't think of it."

A little before eleven, Frank said they'd probably had enough. "Don't want your arm falling off."

He turned to Zoey.

"You said she might be doing a little hunting. She's a fast learner. How about her and me go take a walk in the woods. Back around one?"

"Fine. I brought a book."

At two they hadn't returned. Zoey decided not to worry.

The two archers, bows in hand, appeared at the edge of the gravel pit a little after three.

"Sorry," said Frank. "Didn't expect the little lady to be so right at home in the woods. We did some tracking."

She watched Alison disassemble and put her bow back in the case. She felt a surge of feeling—she wasn't sure what, affection or admiration—as she watched the girl's efficient, deliberate movements repacking the bow. Then Alison reached her hand to Frank with the country formality he'd used when he introduced himself.

"Thank you," she said. "You're a good teacher."

"You're a good student." He took the bills Zoey handed him, gave Alison a big wink, and grinned at Zoey.

"She's a hunter," he said.

The next week Zoey met Alison at the Wendy's near the bus stop Alison used to catch the bus to town.

"You practicing?"

"Every day."

"Okay, something we should talk about. I bought a few things for a deputy once, and he talked to me about his work. He said cops practice shooting a lot because in a real shootout, they forget everything. They can't aim straight, they forget to flip off the safety if their gun has one, they fumble around if they have to reload. If you're really going to do this, you have to practice till you don't even think about it."

"I shoot every day," said Alison. "I won't miss."

"You can't tell anybody about this. Who knows you have a bow?"

"You," said the girl.

Zoey sent a text to a corrections officer named Dana she had done a favor for at the jail. The favor was supplying her with a legitimate Vicodin prescription. She asked if Dana could get her all the information she could about Gary McCord, why he was in jail, court transcripts, witnesses, who his friends were.

"I know you're not supposed to do this," said Zoey, "so I don't want to ask you to do something that gets you into trouble. But I really need some leverage on this guy."

She knew Dana would make an effort. Not only did the guard owe her, but they both understood without having to say anything that if the source of her prescription were made known, Dana would lose her job.

Five days later Zoey received a fat envelope of documents. Gary was down for assault and being part of a theft ring that stole bicycles and sold them to a bicycle shop on Third Avenue in Seattle that police suspected of being an outlet for stolen bikes and motorcycles. Dana's note said the charges appeared to have been reduced through some kind of arrangement with Gary's father, a senior detective in the Port Teresa police department. She included information about two of Gary's friends, accomplices in the bike theft operation. One was serving time, the other had been released for lack of evidence. She would start with this guy, doing a little detective work herself. She had his address. She would follow him, find out where he hung out, and flirt her way into an acquaintance with him and his friends.

CHAPTER TEN

Sam Troshin, notebook in hand, met the PE teacher who served as the PR person for the high-school athletic department at the gym entrance. He carried the notebook because he thought people expected it of him, as though the laminated press pass dangling around his neck wasn't enough to prove he was the sportswriter for the *News*. He rarely wrote anything except scores in the notebook.

The PE teacher had called him a few days earlier to ask if he wanted to watch the girls work out for a group of scouts.

The girls' names were Kirstin and Kelsey, but no one except their families called them that. They were Outside and Setter.

Outside had light brown hair and was a classic beauty. When people first saw her, they almost always stopped and looked a second time. She was six five. Sam had written a story about her. Like most elite volleyball players, she had played for a development club since grade school. Club coaches preferred their girls didn't play for their high-school teams, where the skill level was less and there was a risk of injury. But Outside wanted to support the high-school team, so she played for them during the club tournament off season. She had persuaded an aunt to move to Port Teresa because Kelsey, the best setter in the state, lived there and played for the high-school team.

He couldn't help looking at the girl. She seemed to be without self-consciousness, either about being six five or beautiful or a spectacular athlete. Everyone in her vicinity, he could tell, was aware of her presence. The classic actresses whose pictures he'd seen in magazines, Barbara Stanwick or Grace Kelly, must have had the same effect. It wasn't lust she inspired, though her long athletic legs were just about perfect. It was as though you thought a little better of yourself when she smiled and listened to what you had to say.

"That's them," said the teacher, gesturing across the gym. Four women sat in the first row of bleachers. They looked almost identical, long and lean, hair cut short or pulled back in a ponytail, high cheekbones, clear eyes, confident smiles. They were chatting and laughing among themselves.

"Stanford, UCLA, Oregon, Washington," said the teacher. "Friendly enough, aren't they? Probably all played against each other. But only one of them is going to get Outside."

"When does she have to choose?" Sam asked.

"This is a period the recruiters can have contact with her. She'll schedule visits to the campuses she's interested in."

One of the coaches was working with Setter at the net. The coach lobbed balls; Setter alternated, one set forward, then a backset over her head aiming blind at a five-gallon bucket on the floor ten feet behind her. Half the backsets dropped into the bucket. Sam tried to analyze what Setter did with her hands, but couldn't do it. The lobbed pass fell into her fingers extended above her head. There was an instantaneous flicker of movement, and the ball shot up in an arc to the hitter at the net or back to the bucket. It was like watching the shutter of an old Nikon film camera tripped at five hundredths of a second. He could see movement but couldn't really break down the motion into its parts.

He saw Outside lying on her back at the side of the court, stretching. The coach blew her whistle. Everyone cleared the court. Two aides began setting up orange cones in a row a yard inside the back line, two feet apart. The scouts stopped talking. Outside rose from her stretches and began swinging her arms in loose circles. Setter walked toward the center of the net, bouncing a ball. She tossed the ball to Outside. Outside lobbed a high pass back to Setter. Setter set the ball.

Outside took three fluid steps, rose into the air with no apparent hurry or effort, twisted at the peak of her leap, and struck the ball.

The leftmost cone exploded into the air and slapped against the far wall of the gym.

"Jeez," Sam couldn't help exclaiming.

Setter set the ball again. The next cone went sailing. The drill continued until all the cones were gone. She'd had to take a second swing at two of them.

"Seen anything like it?" said the assistant.

"How much does she practice doing that?"

"Something like this twice a week."

"Doesn't seem like much."

"She doesn't need to practice hitting. They work her mostly on serve reception, a little work on hitting off blocks."

He looked across the gym at the scouts. They watched with silent concentration. He'd watched enough volleyball to know what they were seeing, a rare combination of size and coordination.

"You want an interview?" said the teacher.

"Damn right," said Sam.

O'Gradys was a brewpub popular with the high-school kids because it had the best burgers in town, local beef, and good sweet potato fries, and you didn't have to be twenty-one unless you wanted to drink beer.

"Dinner on me," said Sam.

"On the paper?" Outside asked with a smile.

Sam shook his head. "I don't exactly have an expense account."

"Okay, I'll have a salad."

Sam ordered the salad and a burger for himself.

"I watched you hit," he said. "That's really impressive. You decided which school?"

"I wouldn't be able to tell you that," she said, still smiling. "The school will make the announcement. But I haven't decided, actually."

"I've covered some of your games," he said. "You guys have to be the best team in the state."

"We are," she said. "We're too small for the 4A tournament. But we played the winner in an exhibition in Seattle. Had them in straight sets."

"I guess women's volleyball has arrived. Is there any kind of career after college?"

"There's pro beach ball in California and leagues in Europe, Brazil, and they pay pretty well. I'll probably be able to do that for a few years. But what I really want to do is journalism. I wanted to ask you about that."

"Really? Journalism?"

"I hope you don't mind."

"Not sure I'd advise anyone to go into journalism. You must know print journalism's about dead. I barely have a job here. Need a second job to pay the rent."

"But so much goes on that people need to know about. There has to be investigative journalism."

"Well, you could go into media. You're a, uh, striking-looking woman. You have a good voice. You could probably work on air."

"Are there any internships at the paper?"

"No internships, sorry."

"But what if I had a story idea?"

"Well, if you work up some community story, I could get the editor to take a look at it. Do you have a story idea?"

Her eyes brightened. "Have you ever noticed all those half-finished mansions on Redwell Road, East Blakely, that area?"

"I don't get out there much, but I think I know what you're talking about."

"It just doesn't make economic sense. There must be a lot of money tied up and nothing happening. I asked one of my aunt's friends in real estate about it. He said there's some foreign builders, and how they got the loans he doesn't know. I'm sure there's some big problem there. Somebody's losing a lot of money. So somebody's making a lot of money."

"Hey, babe."

Sam looked up and saw four men filing past their table.

"Hello, Ronnie," said Outside.

"Who's your friend?"

"This is Sam. He writes for the paper."

"Hey, Sam." Ronnie was Sam's height, barrel chest, grizzled goatee, hair long enough to be combed back with some kind of gel. Nodded his head with a swagger. He extended a hand toward Sam but gave him a forceful slap on the shoulder instead of shaking the hand Sam offered. His eyes had the quick shift of someone turned aggressive rather than mellow by alcohol.

"Thought for a second you were dating older guys. But it's newspaper business, right? Another story about our big star, Sam?"

"You've been drinking, Ronnie," said Outside. "You and your friends should go outside, get some fresh air."

"Oh," said Ronnie. "Advice. Do I look like I need advice?"

He turned and planted his feet. He wasn't just being offensive passing by their table, he was going to make a drunken scene.

"Not a good idea to be telling people what to do."

"I'm not trying to give you advice."

"Tha's good. Don't really need advice from a kid. See, big jock lady, I got this idea what you think."

He leaned forward and braced his hands on the table. "That's what being the big star does. No time for talking to the plain old folks like us. Nobody ever taught you manners?" He drawled out the "plain old folks" with drunken sarcasm. "Maybe your newspaper buddy could help you with that."

"You're making a fool of yourself. You should just go."

"A fool, is it? That what you're calling me? You know, you're just a big dumb fucking bitch."

Outside rose from her chair. The blow was so fast Sam heard the slap before he saw her hand move. Ronnie crashed across the next table, sending two pitchers and a bowl of nachos flying. The people at the table jumped up, yelling at Ronnie to watch the fuck out.

It took Ronnie several seconds to get his legs under him and stand up again. His cheek was bright red. He snarled and launched himself at Outside.

And banged into Sam. Sam put a hand on his chest.

"Hey, hey, easy there," said Sam. "Take it easy, pal. She'll tear your head off."

Ronnie stared at Sam, then took a swing at him.

There had been a time Sam did not avoid getting into fights. Then his daughter had died, he beat someone he never should have, and everything in his life changed. Now the bars he patronized were the peaceable type, where most of the customers were older. On the few occasions where he was confronted, he talked the way a person might to soothe an angry dog, with calming, open-handed, unrushed gestures. And if he had to, he would turn away and not care if observers thought he was chickenshit. All but a couple of times in the past several years he had succeeded.

If it had just been him, he probably would have succeeded this time too and calmed the situation by pushing the man's blow aside. But when he swung at the girl, Sam's reflexes took over. He drove his right fist into Ronnie's face. Ronnie dropped like a sack of sand. One of the man's friends stepped forward and swung at Sam. Sam leaned away to dodge the blow, then hit the man in the mouth. The second man fell, dazed, to a crouching position half-across Ronnie.

Sam sucked in air and muttered, "Okay, okay, okay," to himself. He held himself motionless and tried to let the rage bleed away. O'Gradys was not a bar accustomed to brawling, especially as early as the dinner hour. The room went silent, no movement except the baseball game on the TV screens.

Sam bent down, hooked his forearms under Ronnie's

armpits, and hoisted him to a standing position. He pushed Ronnie at the other men.

"Get him out of here," he said. The men with Ronnie looked hard at Sam but didn't want to drop Ronnie. "Shouldn'ta done that, fucker," one of them said. They walked Ronnie out of O'Gradys.

Outside raised her hands to her cheeks. "I'm so sorry," she said. "He's been hassling me."

Sam continued breathing deeply and calming himself. He wondered about a guy this man's age trying to put the moves on a high-school girl. Maybe her height was a challenge to a certain kind of man. Dominating a girl four inches taller than you might appeal to some males. He flexed the fingers of his right hand. Crap. The knuckles would swell and hurt in a few hours. Better get some Advil in his system.

"Okay," he said. "I guess I have enough for a volleyball story."

"I wish things like this didn't happen," she said. She didn't look angry to Sam, just upset and sad. She would always be having an effect on people, he knew.

"That story you're talking about," he said, once he'd collected his thoughts. "If you get a draft, let me know. I can't promise anything, but I'll have the editor take a look."

CHAPTER ELEVEN

Neither Sam nor anyone else in the restaurant noticed the man who entered O'Gradys half a minute after Ronnie's group had walked in. He found a seat and watched Ronnie talking to the tall girl, saw her slap him, and the brief fight between Ronnie and the man the girl was with. When the men with Ronnie helped him out of the restaurant, he rose from his seat and followed. No one had noticed him come in; no one noticed him leave. There was something so inconspicuous in his manner and appearance that none of the waitstaff approached him during his brief visit.

The men got into the two vehicles they had driven to the restaurant. One of them drove Ronnie's truck with Ronnie in the passenger's seat. They parked the truck at Ronnie's apartment and drove away as Ronnie, moving heavily, staggering to his unit.

The man drove to his own apartment.

He had given himself three days to learn what he could about Ronnie's daily life, his routines and habits. He didn't usually have the time to do this, but the timeline for this assignment was flexible. The only limit to the time spent observing a subject was the need to remain unnoticed, and that was something he was good at.

Ronald Brenchlow worked at the order counter of a builder's supply store on Fourth, a strip of auto dealers, trailer hitch installers, and millwork shops. At noon he walked a block up the street to a Subway sandwich shop, the same thing he had done the day before, and took his sandwich back to the store to eat. A little after six, he got into his pickup and drove to a bar. A man whose life had settled into a routine. In the bar Ronnie ordered a pitcher and took it to a group of men at a table. The man followed a moment later and took a seat close enough to hear some of the conversation from the group. Brenchlow's laugh was an explosive snort. He talked with a slight lisp, probably the result of the punch in the face the day before. His conversation was fucking this and fucking that, spoken with a sneer that twisted the good side of his mouth. His words were angry and bitter. At one point the waitress looked apprehensively at their table and glanced at the bartender with a raised eyebrow. The bartender shrugged.

Brenchlow left the bar late, nearly midnight, and drove away. The man followed. Brenchlow did not take the same route he had previously. He parked on a residential street, took something from his truck, and stood looking up the street. The man could tell at once from Brenchlow's tentative but deliberate body language he was doing something that wasn't part of his normal routine. Brenchlow walked half a block, stopped, and looked up and down the street again to see if anybody was watching him. The man knew his car had probably been seen. He continued driving past Brenchlow without changing speed and turned at the end of the block.

There were no sidewalks along the street. The yards sloped to a shallow drainage ditch separating lawns and fences from the street. Trees thick with leaves, chestnuts and maples, arched low overhead, giving the street the feel of a leafy tunnel. Early chestnuts had dropped along the roadway. He parked and walked quickly back to where he could see the man he was following.

For a moment he couldn't find him. But he was there, halfway under the front of a car parked in a driveway. Brenchlow pulled himself out from under the car, took a quick look around, and walked hurriedly back to his truck and drove away.

At six the next morning, the man was parked down the street from the house Brenchlow had visited, waiting quietly. At seven thirty a young woman came out of the house carrying a gym bag and walked to the car. He immediately recognized the tall woman who had slapped Brenchlow at O'Gradys. She was dressed in workout pants and a sweatshirt. Her light-colored hair was pulled back in a ponytail. She was a beautiful woman, stunning.

He made a decision. His rule was to never engage unnecessarily with anyone when he was on a job. He was breaking that rule now. He walked up to her as she was putting the gym bag in the back seat.

"Excuse me," he said. "Is this your car?"

She looked at him with a friendly smile. "It is."

"I was driving home last night pretty late and saw something strange. I saw a guy crawl under this car. It looked to me like he was tampering with it. I think you should have a look before you drive."

"You sure it was my car?"

"I'm sure. I'll take a look if it's okay with you. Could be something obvious."

"Wow," she said. "Okay, thanks." She had a pleasant voice, melodious. Even though he was a stranger with a strange message, she didn't seem to mistrust him.

He dropped to his knees and looked under the car, a five-year-old Taurus.

"I think I see it," he said. "Put it in neutral, release the brake. I'll push you back. Then set the emergency brake."

When he had pushed the car a few feet, he gestured to her to have a look.

"Brake fluid," he said, pointing to a large wet spot where the car had been parked. "Line's cut partway through. You'd drive maybe a half mile, then the brake pedal would go to the floor and you wouldn't be able to stop."

"My God," said the girl. "Why on earth would somebody do this?"

"Maybe somebody is trying to get back at you for something. You think of anybody?"

She looked thoughtful, then sad. "It's possible. This is hard to believe. Should I call the police?"

He could tell her it wouldn't matter, but that would be too much information.

"I probably would," he said.

"Can you stay and be a witness?"

"Sorry, I can't. Just tell them a neighbor saw someone tampering and let you know."

He wanted to stay. He wanted to tell her more, to help her with the car. He couldn't, of course. But he was drawn to her in a way that he did not expect. She was too young, maybe not yet out of her teens, for simple sexual attraction to account for how much he wanted to continue talking with her. He would have to think about why he reacted to her as he did.

CHAPTER TWELVE

Two days after Sam's altercation at O'Gradys, Zoey sat in her pickup on Walnut, a back street where the garbage trucks emptied the Dumpsters of the bars and cafes that fronted on Main. Earlier in the day, she had sent Sam, the reporter doing a story on the book group, a text saying she had the Rawlings glove he'd asked about. He could take a look and see if it was what he wanted. He'd replied that he was meeting some people at nine at the Spruce Tavern to talk about a softball league and asked if she could meet him there afterward.

She replied, "Fine," and decided to kill two birds if she could. A client wanted to meet her somewhere away from traffic to show her some merchandise. She proposed the street behind the Spruce, enough streetlight to see things but not a lot of people wandering around. The client had several things he wanted to sell her. The goods included a tig-welding set, still boxed, a slightly used Browning over-and-under shotgun, long barrels for trap shooting, and a mountain bike. Somebody's basement left unlocked, or more likely a basement unlocked with some mechanical assistance. She drove a hard bargain with the client, saying a nice gun like that certainly had a serial number registered with the retailer that sold it and would just as certainly be reported stolen if it was. Selling them, in other words, would be tricky. The client swore for a minute, then took her lowball offer.

She had texted Sam that she would wait behind the tavern while he had his meeting and see him afterward.

When the client drove away, she put the flashlight she had used to examine the merchandise back in the glove compartment and hefted the shotgun. She could almost understand how NRA types found guns a sensual experience. The solid balance of a good tool designed to be held. The smooth walnut stock shaped for the hands did make you want to raise the gun to your cheek.

A quick movement across the street in the parking lot behind the bar caught her attention. Several men came out a door, pushing another. They began hitting the man, then moved out of the way so that one of them could swing a baseball bat at him. Was it possible the man they were hitting was the reporter? Yes, she was sure of it. She watched the man with the bat raise it over his head and take a swing. They were trying to kill the guy, for God sakes. She had to do something.

Luckily the seller had included a box of shells. She broke open the gun and dropped a pair of shells in the chambers. She closed the breech, pushed off the safety, easily intuitive, then stepped out of the truck and leaned across the roof. The gun thundered as she fired into the ground in front of the men. Stinging dirt, debris, and birdshot splattered into the group. The men froze, looked around, then sprinted for a car parked down the street, not waiting to see who was shooting, and accelerated away.

Zoey took a long breath. She'd sold guns before, and had fired a few of them, but never in the direction of people. Later she would recognize the surge of satisfaction at the power the gun gave her. But now she lay the gun on the truck seat and ran across the street to where the man she thought was the reporter lay curled up in the dirt.

"You okay?" she asked. She could see he was conscious but with his eyes shut and a grimace of pain twisting across his face.

"Jesus," she heard him mutter.

"Hang on, I'm getting help."

She opened the back door of the bar the men had spilled out of and yelled that someone was hurt, to call 911. When she went back to the reporter and bent over him, he opened his eyes. She could see his lips form a silent thank-you. She put a hand on his forehead as a gesture of reassurance.

"Help's coming," she said, then hurried to her truck. No point at all in waiting around and talking with police. Probably there were people nearby who had heard the shotgun, and she didn't want to have to explain.

CHAPTER THIRTEEN

When Brenchlow came out of the shop at the end of his shift, he saw a man standing next to his pickup, admiring it.

"Yours?" he asked, when Brenchlow put his key in the door.

"Yup."

"Nice, really nice. Hope you don't mind me looking it over. I used to have one. Selling it was one of the dumbest things I ever did. You probably hear that a lot from guys, had an old F-100 once and wished they'd kept it."

"True," said Brenchlow. "When I take it to shows, I hear that a lot."

"You know, now that money's not an issue, I told myself I'd get a nice example if I could find one. I don't know anything about the mechanical condition, but what I see, I gotta ask, any chance it's for sale?"

"Nah, it's a nice ride. Not really looking to sell."

"Ah, too bad. Just for the sake of argument, what kind of value would you put on it?"

Brenchlow stood back with one hand on his hip, the other tugging at his graying goatee, and looked at the truck as if he was studying it.

"It's all original. Restoration work done by a first-rate shop in Seattle."

Brenchlow ran a hand along the roofline. "I probably couldn't sell it around here. There's no money. No work in this fucking town. If I want nationwide, I'd get maybe fifty thousand."

"Huh," said the man, as if taking a moment to consider." If I offered you forty-five, would we be having a conversation?"

Brenchlow continued staring at the truck. He hadn't given any thought to selling. The truck had sentimental value to him. But he knew the current market for hot rods and muscle cars sucked. He'd be lucky to get $20,000 for it at the moment. Was this guy serious?

"You really that interested?"

"Well, I have to ask a few questions. We got matching numbers here, or did you drop a 350 Chevy in it like everybody seems do?"

"No, no, numbers all match. This is the original motor. Forty over pistons, four-barrel, mild cam. No front clip, no discs, this is for somebody who wants original."

"I'd want a test drive."

"Easy enough. But I'd need to see forty-eight."

"Forty-seven." The man smiled a benign smile at Brenchlow. "Five."

"Are we talking cash?"

"However you like. We could do a cashier's check at your bank."

"Okay, this is all pretty fast. Give me a minute to think. So you want to go for a drive now?"

"Don't actually have time. I'm not in town that much. Would tomorrow evening around nine work? I know it's late, but it works for me. I'd just like to get in a few miles on a country road."

"Good enough. See you right here, tomorrow at nine."

"You got it."

A little after midnight, the man drove out of town on a winding two-lane road that carved through a dense forest of pines, firs, and maples until he found the spot he was looking for. He parked his car off the road and walked back with a cargo bag over his shoulder. The place he was interested in was a tight, slow-speed curve in the road above a steep dropoff. He climbed over the rail, studied the back of the railing for a moment with a flashlight, then went to work on the railing with a saber saw. He worked quickly so the harsh sound of the saw on metal wouldn't attract attention. Once, headlights appeared, and he slipped a few feet down the embankment where he couldn't be seen. At this point a driver would be focused on the road, not looking around. It took him ten minutes to finish his task. The railing was still in place but greatly weakened.

At nine the next evening, Brenchlow was waiting in the truck outside the shop. The truck had been freshly detailed, the tires glossy with Armor All. Brenchlow was alone, as he expected. Three in the cab would have been a little snug. He wanted to avoid having anyone connect his face with Brenchlow.

Brenchlow got out of the truck and walked around to the passenger side.

"Always starts easy," he said. "Give it a little choke when it's cold."

The man started the engine and drove through town, driving gently to get the feel for the clutch and the three-speed floor shift. He turned onto the road he had been on the night before. "Nice," he said. "Feels tight. You have the bushings refreshed?"

"Oh yeah," said Brenchlow. "Tie rod ends, they did all that."

Thirty yards before the turn in the road where he had worked on the guardrail, the man pulled off to the side of the road and set the emergency brake.

"If it's okay, I'd like to take a look under the hood while everything's running nice and warm."

"Wouldn't it be easier back in town with the lights and all?"

"Yeah, but I wouldn't mind taking a quick look."

Brenchlow stared ahead at the curve in the road and the guardrail, and a furrow deepened across his forehead. He turned and looked at the man as if there was some question he wanted to ask. He shrugged and said, "Go ahead."

The man smiled a sunny, engaging smile, pulled a flashlight out of a pocket, and said, "Come on, have a look under the hood with me. I might have some questions."

Brenchlow grimaced, sensing that something wasn't right. Moving slowly, as if his legs had become very heavy, he climbed with great reluctance out of the cab and shuffled around to the front of the truck to stand next to the man looking at the motor.

CHAPTER FOURTEEN

On the church walkway after Ronnie's funeral service, Candy Brenchlow watched people approach Helen, who was Ronnie's mother, and her husband Neil's first wife, to offer their condolences. Mostly they were Neil's friends and business associates. Neil stood surrounded by people. There was a group standing apart, maybe a dozen, mostly males, who would have been Ronnie's friends. A couple of them wore sports jackets with buttons puckered across the stomach. Fifteen more pounds on the gut since the last time they wore those, she thought. She'd never met any of them. Only one man from the group had the tact to walk across to Helen and say a few words.

She and Helen had never met, but Candy had a pretty good idea Helen knew who she was. It wouldn't be right not to say something, and she was curious. She waited until most of the guests at the service were gone.

"I wanted to tell you I'm very sorry about Ronnie."

"Thank you for saying that," said Helen.

"I can't imagine losing my daughter. I guess you know who I am."

"Oh yes. You're the arm candy."

"It's hard not to make that joke. Actually, I'm flattered anybody would still call me that."

"Don't be hard on yourself. You haven't lost your looks."

"I didn't know Ronnie that well. He hardly ever came around the place."

"You didn't miss much. I'm grieving because he's my baby who came out of my body. How I loved him when he was a ten-month-old baby and smiled at me with his big, lovely smile." She pressed her lips together and gave a single sniffle. "You never forget that. But adolescence wasn't kind to him or me. He went from remote to hostile to smartass. Raising a kid like him is the most thankless job on earth. You probably think I'm a jerk dumping on my child when he's dead."

"Oh," said Candy, not sure what to say. "Kids can be a disappointment to their parents. I probably was."

"Could I have been a good mom? If you have only one and they don't turn out well, you'll always wonder."

Candy's daughter, Anna, at age twenty, had turned out well enough. She was an aspiring actress who stayed in touch with her parents and had gotten through her teens without drug problems Candy knew about or getting into trouble with the school administration or police. Candy didn't take credit for her daughter's life. She had probably been neither a better nor worse mother than Helen. Just luckier.

"So how are things with you?" Helen continued. "How's Neil? How's it going with the two of you? If you don't mind me asking."

"Not at all. Neil's Neil. We're all right. I kind of stay out of his way."

"He still get it up okay?"

"With a pill and a little help. He's sixty-eight, remember. The inspiration doesn't come as often as it used to. I think he's got a lot on his mind these days."

"That doesn't surprise me. He talk to you much about his business?"

"Never did. He gripes about having to travel around so much."

"You interested in getting together sometime and having a drink?"

Candy looked at her in surprise. "Sure, I'd like that. I thought you wouldn't want to have anything to do with me."

"He didn't know you before we got divorced, am I right?"

"No, you were out of the picture when we met."

"So it's not like you were fucking him while we were married. I got nothing against you. You're about exactly what I thought he'd end up with. Why don't you give me your number?"

Helen and Candy met for that drink.

"I wanted to ask," said Helen. "How's Neil handling Ronnie's death?"

"Hit him pretty hard, though he doesn't talk about it. He's drawn into a shell. Talks to me in two-word sentences since it happened."

"He always hoped Ronnie would do something."

Candy nodded. "When we were dating, I know he tried to set Ronnie up with a construction business. Lined up some jobs for him, but Ronnie just hired his slacker buddies. The clients didn't accept the finished work."

"That's Ronnie. So dating. How long did that go on?"

The question didn't sound as snarky as it could have. She decided Helen was simply curious.

"A few months. He can be charming, you know. You think I was a gold digger?"

"Were you?"

"I did like him. I wasn't going to marry somebody without money."

"You got money of your own out of it?"

Candy looked at Helen a moment, wondering where the conversation was going.

"You mean is there money in my own name?"

Helen nodded.

"I guess not really. I spend what I want. I prefer to buy good things. Good quality antique furniture, things that make me feel comfortable. He's asked me about a few things I've bought, but not to complain. Just to let me know he's paying attention. I'd expect that of a banker."

"Can I give you some advice?"

"Sure."

"I'm with the chamber of commerce now, but I still work in banking. You don't know much about his business, but I do. We were pretty much partners when we were married. I've been hearing things. If I were you, I'd lay my hands on everything I can and get it out."

"Are you saying bankruptcy? What kind of things are you hearing?"

"Honey, this isn't bankruptcy we're talking about. There's some new folks with the regulators that are asking questions about some cozy deals Neil and his buddies arranged over the years. I'm betting there's going to be an investigation. I can tell you there are things there for the investigators to find. We could be talking jail time."

"Shit," said Candy.

"No shit. So you don't know about my arrangement with Neil?"

"What's that?"

"I worked at the bank, that's how I met Neil. When we got married, I started helping him. Banks have a process culture. Neil's got a decent head for numbers, but I'm the one who understands how banks work. I'm a process junkie. I showed him how to move money around until it became invisible. I set up offshore accounts for him. So when he started screwing around with the first of his little sweeties, I got to thinking. In the beginning I thought I could deal with it, as long as he came home most of the time. I liked the boat and the nice things. Like you do. But then I decided, no. It was pride, really. I couldn't stand people thinking I was naïve. So we had a little talk. He would give me a divorce, and an annual under-the-table payment. We both knew if I came after his assets, it would blow everything up."

"I had no idea," said Candy.

"There's a construction company shell that buys materials from a couple manufacturing companies he owns with grossly inflated markups. And there's a lucrative business down in the woods in Shelton he wouldn't want anybody knowing about. So I get a generous enough informal alimony, and I keep my mouth shut. But I think those payments are going away."

"Good God," said Candy.

"Yes. So I want to ask. You have any interest in partnering up with me and see if we can't lay our hands on some of that invisible money before it disappears?"

Candy glanced at her wrist, not to see the time, but to appreciate for a second or two the handsome Breguet watch—$45,000. She was quite fond of the watch. It represented other things, the antique furniture and good shoes that she liked.

"What would you want me to do?" she asked.

"I'm going to have you come down to the office. Gal I work with can show you how to get stuff off a computer. Like Neil's."

CHAPTER FIFTEEN

"You up to talking a little?" asked the man sitting beside his bed. Sam must have been sleeping. He let the room come into focus.

"I think so," he said.

"How are you feeling?"

"Give me a minute."

"Take your time. We need to talk about what happened."

"Are you . . . ?"

"Detective McCord, Port Teresa police. These men who were hitting you. You know any of them?"

Sam lay still a moment. He tried to clear his head, fill in the spacious blanks with chunks of memory. He knew he needed to be careful about what he said.

"It's fuzzy. I don't think so."

"That bar, the Spruce, you're not a regular. Bartender hadn't seen you before. What brought you there?"

"I write sports for the *News*. Somebody called the paper and said they wanted to meet the sports guy there, talk about reorganizing the city softball tournament."

"You get a name?"

"No."

"Know any of them?"

"They didn't exactly introduce themselves. There was a Bob. Sorry, not much good with names."

"Mr. Troshin, I see you were up for assault here year or so ago. Is that something that happens to you, getting into fights?"

What should he say? He didn't want to get caught lying, but he didn't want to say more than he had to. "I was in the wrong place, and things happened around me. You can check, the charges were dropped," said Sam.

"But not five years ago. Eighteen months for assault. Doesn't seem like a coincidence you get yourself into another fight."

"We were talking baseball, and they just jumped me. Maybe the bartender saw something."

"We're talking to him. Mr. Troshin, if we find there's something going on here you're not telling us, you could end up with another assault. For a felon with a record, that would not be good."

For the first time in their conversation, Sam turned his head enough to look directly at the detective. Gray hair cut short, in his fifties probably, big solid man, pale-blue eyes that could stare without expression at someone for minutes at a time without blinking. Waiting for the person across from him to become so uncomfortable he would say something, anything. The expressionless expression of a man who knew most of what he was being told was lies.

Sam stopped himself from saying anything further. He knew the medication was making his brain fuzzy. Would it be obvious he wasn't telling the whole story? Go really slow, he thought. This guy is waiting to pounce.

"We were just talking sports. All friendly. Maybe somebody in there saw it."

The detective looked at him in a way that conveyed his skepticism. Maybe cops always looked at people that way.

"I'm leaving you my card. Anything clears up, you call, all right? I'll probably check in with you again."

He stared at the card and let his eyes come into focus. Detective M. McCord.

"Anything comes back I'll sure let you know."

"Good. You do that."

If the detective had done enough homework to discover he'd knocked down two of the men waiting at the bar a few nights previous and asked him if there was a connection, he would have told him. But he didn't want Outside involved. This detective was ready to make him responsible for what happened because he had a record. He'd be courteous, but he was done talking.

He knew from experience that the numb sensation that left him feeling he was floating in the bed would be replaced with pain before long. The emergency doc released him the next day. The staff insisted on wheeling him to the exit in a chair, though he could have walked just fine. Pretty much. Molly from the paper was there to give him a ride to his apartment.

He let her hold his arm climbing the stairs to his unit. He could manage okay on the flat, but stairs were tricky, and the place didn't have an elevator.

"Is there food here?" she asked, and opened the refrigerator. Two frozen Swanson tuna noodle casseroles, leftover rotisserie chicken in a Safeway package, a carton of orange juice, a carton of milk, a half a package of bacon.

"Good God," she said. "I'll go shop. Back in half an hour."

"I'll be fine," he said.

"You're concussed if you think you'll be fine with that," she said, waving at the refrigerator. "You're going to be here awhile, mister."

Molly served as the city editor at the paper. She wasn't Sam's boss, but he saw a lot more of her than he did of the editor. She made suggestions, and he usually took them. She was a thin, homely young woman, with an overbite and narrow receding chin, though her eyes were vivid brown and long-lashed, striking even without makeup. She was a hard worker and seemed to have found a good journalist's balance between skepticism and cynicism.

When she was gone, he turned on the television and sat down. As he anticipated, the dull ache was becoming less dull. He was beginning to hurt like the day after the game with the Idaho Vandals, when he spent the afternoon tackling a 240 pound running back who his teammates channeled in his direction rather than trying to tackle themselves. His left forearm was broken and in a soft cast, he had a blackening bruise on his thigh that looked like a map of Africa, and a ringing in his ears came and went. His memory of what had happened was hazy, though not as hazy as he had let the cop think. He knew when he recognized Ronnie Brenchlow in the group at the bar that talking about softball wasn't the agenda. More like hardball. When they were hitting him, they'd suddenly stopped though and disappeared. Zoey, the woman from the book group he was meeting, must have been waiting behind the tavern. She saw what was happening, and whatever she did brought a quick end to the beating. He'd missed a meeting of the book group while he was in the hospital. He'd be at the next one and ask her what the hell she'd done.

He didn't like taking pain pills for any extended period. The story of Alonzo Mourning, the Miami Heat basketball center who took ibuprofen before every game and needed a kidney transplant by the time he was forty, had made an impression. But whatever they'd given him that morning was wearing off. He poured a glass of orange juice, took two Vicodin, and waited for Molly to come back with too much food.

He passed the next two days reading through the magazines Molly had brought and watching movies on cable. He wished there were games on the TV during the weekdays. Watching sports was his refuge. His routine was to let the games draw him in and for a few hours was free from the weight of his memories. Football games were good, basketball games, college games more engaging that the pros, hockey, baseball less so. Baseball depended too much on the nattering of the announcers to hold his attention. His ability to let himself be absorbed in the moment of a game was probably why he'd become a decent sportswriter. One unexpected distraction was a thick history of WWII Molly had dropped off, which he began reading and found engrossing. He tried to imagine being a soldier in a war. What would it be like marching forward with a group of men knowing some of you would be shot dead or blown to red meat before the day was over?

On Saturday he felt well enough to drive to the college and sit in on the book group meeting. He told the school office he would be back to his custodial duties on Monday.

As he walked into the classroom, he wondered whether a weekly book discussion had much value. The way Leah talked about it, he knew she wasn't expecting miracles. Maybe she and the judge thought doing anything was better than ignoring the lives of young people caught up in the meshes of the system. The two girls, Alison and Zoey, he could tell, thought about what they were reading and could talk about it. But they were both intelligent. He didn't think they were typical of the whores and druggies in the jails.

"My God," Leah exclaimed when she saw him. "What happened to you?"

"Didn't watch where I was going," he said.

She looked at him expectantly, but he just shrugged and didn't explain further.

The assignment for today, she briefed him, had been to write an essay. Write about a time of innocence, she'd asked them. When everyone was in their seats, she asked Alison, the teenager, to read what she'd written. The girl stared stone-faced at her notebook, then began to read. Slowly at first, but after a few sentences more forcefully, as if she was driving the words through her teeth. She had written about how the game in *The Hunger Games* was like life—complicated rules that made no sense, or changed if you tried to take advantage of them, the requirement to fight if you wanted even a chance to survive. She spoke as if the world of Katniss was real. What's she been through, Sam wondered, to see things that way at her age. The age his daughter had been.

When the older guy, Barrett, began talking, he saw Leah's eyebrows lift with surprise. The man had rarely said more than two sentences in a row at the earlier sessions. Squinting at his pages, he began talking about fishing with his older brother in the Feather River in California. The brother was a fly purist who criticized Barrett for being a meat fisherman. Barrett described turning over stones in the river and peeling off caddis larva for bait, and he said he was the one who provided most of the trout for the dinner they fried over a fire that evening.

"Bait fishin's easy," Gary interjected. "Probably couldn't tie on a fly if you wanted."

Barrett looked down at the floor. Could be true. Sam had done a little fly fishing and knew tying a trout fly to a leader tip required some dexterity. What a jerk this guy is. Sam looked at Barrett with admiration. He liked fly fishing but would have been at a loss to explain why he enjoyed it beyond the soothing sensation of water flowing around his legs. Write about a time of innocence, Leah had told Barrett, and he'd found it.

Everyone had a time of innocence, he thought. Did it do any good to recall it? Things happened, and you weren't innocent anymore.

But writing about it, look at the guy, Barrett; he'd come to life. Sam's English-major girlfriend in college tried to convince him it was good to write down and express what you were feeling. Maybe it worked for some people.

Gary read a brief page of sentence fragments about the high-school football team he'd played on. No insights, just the scores. The rest of the session Gary watched the others with a patronizing grin. But he wasn't making the snide smartassed comments Sam remembered from the earlier session.

The painkillers in his system gave Sam the sensation that the faces he was seeing and the mouths moving were detached from the voices he was hearing. When Zoey spoke he tried to concentrate on the sound of her voice. Her essay was a tribute to a girl she'd hired to work at her booth at community fairs last summer. The girl was beautiful, gracious, and very tall. She was a volleyball player, the best-known athlete in town. She was also a great salesperson because she learned about the products and could answer questions but never pushed. People bought things because they liked listening to her.

So she had hired Outside to help her during the summer. As she listened to Zoey describing Outside, he closed his eyes so he could concentrate on the sound and inflection of her voice. Lying in the dirt behind the bar, that was her he had seen. That was her voice that said help was coming.

When the session was over, Leah handed Sam a manila envelope.

"You asked me to write something up about the group," she said. "Won't hurt my feelings if you don't use it."

"No, I appreciate it," he said.

"My husband's in TV. I thought this might be a good community news story, but he wasn't interested."

"What's he do in TV?"

"Six thirty anchor. Scott Sound, you've probably seen him."

"Oh, sure," said Sam. "So that's your husband."

"Yup."

Scott Sound. He played ball sometimes in the Tuesday evening pickup basketball game Sam had found. Took too many shots, didn't pass the ball enough. Handsome, nice thick hair, well-modulated voice, affable manner on the air. On the ball court, he snarled a curse when he missed a shot but otherwise was brusque and almost affectless, as if he was saving any effort to communicate for the camera.

Leah looked like she wanted to talk more. Sam told her he needed to catch Zoey before she left.

Sam remembered Zoey and the younger girl leaving together after the previous book sessions. This time he saw Zoey standing alone inside the glass doors, looking out.

"I recognized the girl you were describing, the one you hired. That's Outside, isn't it?"

"You mean Kirstin?"

"Yeah, Kirstin Kelly. She's a fantastic volleyball player. I've written a couple of stories about her. At the school they call her Outside. It's her position."

"I didn't know about the nickname. I did know she was a volleyball star, though. That's why she wanted a weekend job, so she could train during the week. I was lucky to get her. You know her as an athlete. I just know her as a person. You could probably tell, I really like her."

"I do too; I really admire her," said Sam. "That was you that saved my ass, wasn't it?"

She turned and looked at him but didn't speak.

"What'd you do? They were beating on me, then they were gone."

"I saw them hitting you with the bat. I had a shotgun and let off a round."

Sam shook his head as if he was having a hard time believing what she was saying. "Jesus," he said, "a shotgun. You usually carry a shotgun in your truck?"

"No," she said, "that was just luck. It was trade goods. I'd just bought it from a guy."

"Sorry, I guess I lost my interest in that baseball glove. I won't be catching any balls for a while. I owe you big-time. Can I buy you dinner or something?"

"Maybe," she said. She smiled, but the smile didn't last. He realized she had been staring out the door with a hard frown on her face, only half focused on their conversation.

"Put my number in your phone," he said. "Dinner, okay?"

She nodded and entered the number he gave her. He thanked her again and headed for the parking lot.

When he got back to the editorial room, he looked over what Leah had written. She was a good writer. Her main point seemed to be that reading stories gave the parolees a chance to use their imagination to dip into the lives of people who were different from them and yet like them. He knew how people with jail histories could be both street savvy and lacking in self-awareness.

Did self-awareness lead to reform? What had she said to

the slope-shouldered jerk in the group? Only you can reform yourself. Or was "reform" just a word left over from childhood? Reform school, the juvie was called.

Did he believe that? Did she believe that? Maybe she was being a typical teacher, putting the best spin on what she was doing. A young teacher trying to keep her idealism alive. He hoped she would succeed.

CHAPTER SIXTEEN

"So how did you get into sportswriting?" Zoey had asked him while they sat in her pickup after rolling Gary's body down a twilit hillside.

Sam's older brother Nolan played football. He was good in spite of whatever screwing around he was doing with drugs because he was big enough, fast for his size, and had a mean streak. He expected Sam to play, so Sam did.

The first time Sam tackled a running back in a high-school game, he needed a moment before he could regain his feet, shaken to the core. He'd tackled teammates in scrimmages, but those were drills. In the two seconds of clarity as blockers cleared a path between Sam and the fullback, Sam saw the back, who outweighed him by twenty pounds, make the decision not to juke but to run over him. The back compressed himself for contact, and Sam bent and drove at the runner's middle.

Christ, he said to himself as he sat clutching his helmet on the bench. That hurt. Nolan and other guys talked about how they loved to hit. Either they were short a few nerve endings, or they were overtaken by some kind of fury that distanced them from the pain the way a half bottle of bourbon did, a form of painkilling Sam had recently experienced with Nolan's friends.

The defensive coach came by and punched a fist on Sam's shoulder pad. "Nice stop, Troshin," he said. Maybe that was it, pride. Or was it not wanting to disappoint expectations? He had, after all, dropped the runner in his tracks. It was an equation. If you hurt, but the other guy hurt a little more, the plus was on your side. The plus was the glory, or the satisfaction, or whatever it was exactly. He would have to think about that.

He worked out at the school's tryouts day. One of the Division I coaches rating players told him he needed to either add ten pounds or knock two tenths off his forty-yard dash. He would never have Nolan's size. But at six feet and 190, he was fast enough to play safety at the Division II level, and he picked up a modest scholarship at Central State.

Big school or small, people paid attention to the football players. There was one set of cute girls, he noticed, who studied in the library in Spellman Hall, where the prelaw students did their homework. Not hard to figure what was going on there. Landing a guy with a good probability of a healthy income. Not concerned at this point he would also have good divorce skills. Another set of cute girls liked being around the football players. Sam didn't need much in the way of social finesse to meet them. Flash a grin at one, and she would come over and talk. He liked that he could have sex with a girl and not worry she'd start planning for a family. The prelaw guys in Spellman probably had a little more hinting along those lines to deal with. In fact, there were girls who just wanted to brag they'd fucked a football player and that was it. He compared notes with a couple of teammates and found one chick who'd done the whole starting defense, him included. Which was surprising, considering the offense was where the glamor was. Maybe she'd done them the season before.

In his junior year, he hooked up with Penny, an English major who wrote for the school paper. She persuaded him to write an article for the paper about playing football, covering the game from a player's point of view. He objected that it would look like a big ego trip. Penny said, "Okay, talk a little about yourself but mostly about other players."

The editor liked the story and asked Sam for more. "What do you know," the faculty advisor said. "A jock who can write a complete declarative sentence."

The town paper picked up a couple of his stories. By the time he graduated he had a portfolio of stories, and the portfolio got him a job at the sports desk of *The Spokesman Review* in Spokane.

Sportswriting was easy for Sam. You named the winner and picked a couple of game highlights, then unfolded the event chronologically with the lesser highlights. With bios, you described the guy's skills and let him talk about how he got to where he was. This usually involved either hard work and an influential mentor, or overcoming hardships. Sports-page editors were never bothered by the formulas you could use over and over.

He settled into a routine of drinking after work with the unmarried sportswriters, playing pickup basketball to stay in shape and, during the football season, spending home-game weekends in Pullman covering the Washington State games. He had relationships that lasted from a few months to nearly a year and ended in a similar way. Sometimes the word was used, and sometimes it wasn't, but the women were looking for commitment. He didn't understand why a man and a woman who had a good sex life, enjoyed the time they spent together, and took some interest in one another's lives couldn't have a stable relationship. He felt he was learning a universal principle, that relations between the sexes weren't so much unstable as they couldn't remain static. In life, today was not the same as yesterday. Marriage was something other people did, mostly unsuccessfully.

CHAPTER SEVENTEEN

Gary McCord's body was discovered sooner than Zoey had hoped by someone walking with a dog. She watched the TV news coverage. The video angled downward from what must be almost exactly the spot she and Sam had dragged Gary's body over the railing. Two men in dark-blue coveralls and white gloves prodded through the brush. She tensed. She was getting a glimpse of a systematic, professional process. Had she overlooked something? She calmed herself and walked in her memory through each step they'd taken. She'd run a flashlight along the roadside when they were done. No receipt spilled out of a pocket, no Vibram sole indentations in the dirt. The investigators here weren't Nick and Sarah; they weren't going to perform any CSI magic. But they could know more than they were saying. She was just going to have to wait.

The next Saturday Leah told the class in a subdued voice about Gary's death. Barrett and Denton hadn't known. The discussion had an odd solemnity, as if the death of a member, even if he was someone nobody liked, gave the discussion a weight it hadn't had before. Zoey watched Alison carefully for signs of nervousness or other reactions to what had happened. The girl spoke in a low voice that mirrored Leah's lead. She's handling it, Zoey thought. I'm handling it.

As they were wrapping up their discussion, someone from the office put her head in the room and said there was a police officer who wanted to talk to Zoey and Alison.

"Stay cool," said Zoey as they went to the door. "Let me talk."

The officer was dressed in a tie and sports jacket. He was big, with a once-square jaw rounding off with flesh. Zoey took a quick look at his hands. Big, heavy knuckles. Probably hit a few people in his day.

"You heard about Gary McCord," said the officer. "We're talking to people who knew him. He was in your reading group. I understand he had a relationship with one of you."

Alison and Zoey looked at one another.

"Yeah," said Zoey after a long second.

"You?"

"Yeah."

"Your name is?"

"Zoey Franco."

He looked at Alison. "You can go."

Alison looked at Zoey. Zoey made a quick gesture with her head. Alison turned and hurried away.

"Okay, Zoey, let's go out where we got some privacy. We can sit in the car."

Zoey didn't like sitting in the cop car. Ugly, computer on a swivel mount, shotgun in a bracket against the dash, Plexiglas behind the front seats. Cheap, thick plastic seat covers. Probably got puked on. Stale smell, BO, like nobody ever drove with a window open. Could cops smell their own cars?

"So you and Gary," he said. His iron-gray hair was trimmed short. A thick lower lip drew down to one side when he talked. "How long were you seeing him?"

"I don't know, maybe a month, little after the book group started."

"You didn't know him before the group?"

"No."

"How much you see of each other?"

She shrugged. "You know, here and there, after the group mostly. Not really what you call dating. Just hung out."

"Hung out where?"

"Oh, like I say, here and there. The school, drive around some."

"So you had sex where?"

Oh, are we right to that? she thought. I knew it. This asshole's his dad.

"Like I said, here and there. In the car. We'd go park."

"When is the last time you were with him?"

She thought ahead, working out what to say to the questions she knew he'd ask.

"Must have been here. We hung out after class, had some lunch. Didn't hear anything, then he wasn't at the next meeting. Then I heard about him being found."

"Did that bother you?"

"What do you mean? Of course it did. It was shocking. Why would somebody do that to him?"

"You in love with him?"

Zoey shrugged again and made a "whatever" wave of her hand. "I liked him. He was funny. We just hung out. That was all."

"So that's what you did, you hung out?"

"Yeah."

"Yeah. Okay. The thing is, Gary's a guy who never really had a girlfriend. He had some problems there. All of a sudden, you're there, he gets a little worked up, and he's dead. Just like that. Here's what I think, Zoey. I think there's more you need to be telling me. Looks like you're the last person to see him. I'm pretty sure you have more of an idea what happened than what you're telling me. You need to tell me about it."

Wonder why we're doing this in the car, she thought. This prick would rather be staring me down across a desk.

"I'd like to give you a couple of days to think about it. Go over what you remember in detail. Then I'd like you to tell me what happened. Think about your life in general, where it's going from here. You're down for sale of a controlled substance. You're skating close to being down for more controlled substances. There's a risk things could be found in your vehicle, isn't there? There probably won't be any easy book-group paroles next time. Think about it. Whatever happened is probably not as bad as what you could be doing next. You understand what I'm saying?"

"What are you hassling me for? I didn't do anything. I don't know anything."

"I don't think that's true. You had a whole lot of questions for Bob Riddell about Gary, didn't you? Picked his brain. Why'd you do that?"

It was true. After looking through the records Dana had provided, she'd located a couple of individuals listed as Gary's associates. She did pick their brains, trying to learn something that would give her some leverage with Gary. Blackmail him into leaving Alison alone. She was still working on it when Alison had shot him. The day after Gary's death, she had sent a text to Dana, thanking her again and telling her that due to the unexpected passing of the person she was interested in, there was no longer a need to gather information about him. She didn't want Dana finding Gary's name in the newspaper and wondering if there was a connection between the death and the research she'd done for Zoey.

"Sure, I talked to him. Isn't that normal, to be curious about a guy you're hanging with? You're his dad, aren't you?"

"What did he tell you about that?"

"Said you were a cop. That's all."

"Yeah, Gary was my kid. He had some issues, but he was my kid, and I'm going to find whoever killed him. You are going to help me. All right, we're done for now. I've got your cell number. Answer it when I call. And don't leave, because that would tell me you don't want to talk to me."

Prick, she murmured to herself. Father and son alike. She was relieved he hadn't pushed her harder. A little surprised he was giving her time to put a story together. Her idea of police interrogation was they pushed you fast so you couldn't think clearly. She thought she'd done okay, not given him anything that could be verified by witnesses. She'd work up a good story about that last day, put some details in like she'd struggled to recall everything. Maybe she could get some information out of him. Who else in Gary's life didn't like him? Had they figured out it was an arrow? She needed to have Alison get rid of the bow.

And she wanted a plan B in case he didn't believe her and came after her with a phony drug charge. She had no doubt he could do it. She'd get out on the network and see if she could find anyone who knew anything interesting about Officer Mac McCord.

CHAPTER EIGHTEEN

The connection of Ronnie Brenchlow's death in a fiery truck accident with events from thirty years earlier in Port Teresa's history may never have been discovered if Sam Troshin hadn't been asked to cover the Fifth Annual Port Teresa Rotary Club Car Show.

Sam wasn't sure why covering the local car show fell to the sportswriter. He'd never been much into the car culture. But Molly knew he ritually washed his Toyota two-seater every weekend, and probably assumed he was more of an enthusiast than he was. He was glad enough for the work. He asked a pub friend, Nick, to go with him. Nick did know about vintage cars. He owned a 1966 Jaguar, an E-Type with an edgy exhaust note and a nicely buffed British racing green finish. Nick could tell him what he was looking at.

Rotary volunteers began lining up the cars on the park lawn at seven. By ten o'clock, when the show officially opened to the public, there must have been two hundred cars in rows along the grass. Vendor tables and awnings were set up next to the sidewalk selling sports drinks, novelty key fobs, and car-themed

T-shirts. Owners gave their vehicles a final dusting with boar's-hair brushes or microfiber towels.

"What you have here is Porsches and Lamborghinis from the tech guys in Seattle, the old guys with the muscle cars and hot rods, and the vintage sports car guys."

"Beer guys and wine guys," said Sam.

"Craft beer, Bud, and Willamette Valley Pinot would cover it."

"Your Jag is very cool," said Sam. "I'll have the photographer get a shot."

Sam was drawn to a pickup in the center of the park. Highlights in the maroon finish glowed in the midmorning sun. The chrome trim looked fresh out of the plating bath. Under the open hood, which had been modified to swing forward, a large acrylic photo had been placed. The photo was an enlargement of a black and white shot of two girls, maybe eight and ten. Lettering above the picture read "Brian's Girls Love Dad's F-100." The owner, a tall, lean man in his sixties, was talking to three or four people, gesturing toward the sign.

"Nice truck, huh," said Nick. "That's Brian Porter. Brings it to all the shows."

"What's with the photo?" Sam asked.

"The older daughter, that's her over there in the red jacket at the coffee stand. The younger one was raped and killed when she was sixteen. Must be twenty-five years ago. What he tells people is the two girls loved the pickup. They'd drive it around the farm with the older one steering and shifting and the younger one sitting on the floor working the pedals. The truck's his memorial. Taught himself painting, machining, welding, everything. Hundreds of hours he put into learning the skills and doing the work, like his therapy."

Sam looked away. One way to memorialize a dead daughter. Not a bad one. He couldn't have done something like that. He didn't know enough about Ella's life.

"Sam?"

"Maybe there's a story there," said Sam.

"Somebody from the paper wanted to do Porter's story a few years ago. He asked them not to."

"Old pickups are popular."

"I guess if you grew up rural, that's what you remember from being eighteen," said Nick. "Speaking of pickups, here's a story for you. Remember the truck crash, fire, a week or so back? A guy named Brenchlow."

"Yeah," said Sam. "I know who he is."

"So, the truck he was driving? A nice old Ford F-100, lot like this one. That exact same truck was in another crash and fire, twenty-five, thirty years ago. Big to-do. The girl the truck belonged to said she was raped after the prom, truck was torched by the guys that did it, with her in it. She survived. Here's the thing I don't think anybody caught. Brenchlow crashed same road, same exact curve as the where the girl went off. We're talking in the exact same truck, restored. And Brenchlow? One of the accused rapists. You believe that? Right out of Stephen King."

Sam didn't include Brian Porter's story in the piece on the car show he turned in the next day, but he thought about it. Teenage girls were so fucking vulnerable. Porter's daughter, Alison from the book group, the high-school grad Nick told him about who owned the pickup. Ella. Fathers want to believe they can keep their kids safe, but they can't. Was that all you could do, find some way to grieve that kept your hands busy and try not to spend your nights imagining what your child's final minutes must have been like?

He couldn't let himself think about any of this. He was doing all right, getting through his nights better than he used to. The night job at the school had turned out to be a good thing. If he went to bed tired at two and made himself get up at seven thirty, he could get through most of his nights without meds. During the day the goal was to stay occupied. He watched games, wrote sports stories, played pickup basketball, talked sports over a beer.

He should have let Porter's story go, and not given any more thought to the coincidence of Ronnie Brenchlow's death. But a morbid curiosity about the death of the guy who'd tried to kill him with a baseball bat didn't go away. He decided to spend some time scanning old issues of the paper in the microfiche files and learning what he could about the two rapes Nick told him about.

When he worked for the metropolitan daily and people asked him what he did, he said he was a sportswriter for the *Review*. Now when they asked him, not that anyone asked very often, he didn't call himself anything. He just said he covered sports for the *North Coast News*. What he definitely was was a custodian. He had specific duties, performed at specific times, and no one else did them unless he swapped times with Horacio. But when he was sitting at his desk in the newsroom not working on anything, was he a newspaperman? He didn't have to be there. He wasn't being paid to be there. He was paid for his stories. But they'd given him a desk. He heard that when they took your desk in the newsroom away and made you work at a table, you were on your way out.

He'd never used the room they called the library, where back issues of the paper had been microfiched and stored. Neither did anyone else, judging from the dust on the tops of the gray metal file cabinets.

The rape stories, he guessed, would make the front page. He'd only have to scan front pages.

He worked his way through three months' worth of microfiche pages before the needlepoints of an incipient headache began to push into the backs of his eyeballs. It took him two afternoons before he came to the story of the death of Porter's daughter. He read backward from the conviction of the rapist, an ugly man with a heavy-jowled, brutal face who lived in the area, to the police investigation, involving blood spatter and a tracking dog, and finally to the initial discovery of the girl's body.

He experienced a welling of grief. It was easy to imagine the anguish of the man he'd seen at the car show. Porter wasn't trying to blank the memory of his daughter's death out of his mind. By showing the truck and the photo of his daughter, he was trying to share the memory of her with others, a way to keep the memory alive. Accepting his pain.

He shook his head to bring his attention back to the present. He threaded the next reel and pushed the back button. The reel squeaked, maybe a little WD-40 needed, carefully applied so it didn't contaminate the film. He came to the first story about the acquittal of three high-school boys at the end of a rape trial three years before the Porter girl's story. He did a quick scanning scroll back, skipping from Monday to Monday, until he found the first articles because he wanted to read the story chronologically from the beginning. The trial lasted a full week. He began with the alleged rape and the truck fire. The event took place the night of the Port Teresa high-school prom. Police found Claire Draghici, a graduating senior with top grades, badly burned near the wreckage of her pickup. When she had recovered enough to talk, she said she had been raped by three schoolmates, who had pushed her truck off the road and set fire to it.

The trial, which began two months after the event, filled the front pages. The girl claimed she had been a virgin. The attorney for the accused boys said there had been consensual sex, and that she had driven away afterward in the truck. The critical testimony seemed to be a man a few years older who said Claire was a well-known party girl with whom he'd had casual sex a couple of times.

The jury acquitted the three boys.

Now that he was learning to think like a reporter, Sam picked up a couple of phrases in the coverage that suggested the reporter accepted the view that Claire had indeed been a party girl.

The reporter with the byline on the trial coverage was Dexter Preedy. This must have been five years or so before he became the editor.

Ronald Brenchlow was one of the three boys accused. Sam read the names of the other two boys several times before a second name jumped off the microfiche screen. Carl Tillis.

Carl Tillis was Setter's dad.

Two days before Sam began his search of the archives, Outside and Setter had come looking for him at his desk at the paper. Outside looked serious, Setter distraught.

"Can you help us?" Outside asked. "Kelsey's dad disappeared."

"He left a note," said Setter. "He said he had to leave for a while. I called my uncle and my mom. They don't know anything. Something's wrong."

"How do you think I can help?"

"You're a reporter," said Outside. "You know how to find things out."

"I'm a sports writer," he said. "Have you talked to his friends? Where he works?"

Setter's face was compressed by the effort of holding back tears. "He doesn't have many friends. The guys he works with, I guess."

"You want me to talk to them?"

"Would you? You'd be more clearheaded than me. Oh my God, thank you."

"You go to the police?"

"We were just there," said Outside. "They let us talk to a detective. We showed him the note. He said it was probably some personal issue. He said it happens a lot. All he did was take the name and told us to call if we learned anything more. He wasn't very helpful. But something's wrong, Sam."

"Okay," he said. "How about if I go over to where he works in the morning and talk to people?"

Outside gave him a thankful smile.

He doubted he would be much help. He knew nothing about Carl Tillis except that his daughter said he didn't have many friends.

Now he knew something more about Carl Tillis. He refiled the microfiche reel and went in search of the editor.

Until a few months ago, Dex Preedy would spend time wandering through the newsroom talking with staff about their stories. But recently he'd become almost invisible, sitting in his office with the door closed. Sam asked Molly if there were maybe health issues. Molly said nothing she knew about. Sam overcame a moment of reluctance and tapped on the door of Preedy's office.

"Yeah!"

Sam put his head in the door.

"You remember much about the Claire Draghici rape trial, thirty years ago?" he asked. "You covered it."

Preedy looked up from what he was reading and glared at Sam over the top of his glasses. His jowly face was almost as red as his polka-dot bow-tie.

"Why?"

"You think maybe they raped her and got off?"

"Why are you asking me?"

"You know that truck Ronnie Brenchlow was driving when he crashed and burned a week ago? That's the exact same truck the girl was driving. Somebody must have restored it. Brenchlow must have bought it. I got curious and looked up the story."

"You got curious. What does that mean?"

"The car show last weekend. Somebody told me about the truck and the old case. They said Brenchlow's truck crashed at the same curve where the girl crashed. Doesn't that seem just too much for coincidence?"

Preedy's mouth pulled back in a snarl. Sam thought he was going to tell him to fuck off, stop wasting his time, and go cover the track meet coming up. Then Preedy's already hunched shoulders drooped further. He swiveled his chair, searched for a moment in the file drawer behind him, and pulled out a manila folder. He handed Sam a newspaper clipping.

"Obit from a Florida paper. We ran it a month ago. You wouldn't have noticed. Came in the mail, no idea who sent it. Addressed to me personally, not the paper."

"What am I looking at?" Sam asked.

"Go back to your desk and read it, for Christ sakes."

The obit was for a man named Ray Westingale who had died in a fire in trailer camp near Tampa. He'd worked construction jobs after moving to Florida twenty years earlier. He had family in Washington State, where he'd grown up.

Now Sam knew what he was looking at. Ray Westingale. Alleged rapist number two. Burned to death a month ago in a fire. Alleged rapist number one, Ronnie Brenchlow, burned to death two weeks ago in a very peculiar truck fire. Alleged rapist number three, Carl Tillis, disappeared. Maybe that was why Tillis was gone. Maybe he'd read about Brenchlow's death and was frightened that after thirty years Claire Draghici had come back to avenge herself.

Tillis differed from Ronnie Brenchlow because he had a daughter who cared about him. She cared about him, and he had abandoned her.

Abandoning your child. Sam knew what that felt like.

CHAPTER NINETEEN

In the morning Sam drove to the Peninsula Salvage Yard, where Carl Tillis worked.

"He hasn't come in for a couple days," said the woman at the counter. The reception area was much tidier and more finished that he expected at a junk-yard. The counter was ornate walnut, maybe a bar-top salvaged from a nineteenth-century saloon. Framed photos on the wall featured grinning crews of mechanics surrounding a stock car sponsored by the business.

"Anybody I can talk to, a friend, maybe somebody heard something about where he's gone?"

"He works with Jules out at the car compactor. You can go ask him. Here, wear a hard hat if you're going out there."

Sam thanked the woman, who had a pretty face and Russian accent. She pointed him in the direction of the car compactor.

The compactor was an open-faced steel box the size of a freight railcar. The big diesel that drove the compactor's hydraulics throbbed like a tugboat motor. He watched as the massive steel top of the compactor descended on an SUV in the box. The SUV folded like a toy, metal popping and screeching until it was a crumpled mass three feet thick. The lid stopped, reversed, and rose to the top of the framework. The operator stepped away from the control panel and headed toward a forklift.

"You Jules?" Sam called out.

The man turned and looked at him.

"What can I do for ya?"

"I'm looking for Carl Tillis. His daughter's worried about him, hasn't heard from him for a couple days. He tell you anything about going away?"

"Nah," said Jules. "Carl's a quiet guy. Did look a little stressed last time I saw him. He never said anything about leaving."

"What's he do here?"

"The bleeder," said Jules.

"The bleeder?"

"Sure. You know, gotta drain the fluids before you break 'em down. See the big tray over there with the rack on it? If you don't get the fluids out, it's a mess. Gas, oil, transmission fluid, brake fluid, power steering, coolant. He pulls the cat converters too."

Sam looked at the rows of stacked crushed vehicles. "This is a big operation."

"Biggest compactor operation in the northwest," said Jules.

"What happens to the cars?"

"Straight to the boat. Like that one I just crushed? It'll be coming back this way on the boat in six months, new Hyundai Elantra or something."

Sam gave Jules a business card the paper had provided him with and asked Jules to call if Carl showed up. He returned the hard hat to the office. There had been something hypnotic about watching the descent of the crusher on the unresisting vehicle. The end of the life cycle of a car. He'd never thought about it. Axles to axles, rust to rust. An irony, he realized, Carl's life turned upside down when he tried to destroy a truck as a kid, and now it's what he does for a living. Bleeder. Had to be a coincidence.

So maybe Tillis was dead. Burned in a fire somewhere. Or maybe after hearing about Brenchlow's death he had just taken off. He was going to have to decide what to say to Setter.

But the first thing he had to do was take his screenshots from the microfiche files to the editor.

He lay out what he had on Preedy's desk.

"Is it her?" he asked. "Her family maybe?"

"There's no family," said Preedy. "I checked."

So he knows about this. Been thinking about it.

"You going to have somebody work on this?" he asked.

"Yes," said Preedy. "You."

"Me? I'm the sportswriter."

"You found it. You do it."

What? Was this a promotion? Preedy made it sound like he was being punished for nosing into an old story.

"It's going to come out," said Preedy. "We'll look stupid if we're not in front of it."

"You're giving me the hours?"

"I'll put you on the clock. You're still doing the sports page stuff."

He nodded and backed out of the editor's office, wondering at Preedy's irritated lack of enthusiasm for a story that could sell a lot of papers.

"I need help," said Sam to Molly. "He just put me on the clock and told me to go do it."

He handed her the sheaf of printouts from the trial coverage.

"Whoo," she said ten minutes later. "Two of these boys die in fires in the last month."

"And the third one just disappeared," he said.

"So how are we going to write about it? Coincidence, question mark? Is the woman a suspect? Does anybody know where she is? You talked to the police yet?"

He rubbed the top of his head. This was him being indecisive.

"I haven't talked to anybody yet. I guess we start with the police?"

"I guess you do. Welcome to investigative journalism."

Matt Moore did public relations for the department. Matt had been friendly but cool until Sam said that he'd covered the Seahawks for the *Review.*

"Wow, what was that like?" Matt asked.

Sam related a couple of incidents involving Seahawks players, and in ten minutes Sam knew he had found a friend in the department who would be willing to talk to him.

"You do PR full time?" Sam asked. Matt said the department wasn't big enough to support a full-time position. He was a beat cop who did a few partial shifts a week. Molly had questioned Moore a few times in the past and said he didn't usually have much information to offer. His real job, she said, was probably to be a buffer between the public and the workings of the police.

Sam outlined the story and asked Moore if the police were looking at the death of Brenchlow as suspicious.

Moore made an uncomfortable face and said, "Give me a minute."

When he returned he said Detective McCord would talk to him.

Detective McCord. Sam wondered how many detectives the Port Teresa police department employed. Maybe this man screened everything and delegated what he wanted somebody else to deal with. He sat behind a desk looking at a computer screen. There was nothing on the desk except the screen and a phone set. Either the detective was compulsively neat or he didn't do anything in the office except look at the computer and talk to people.

If he recognized Sam from the hospital, and he probably did, he gave no indication of it. He didn't rise or offer to shake Sam's hand.

"You're asking if we investigated Ron Brenchlow's death. We did. The investigation showed it was an accident. Yeah, you got a coincidence here with the connection to that trial thirty years ago. But we look at the evidence for each death. We focus on the evidence. It was an accident."

"I noticed your name in the trial coverage," said Sam. "You remember anything about that girl, Claire? Could she turn into somebody who'd come back and kill people? I got the sense reading the coverage you thought she was kind of a lowlife."

The detective stared at Sam a few seconds before answering. "As I remember the case, I had no opinion about the girl. That was decades ago. My job was to talk to people who knew her and report what I learned."

"Okay, well, thanks," said Sam. "I just wanted to find out if there was an ongoing investigation. And give you a heads-up. We'll be running the story next day or two. You could be getting calls about it."

"Nothing to investigate further at this point. I appreciate the heads-up."

Sam rose and tried for a disarming smile but got a look with no expression. The detective didn't reach across the desk to offer a hand.

CHAPTER TWENTY

Dectective McCord liked being the big carp in a small koi pond. He had trod on the toes of several individuals in Zoey's network. Two friends Facebooked her about narcotics planted where they lived. One encouraged her to check out the history of an Angel Valdez. In exchange for not having a package of meth discovered in the trunk of his car, Valdez gave up a couple of names to McCord, pieces in the pipeline. Because he talked to McCord instead of doing the time, somebody left Angel in a Dumpster in Tacoma after opening a carotid artery with a sharp blade. The most interesting one though suggested she talk to a man named Zumholtz at the Cresthaven Retirement Home.

There was indeed a Morrie Zumholtz at Cresthaven, twenty miles up the highway in Cotlam, a community tucked in the rain shadow of the Olympic Mountains, where half the teachers from southeast Alaska came to retire out of the rain. When she asked if Morrie saw visitors, the receptionist said if she was lucky and got him on a good day.

"You family?" she asked.

"No."

"He might see you then."

She made the drive east along the strait to Cresthaven. The building looked like an upscale motel or winery set on a hillside overlooking the highway and the strait beyond it. A staffer in a light-blue dress pushed a man in a wheelchair along a walkway that led to a well-maintained flower garden. Nice grounds, couldn't be cheap to leave a relative here.

An aide took Zoey to the recreation room. There were maybe twenty people in the room, some playing cards and board games, a few reading, someone working with a very furrowed brow on a crossword puzzle, some just sitting in wheelchairs looking blankly across the room. She caught the eye of a woman looking at her. The eyes were kind and mild, not unintelligent, a grandmother with sympathetic counsel and cookies for grandchildren. But her mouth hung down over her throat, giving her a look of senile idiocy. They said the eyes revealed a person's true nature. But whatever feelings she was reading in the woman's eyes was overwhelmed by the appalled expression of the dangling jaw. You had to brace yourself before coming to a place like this, she realized. A glimpse of your own future if you lived long enough.

"Stay here and I'll go see," the girl said. She crossed to where three men were playing cards and spoke to one of them. All three turned and took a long look at Zoey. A grin spread across the corrugated features of the one the aide had addressed. He hoisted himself out of his chair, lined himself up behind his walker, and shuffled across the room to where she waited.

"Hello sweetheart," he said in a voice that sounded like it was being dragged along a garage floor. "Do I know you?"

"No."

"Well to what do I owe the honor?"

"There's somebody I'd like to ask you a few questions about, if you don't mind."

One disheveled, hairy eyebrow rose up toward Morrie Zumholtz's bald pate. "Ah. People with questions about my old friends are often looking for negative information."

"It could be," said Zoey.

"And what old friend would we be talking about?"

"Maybe not a friend. I want to ask about Mac McCord."

"Detective McCord. Yes, we are, I would say, acquainted. Looks like a fine day outside. What do you say, take a walk?"

Zoey adjusted her pace to Morrie's short shuffle-steps and walked beside him out a glass door to a concrete walk that crossed in front of the rec room windows.

When they were halfway along the walk, Morrie said, "Okay, sweetheart, indulge me a little here."

She felt a surprisingly large hand grasp her buttock and give it a vigorous squeeze.

"Hey!" she reacted.

"Big smile, dear. Give me a big smile here."

"Okay," she said. "This is for your friends, right?"

"Pretty girl like you with such nice boobies, they are eating their hearts out."

"Aren't you guys a little old for that?"

"My dear girl! This is a misconception. My friend Tommy and I take turns seeing Louise Backermann, second floor. A little lean in the haunches, but you can have your way with her. Just have to wear a shirt and tie. She has her ideas what a gentleman is. I take flowers or a bottle of rosé. You're expected to wear a tie. Can't seem to tie a goddamned tie anymore, though. Had to have them bring me a clip-on. The mortification of age, a clip-on fucking bow tie."

"I bet you like that blue pill," said Zoey.

"A blessing of my life I lived long enough for someone to invent it. But what a rip-off. They were ten bucks when they came out. You know what those assholes at Pfizer are squeezing our dicks for today? Can't get 'em for less than thirty now."

"I could get you some at eight bucks apiece."

"You could?"

"How many would you want?"

"You talking some Asian rip-off?"

"Straight off the Pfizer truck."

Morrie twisted his thickish lips to one side in a grimace of calculation.

"A hundred?"

"A hundred?"

"You're laughing. I can be an optimist, can't I? Anyway, I can offload some on Tommy. Fifteen bucks, he's getting a screaming deal."

"Detective McCord. I heard something about a real-estate deal that was maybe crooked."

"Interesting somebody told you that. Can we sit on that bench? I'm getting a little winded."

Morrie dropped onto the bench with a heavy sigh. Zoey sat beside him.

"So, I'm sorry, remind me of your name again. Can't seem to hang on to names anymore."

"I'm Zoey."

"Zoey. Is that short for something?"

"It's long for something. Zoe."

"Does that mean something?"

"Life. You know, like zoology."

"So Zoey. You know where a cop has his power? It's not that he can arrest you for something. It's that he can choose not to arrest you for something. Back in the day, Mac McCord was Neil Brenchlow's foot soldier. Brenchlow's a banking guy. Asked McCord not to go after one of his friends who did a no-no. The reward was a very nice piece of view property over in Port Townsend. Quitclaim for an incapacitated owner. There's a document in that transaction with the signature of a state official. The official would never have signed that document, which amounted to giving the property away. Brenchlow has a lot of people who don't like him. They would love to know about that forgery. I don't know if McCord has sold the property since then. If he still has it, he'd lose it. If he sold it, the state would come after the proceeds. There's some other shady shit I could tell you about, but that'll be the one your friend was referring to."

Zoey nodded and thought about the directions a conversation with Detective McCord might take.

"How is it you know all this?"

Morrie grinned and winked at her. "I was a CPA in that town for many years. There's two ways to know about somebody's business. One is the bullshit PR that comes out of their mouth. The other is the numbers. I had ways to see the numbers. Okay, sister, I'm gonna have to lean on you a little here. You okay with that?"

"Sure," she said, rising from the bench. "Maybe don't grab my ass this time."

"Maybe just a pat for the fellas. You're not going to forget about the pills?"

"A hundred pills. That's eight hundred bucks. You good for that?"

"Hey, look around, sweetheart. Sorry, tell me your name again."

"Zoey."

"Zoey! Right, of course. Zoology. So look around. Very nice place, am I right? Lovely view of the strait, place is always clean, quality help, Filipinas, they're all sweethearts, no Somalis with crap English, wide-screen in the entertainment center as big as Ken Griffey Jr.'s. Most of the people here are here because their families feel guilty about dumping them in a rest home and pay up for a good one. Me, family couldn't give a flying fuck, but I foot the bill here no problem. I'm gonna see you in the week?"

"In a week, yes."

"The check'll be good. If not, you know where to find me. Hah! That's a joke."

CHAPTER TWENTY-ONE

When McCord called he gave Zoey a time in the afternoon to meet him at the police station. She half-expected him to do a power number and keep her waiting for an hour or two, but she was led immediately into what she guessed was an interrogation room because it looked just like the one on *CSI*. The Las Vegas one, she had no use for the obnoxious cop on the Miami *CSI*. McCord came in a moment later, sat down, and leaned back in the chair with his arms folded, as if he expected her to become uncomfortable and say something. She looked at the table and did a mental exercise of moving her awareness through different points in her body, as she had learned to do in yoga class, except she was doing it now across her face, checking to see that the small muscles weren't holding an expression.

"You thought about the last day with Gary?"

"I have, actually," she said. "The last couple times I saw him. I tried to remember everything, like you asked. So he didn't seem upset about anything, like being pissed at anybody, or anybody being pissed at him. He didn't say anything about what he was going to do the rest of the day. Since he didn't tell me anything,

I just figured it was going to be an ordinary day, no particular plans. I think he must have just run across the wrong guys at a bad time. Nothing he was expecting, I'm pretty sure of that."

"You're not bad," said McCord. He looked at her, matching her expressionless face with his own. His silence made you want to say something, anything. He was good at it, but she held herself and didn't say anything. "But you're lying to me. You fucking know what happened to him. I think we need to strap you up to a lie detector. You and I are going to work our way to the truth, however long it takes."

"A Keeler machine? Nineteen twenties technology. The only reason those machines work, sort of, is they intimidate people. You know why they never worked on Russians? Because they don't believe in them. Now voice stress analysis technology, if you had that, that's a little stronger."

Zoey stopped herself. It was a weakness; she loved doing this. Listening to somebody act like they knew what they were talking about, then topping them with her Wikipedia knowledge. Some evenings she lost herself cruising the links through random information until it was long past time to get some sleep. The University of the Internet. She reminded herself of her purpose here: to find the right balance between appearing intimidated and doing a little intimidating herself that would get this jerk off her back.

"You are sassing me. Keep doing that, and you will just not like what happens."

"I'm not sassing you, sir. You want information, and I'm trying to give you all I can."

"So let's get the machine in here and see if you're smarter than the lie detector."

"I'm asking this with all respect. You're recording our interview, aren't you?"

He gave her a long, flat look. "Does it matter?"

"I think you are. That's why you haven't repeated the threat to plant narcotics in my truck. But I hope you'll switch it off for a few minutes and we can talk."

He didn't take his cold eyes off her, but she saw movement. A floor switch.

"Go ahead," he said.

"Okay," she said, "here's the problem with giving me a lie detector test. First, you won't learn what you want because I don't know anything that will help you. Second, I'd get nervous and start saying things you wouldn't want me to say, and the graph would show the things I was saying were true."

"You're fucking with me. Why do you think that's a smart thing to do?"

"I'm not. I'm a little scared, actually. What I'm afraid of is I might start talking about that property on Cypress Street in Port Townsend. You know, that sweetheart quitclaim giveaway the state would never sign off on, so somebody faked a signature and notarized it? I hear it's not a good fake. I'm guessing with the bad publicity the banks are getting around here, the people in Olympia would be interested in checking out that signature. I just don't think I should be talking to a lie detector about all that."

H gazed at her with an impassive expression. "You're digging a hole for yourself."

"Look, Officer McCord, I don't understand why you're pushing me. It's terrible about Gary. I'm sorry you lost your son. But you want me to tell you more, and I can't. I don't know anything. I have no reason whatever to go to the newspaper or anybody else with any of this unless I need to defend myself. You and I should just carry on and leave each other alone."

"You know what, Zoey? Your future sucks. You can go."

"Okay. Just one thing, because I know you're a powerful person. I'm not going to the newspapers or anything like that. But in case you think I'm blowing smoke out my ass, all this I'm talking about is out there, tucked away in the cloud. I've got a lot of Internet friends. I'm part of a big community. Say I had an accident, or disappeared, there are people who would put two and two together, and that bit of digital information out there would be accessed. Maybe you know how fast things go viral. So. Really best we let each other get on with our lives."

She stood and left the room and the police station, past a front desk not being staffed at the moment. She was a little surprised he'd let her have the last word. Maybe that should worry her. She should be okay, though, she thought. To old-school guys like McCord, who had no clue what the cloud was, the digital world was intimidating, basically the contemporary form of magic because they didn't understand what it could do. Asshole.

CHAPTER TWENTY-TWO

How was he supposed to tell the girl about her dad? Maybe he was a rapist. Maybe he'd tried to burn a girl alive. Maybe he was dead, the third and last of the perpetrators. Maybe he feared for his life and had run away. Were there other alternatives? Sam couldn't just let her read it in the paper. He had to talk to her.

But Kelsey didn't respond to his text and phone message. And the trial story didn't run the next day. In the midafternoon he looked up from his computer to see Molly standing at his desk. She looked grave.

"You better come," she said.

"What?"

"That beautiful girl, the volleyball player you wrote about. They found her last night."

"What do you mean they found her?"

"Somebody killed her."

He shook his head. No. Not possible. Outside couldn't be dead. If anyone possessed the immortality of youth it was her.

"Where?" he asked.

"Behind the mall. Police news conference at three. We should be there."

He rose from his desk and walked out of the newsroom. He didn't want to talk to anybody right now. This just shouldn't be. He walked down the street with only a minimal awareness of traffic lights and other people. He visualized her rising above the net to smash the ball. Later, the lightning slap across Ronnie's face. Flashbacks triggered by this news he could only grasp by degrees.

Port Teresa seemed like a normal town when he moved here. People went to work in the morning, the hair stylist, the dental hygienist with the brusque manner, the Toyota service writer, the paralegal waiting to learn if she'd been accepted by the law school at Gonzaga, the owner of the ski shop. They had families, picked children up after school, golfed or played tennis, sailed on the strait, weeded their flowerbeds, tried the occasional recipe from the weekend section of the newspaper. Not innocent exactly—probably everyone had done a few things they were ashamed of—but nothing preventing them from going about their business without worrying that events from their past would be exposed and ruin their current comfortable lives. But there was another life here, outside the boundaries most people lived within. The neighbors' son watching the younger Porter girl, waiting for an opportunity. The graduating senior Claire pulled out of her truck, assaulted, and burned by three classmates. Alison the parolee, cornered and raped by a cop's son. Outside. Women, girls, victims of male malevolence. It wasn't just a few bad men. The four hundred women he'd read about working in the *maquiladoras* of Juarez raped and killed weren't murdered by a few serial killers. The arrogant macho viciousness wasn't individuals, it was a condition. Since the death of his daughter, he had held these thoughts at a distance, escaping into sports events, tiring himself out playing pickup basketball and not getting enough sleep. But events had overtaken him. Helping Zoey with Gary McCord's body had made him more conscious of the streets, the weather, people around him, wondering if anyone was watching him. As he walked among the shoppers and tourists on Main, he realized how much Outside's death had shocked him. Why had someone done that?

Then he remembered the e-mail message he had received from her the day before. He walked quickly back to the newspaper office, sat at his desk, and opened the message.

Outside said she was sending him notes outlining what she had learned about the unfinished mansions. She had found and interviewed a Russian, Alexei, whose name she heard from a couple of people she had met.

"He said he helped a couple of Russians get construction financing," she wrote. "He wouldn't be more specific. He asked me a lot of questions, how I'd found out what I knew. He made me a little uncomfortable. I thought I'd better get this typed up and off to you so you know what's going on. Can we talk about my next steps?"

He read again through the attached pages. She had located a Russian woman who taught Russian at the college, and brought her a copy of a local Russian newsletter.

The ad in the classifieds, the teacher said, offered Russians easy financing for home construction. The ad said anyone with general contractor skills could get a loan without collateral. Organized by a Russian group that wanted to help the local Russian community prosper.

Sam had e-mailed back that he was giving her notes to the paper's business writer for his thoughts. She should be careful, he wrote. If there was some kind of racket going on, she could be threatening these Russians with exposure.

Oh Christ, he thought. Did they do this? He should have stopped her. He should have gone with her, not just let her go to see what she could find out. Please let this not be the reason she was killed.

At the news conference, Molly pointed out newspaper and TV people from Seattle and Olympia. "Hungry bastards," she said. "Takes a beautiful girl being murdered to get them here."

Matt Moore came into the room and scanned the crowd. "I better get a mic," he said to the front row, and went back to his office. When he returned he set a speaker on the table and inserted a microphone in the podium holder.

"Check, check," he said, then cleared this throat and began what he had to say. Kirstin Kelly, a high-school senior and star volleyball player, had been found covered with a plastic tarp by the Dumpsters behind the mall. Her body had probably been moved there. The initial exam showed two blows to the back of the head. One had probably knocked her unconscious, the second killed her. No signs of sexual assault. The wallet she was carrying hadn't been touched. There were no suspects, no witnesses. The police hadn't yet found a motive.

The expected questions came. Was there a boyfriend? Any of her friends have any ideas? Any crimes committed that night she might have stumbled into?

"Nothing like that we know about," said Moore. "We're talking to her friends. She lived with an aunt. We're talking to her."

As the press conference broke up, Sam followed Matt to his office.

"I don't know if this is relevant," he said, "but it could be. She was working on a story for the paper, unofficially. She told me she found what looks like a Russian bank loan scam. I brought a copy of what she sent me. You should have the detective working on this take a look. If they have questions for me, I'll be at the paper."

"Anything could help," said Matt. "I'll pass it on."

While he and Molly were walking back to the paper, she told him she knew how much he admired the volleyball player.

"At her age she was probably the best athlete I ever saw, any sport. I'm having a hard time with this. You know she wanted to be a journalist?"

Molly reached out and gave his arm a squeeze.

Molly wrote the story about Outside's death. She asked him to add a sidebar about her athletic career. By the middle of the afternoon, he was still staring at a blinking cursor on his screen. How could he write her story? All the potential coming to an incomprehensible end. An athletic career he would have followed beyond college. A hope, maybe that was it. He had let a hope develop that she might have become the elusive ideal he wanted to believe in, the world-class athlete who remained modest and open in the crucible of media attention. Roger Federer, Derek Jeter maybe, but there weren't many.

He had contributed to that media attention. But this obituary would be the end of it. He tried to express his admiration for her in simple words. When he was done, he read though what he'd written and saw he'd let himself become angry. He wrestled with his language, trying to edit out the anger. After an hour of concentration, red-eyed from the effort, he took his pages to Molly. Maybe Molly would tell him he'd fallen into bathetic sentimentality. But she read his pages and just nodded and said it was good.

CHAPTER TWENTY-THREE

No visitor passes were required the morning of the memorial service at the high school. Though it was the middle of the summer vacation, the entire student body and staff appeared to be present. The volleyball team stood in a line in front of the stage. The backs of their lilac T-shirts read "Beautiful Kirstin—Love and Power." In death, Outside the athlete had become Kirstin the young woman. The principal spoke first. He asked the students to take staying strong for Kirstin's sake as a challenge. He had the sense to turn the mic over quickly to the students. Several of the players spoke. They stumbled with their words, some of them, looking down at their teammates or just down as they bent over the microphone, but without self-consciousness, willing to share their hurt. The teachers, more experienced with audiences, removed the mic from the stand to look up and speak more vigorously to everyone in the auditorium. Their words were about love of life, team spirit, and grace. That seemed to be the word that came to people when they talked about her—grace. Kelsey fought to keep her trembling voice steady and talked about Kirstin as a loyal friend who was a life model for her. There was much repetition in the speeches made by the girls and several young men, but nobody was trying to say anything novel or clever. The service lasted a long time. Many felt compelled to speak. I could be up there myself, he thought. But I said it the best I could in the story.

There was no restlessness or impatience in the audience. These were people too young to have much experience of random death. Students and teachers, giving one another the chance to express their feelings. No one referred to catching the killer and avenging her death. But Sam heard the grim-faced volleyball coach struggling to mask her rage, trembling visibly at one point, forcing herself to channel her language into an upbeat message.

"Why did this happen?" Zoey asked. He had been so focused on the speakers he hadn't noticed her sit down next to him. He'd found a seat in the back of the auditorium, reluctant to intrude his presence.

Sam just shook his head. "She was an amazing person. People loved her. I was lucky she wanted to work with me."

Zoey's face was pale. Her eyes were dry but looked bleached out. He was surprised to see that this strong-willed woman had been crying.

When everyone who wanted to speak had their chance, Sam tried to get to the front to talk with Kelsey. This was a crappy time, but he had to tell her about the story that was going to appear. No, it was worse than a crappy time. He couldn't do it now.

The volleyball team was surrounded by a pressing mass of young people. He wouldn't have gotten through without rudely using his size.

"You knew her because you wrote about her," said Zoey.

Sam nodded. "You know when you saved my ass? That was actually about her. I was interviewing her at the pub, and this guy started hassling her, really pushy. She decked him. You would have loved it."

"I can't picture her angry. Even when she ran down an asshole that robbed me."

"This guy came after her. I had to hit him. He and his buddies set me up at that bar."

"Could it have been him …?"

"No."

"You sound sure."

"You read about the guy crashed his pickup last week, caught fire?"

"I remember that, yeah."

"That was him."

"You mean the guy's dead?"

"Yeah."

"Well that's weird."

"You know she wanted to be a journalist? We talked about an idea for a story," he said.

They worked their way out of the auditorium. Students and parents moved around them, many with their heads down, more solemn and subdued than they would ever be again at this place.

"I hope that didn't get her in trouble."

"What do you mean?" Zoey asked.

"The story idea was she'd noticed a lot of unfinished houses out to the east. She thought maybe there was some kind of banking scam going on, fake real-estate loans."

"Funny bank loans for real estate?"

"Yeah."

"You gonna find out more about that?"

"I hope so. I'm getting the business writer to look at what she wrote me."

"You're saying this was serious enough somebody might kill her?"

"I don't know. I wish I'd found out more about it."

"Could you maybe get me a copy of that? I've got somebody in the real-estate business who knows a lot about what goes on. I could see if he knows anything."

"Come on over to the paper. I'll print you a copy."

"I just talked to somebody about Detective McCord being

involved in a fraudulent real-estate deal. You think there's a connection?"

"McCord must have some kind of tie to this banker, Brenchlow. You thought a lot of her."

He saw her swallow and realized she was fighting a fresh welling of tears.

"You know what? I liked her a lot. And you know what else? I don't trust the cops here. I don't think they're going to do shit. I'm going to find out who did it."

At the Language Arts office at the college, Sam was told that Oksana Yulets's last class was done at three o'clock. This was how it worked. You got a name, you talked to someone and got another name, you talked to that person and got another name. You were affable and non-threatening, and you nodded your interest though you were actually processing information more carefully than it looked like you were. You didn't furrow your brow in concentration, you smiled. When he pushed his mop through the classrooms he felt he had a purpose. It brought him a dependable kind of satisfaction, the oily mop flowing smoothly over the tiles, leaving a clean path behind it. The newspaper work, it was just something he did because he could do it adequately and somebody gave him a small paycheck to do it. But things were changing. He felt something he hadn't felt in years. Maybe ever. There was a purpose in what he was doing. Sam Troshin had found a job to do. Though it would be more accurate to say the job had found him.

He met her in an office with three desks. He was familiar with the room. Eight hours later, he'd be back in this room to sweep and empty the garbage.

"You talked to Outside—Kirstin—about a story she was working on," he said. "You heard what happened to her?"

"No. What was that?"

"Someone killed her a few days ago."

"Oh no," exclaimed the teacher, a thickish woman with short, vividly dyed bronze hair and glasses with heavy black frames fastened to a cord looped around her neck.

"She was the volleyball player, wasn't she? Oh, I didn't know that was her. *O Gospodi—boje moi!* That's horrible."

"She left me some notes. She said you called somebody who advertised in the Russian paper. About construction financing."

The teacher nodded. "She wanted me to ask them for more information. I wanted to help. I called and spoke as if I was calling for some Russian friends who were interested."

"Her notes talked about what you learned. She didn't have any names. Did you get any names?"

"Person I talked to was Alexei. He was a little evasive, wanted to meet in person. But he said yes. Loans could be available."

She stopped speaking and brought a hand to her cheek. "You don't think that's why somebody hurt her?"

"I hope not."

"Oh, that poor girl. She was so beautiful."

CHAPTER TWENTY-FOUR

Dieter, the stage manager, paced the front of the stage and threw up his hands with a dramatic shrug. "What's happening?"

"Hang on," Shelley called out. "It's just Anna's late."

The troupe was five days from the opening of the play. Two actors were running lines out in the lobby. Somebody was doing "bibbidababbadabobboda" backstage to warm up her voice. This afternoon was the tech rehearsal, the stage manager's day to fine-tune the prompt script and make sure the blocking, prop spikes, and light and sound cues were right. The stage manager was nervous as a cat.

"Oh, where is that girl?" Shelley complained to Candy. Everyone knew Anna was Candy's daughter. Candy had been more passive and keeping herself in the background than in previous plays Shelley had asked her to help with. She was trying to behave as if her daughter was just another actor. She shook her head and shrugged in Shelley's direction.

Just then Anna came hurrying down the aisle.

"Oh my God!" she cried. "Have you seen this?" She waved a copy of a newspaper in the air.

"Now what?" said Shelley.

"You see this story? Thirty years ago there was a rape trial in Port Teresa. It's just like the play. Unbelievable—you have to read this."

"We don't have time. We have to get this rehearsal going," said Shelley.

Anna gave her an anguished look. "I can't. I'm telling you, you've got to read this. I mean now."

"Oh, for God's sake," said Shelley. She took the paper from the girl and unfolded it on the edge of the stage where the light was better.

The story described the trial of three high-school seniors for the rape and attempted murder of a classmate on prom night. The boys were acquitted, apparently as a result of what one of the boy's fathers had done, paying for good lawyers and getting someone to testify the girl was promiscuous. The man who testified was subsequently given a job with the father's bank. A policeman testified that the girl was a known party girl. Testimony supporting the girl's character appeared to have been squelched.

The story had come to light now because two of the three accused rapists had died in fires in the past two months. The article raised the question whether it was possible to believe this was a coincidence.

"Mom?" said Anna, breaking the pretense that Candy was just the assistant director. Candy scanned the story. Oh dear God. Good old Ronnie. Good old Neil.

Ten days earlier, though things happened so fast it felt like half that, Candy Brenchlow had a call from Shelley, the high-school drama teacher. Shelley, who could be a drama queen, was so excited Candy had to hold the phone away from her ear to make out what she was saying. The Port Teresa Community Theater had been approached about performing a new play written by a Hollywood screenwriter. Candy's daughter Anna recruited for the lead, and funding! Money for everything! The catch was they had to do it all, call for actors, auditions, table read, blocking, rehearsal, tech, by like next week. Could Candy help with auditions Friday?

Shelley had discovered a few years ago, maybe from Anna when she had been in Shelley' high-school drama class, that Candy had been a professional actress. She had pleaded with Candy to help with auditions and rehearsals for the drama department's plays.

Candy had performed for one season in a soap opera when she was twenty. She never had many lines. What her character did mainly was gaze adoringly at some guy with slick hair, or scream when somebody tried to strangle or knife her. Her scream was convincing, probably her best attribute as an actor.

Shelley seemed to value her judgment at auditions. Candy wasn't sure why. She had only two expectations of stage actors: that they were loud and clear enough to be heard and that they were remotely convincing as a character. Shelley deferred to her occasional suggestions during rehearsals, maybe because the young actors, knowing her background, paid attention to her. She hoped no one ever dug up any footage from the soap opera days.

Before the auditions Shelley breathlessly filled her in. Generous stipends for the actors, so she hoped to get a strong showing from the Seattle theater community. The script was good. The play was titled *The Acquittal.* It was about a trial for rape.

"What's the rush?" Candy asked.

"I don't know. The producer paid enough of a premium to rent the theater, they postponed what they had scheduled. Never experienced the power of money in the theater like this. I love it!"

"I never heard anything about this," Candy said to her daughter.

"We're on the clock here, people," Dieter called out. "Can we start?"

"We have a crisis," Shelley called back. "Give us a minute."

Candy raised her hands to her cheeks. "She's right. Our play is this story."

"So who the hell wrote it?" Alan, the actor playing the father, demanded. "Does anybody actually know?"

"All I know is somebody's paying a lot of money for us to do this play."

"It's her, the woman who was attacked," said Alan. "She's come back, and she's paid for this play to show the town it screwed her over back in the day."

"Can't be a coincidence," somebody said. "I think Alan's right."

"Oh God," said Shelley. "Okay, everybody on stage in five minutes."

When the actors had gathered on stage, Candy saw that a couple of them had copies of the *North Coast News* in their hands. A couple of others were scanning their phones.

"All right," said Shelley. "It looks like our play is, what, a re-creation of something that happened here years ago? Seems like some of your parents might even have been involved. Maybe that's why it's all so fast. Maybe Alan's right, somebody wants us to deliver a message to the town. So we need to decide right now. Are we going to go ahead?"

The actors looked at each other.

"Anna, what are you thinking?" Shelley called out.

Anna's hands were visibly shaking. She was a very attractive young woman, even when she was distraught. She had Candy's full, well-shaped mouth, cleanly cut chin and cheekbones, wide-spaced blue eyes.

"If this is right, if this is right, my dad did something really awful. To the woman I'm playing. This really sucks."

"So are we doing the tech?" said Shelley. "You want me to find a replacement?"

"No!" Anna cried out. "I can't let everybody down. I'll try to do it."

Shelley stepped up to Anna and put her hands on the girl's shoulders. "Living authentically in imaginary circumstances.

That's what we do. When you walk into this building, Alan here is your father. He has nothing to do with your real dad. On this stage, your relationship with Alan is the only one that matters."

Anna began a slow nod. "I just need to focus on the lines and Alan. Put everything else out of my mind."

"That's what a good actor does. You can do it, Anna."

CHAPTER TWENTY-FIVE

The Port Teresa police department was better prepared for a crowd of reporters at the second news conference to update the press about the police investigation of the death of Kirstin Kelly. Rows of folding chairs had been set up, and bottled water and coffee were available on a table in the back. Matt Moore sat near the front, chatting with reporters. He'd been told at the first news conference that two o'clock was a good time to schedule those conferences. The department would have most of the day to get their information together, the radio people could get any developments of interest into the drive-time broadcasts, newspaper reporters could get their stories done, and TV could decide if anything qualified as breaking news. At two Moore ran a hand through his hair, stepped to the podium, and thumbed on the mic.

Information had been received, he began, linking the girl with a group of Russians in the area who appeared to be defaulting on home construction loans. She was working as an intern for the paper. "Shit," Sam muttered, "that's not what I said. She was doing the story on her own."

One of the Russians, Moore continued, was considered

by the police a person of interest. He had apparently fled the country and was reported to have returned to Russia. Moore emphasized that there was no firm evidence linking this man, whose name was Konstantin Stivits, to the murder. A Russian-speaking investigator from Olympia had been brought in to help question members of the Russian community and try to determine where Stivits was the night of the killing.

"What do you know about the loan defaults?" someone asked.

"I don't have any information about that," said Moore. "Like you, we're waiting to hear from the bank regulators."

When the conference was done and the media people were packing up their gear, Sam asked Moore if he had a minute. Moore told him to wait around so it wouldn't look like he was getting special treatment. When the lobby was mostly empty, he waved Sam toward his office.

"That was a great story the paper did on Kirstin," said Moore. "I felt like crying when I read it."

He nodded. "I felt like crying when I was writing."

"So what'd you want to see me about? I can't really give you any more info than what you heard out there."

"Nah," said Sam. "I just want to get your take on how it's going. If it was the Russian loan thing, I could be responsible. I should have realized she might go talk to those guys."

"You probably didn't have the time."

"Shit. I wasn't thinking. So let me ask. You working toward detective?"

"It's what I see myself doing."

Sam leaned back in his chair and puckered his lips in thought. Stay affable. People will want to tell you things. "Really off the record here. I'm asking because I feel sick about what happened. What do you think of how the investigation's going?"

"How do you mean?"

"If you were the lead detective on this case, what would you be doing?"

"You looking for me to criticize McCord?"

"Just interested in hearing you think like a detective."

"I'd probably have more guys out on the streets talking to people."

"What I'd do too. If it turns out to be this Russian, I guess we're screwed."

"If it's him we are fucked. Extradition from Russia? Right."

CHAPTER TWENTY-SIX

Candy texted her daughter more now than she called. Texting was less invasive. You never knew what people her daughter's age were doing. A phone call might be interfering with some moment of concentration, or intimacy, for God sakes. A text was just a little beep. And Anna always answered her texts in a reasonable time. The life of a twenty-two-year-old seemed so dense. At the rehearsals she didn't want to interfere with Anna's life. She knew a powerful bonding among the cast was part of the process, especially when there was a time crunch.

She sent Anna a message that she and Neil would be in the audience for the opening night performance of the play. Once the dress rehearsals were underway, Candy stayed away from the theater, feeling she was more useful in the early stages of preparation. She was surprised when Anna responded that she'd see her at the cast party, something Candy wasn't sure she should be part of.

Candy usually saw her daughter once a month. Anna's father hoped to keep her visiting the home, and expected Candy to serve good dinners prepared with what they knew about Anna's tastes in mind. Anna had announced a year ago she was a vegetarian. Candy was relieved to learn after spending some time online that a vegetarian wasn't as radical as a vegan. Candy could broil a decent sirloin and fry a chicken, but her skill with vegetables didn't go beyond corn on the cob. She had no idea how you made squash or Brussels sprouts appealing. So she hired a chef to come by the mornings Anna was visiting and had him prep everything and leave her with detailed instructions about the final steps before serving. Usually Anna didn't notice, but at one dinner had gestured toward the coconut oil Thai curry on her plate and said, "That's good. What's in it?"

"Uh, cumin and a pinch of sorrel is what makes it," said Candy. She was relieved that Anna didn't ask for further details.

Her father encouraged Anna to bring her friends, and he would adjust the date if another time fit Anna's schedule better. Without Neil's invitations, Candy didn't think she would see much of her daughter. She was fond of Anna, but once her daughter had passed through adolescence they didn't seem to share many interests except the theater. Their conversations at the dinners were mostly Candy asking Anna how her friends were. She made a point of keeping the names and activities of half a dozen of Anna's friends straight so Anna wouldn't have to roll her eyes and repeat their stories from one dinner to the next. Candy was a little sad that Anna showed no interest in anything she was doing, but realized it was probably normal for a twentysomething to be absorbed in her own life.

So Candy was surprised that Anna wanted to share an important event. She was gratified but a little apprehensive.

Opening night for *The Acquittal* had been a great success. A filled house, and standing applause had brought the cast out for a second bow. There was enough buzz that Candy was sure a professional publicist had been at work. The cast party took place in the banquet room at the Olympic Hotel. Tables at one end overflowed with fancy finger food, a more lavish spread than the last wedding Candy had been to. She didn't think amateur theater groups had the kind of money for something like this.

Anna saw her mother and broke away from an animated conversation with several of the cast members.

"Hi, Mom, what did you think?"

"Sweetie, you were terrific. Your high-school plays were all comedies. As a serious actress, you're the real deal."

Anna's smiled a happy smile at the compliment. Then the smile disappeared.

"What did Dad think?"

Candy winced. "He left halfway through. You can understand. He was pretty upset."

Candy had known she would have to bring up the subject of the play at home. Neil was aware his daughter was rehearsing for a play at the community theater and wouldn't want to miss it. She wasn't sure how she'd respond when Neil asked her what the play was about.

"You've been reading this story in the paper about the rape trial. Ronnie's death."

"Yes," said Neil. He didn't elaborate.

"Well, that's what the play's about."

"About a trial for rape? Or the particular one that happened here?"

"No, it's this one."

"Why is somebody writing about that?"

"I couldn't find that out. They seemed to know about it before the newspaper stories came out."

"Are the parents of the accused rapists in there?"

"The father of one of them."

"The one who paid for the lawyers."

"Yes."

"Well that's fucking great. You going to tell me how Anna got involved?"

"She auditioned. She had no idea what the play was about. None of us did."

Neil Brenchlow gave his wife a long look but didn't say anything more.

Midway through the performance Neil had leaned over to

Candy and whispered, loudly, that it was all bullshit. Then he stood abruptly and told Candy to take a taxi home. She wasn't surprised. He pushed his way through the legs of the people in his row without giving them time to twist their knees aside. She'd heard several people say "easy there" to him. But Neil never paid much attention to people's complaints.

"You think the whole thing's true?" Anna asked her mother.

"God, honey, I have no idea. Nobody told me any of this. I'll talk to Helen when I get a chance. She would know."

"I'm going to ask him if it's true. If he really did that. And Ronnie. My God. Did Ronnie rape a girl?"

Anna was speaking rapidly. Candy hadn't seen her so overwrought since she was fifteen.

"I never asked. You know exactly how you got cast for this?"

"Shelley just offered it to me."

Two women suddenly grabbed Anna, flashing apologetic smiles at Candy, and pulling her into an exuberant crowd that immediately clustered around her. "Go ask Shelley what she thought," Anna called over her shoulder. Candy felt the room filled with the exhilarated energy and relief of people who had worked hard at something that had turned out a success.

"Hello," said a woman who had moved next to Candy. "You must be Anna's mother."

"Candy," she said. "I was just telling her I'd never seen her do anything but comedy. Are you part of the production?"

The woman was thin and slightly stooped but had strong cheekbones and striking dark eyes. "I'm helping as producer. I know you helped Shelley with directing."

"Producer," said Candy. "I never knew exactly what that was. In the soaps it was just these people you saw around from time to time."

The woman smiled. The skin around her smile was taut and fragile.

"Mostly it's seeing that everything gets paid for."

"It's probably as complicated as any business."

"You're right. There's an entrepreneur behind any successful play. So you must be Neil Brenchlow's wife."

Candy nodded, surprised.

"Is he going to see the play, do you know?"

"He saw some of it tonight. He left halfway through."

"I wonder what he thought of it."

"This play is weird. For him it had to be personal. I really don't know what's going on."

"These days dramatists like weird. Some theater is like reality TV raised to a higher level."

"Do you know Neil?"

"Not as an acquaintance, no. I'm sorry, I didn't introduce myself. I'm Mrs. Farres. It's a Lebanese name. My husband passed away a few years ago."

"I'm sorry," said Candy.

"Thank you."

"People here are asking how the play was written before any of this story about the trial came out."

"The story has been there all the time. People have recently become aware of it."

"My stepson getting killed in that crash. When I read about the same truck at the same spot in the road, I wondered if something was going on."

"I read the story. I know what you're talking about."

"This is a first-class party," said Candy. "I've got an idea what the Olympic charges to put on something like this. I can't help thinking. This is a small play in a town with a small-time theater. Where's all the money coming from?"

"That's an astute question. Neil Brenchlow's wife would pay attention to something like that."

Candy looked at the woman. Probably a little older than she was. She held herself like someone who didn't make thoughtless movements. Poised. A fragile but powerful presence being held in check. Pleasant on the surface, wound up tight inside. She didn't really seem to be sharing in the celebration. She was observing. Candy realized the woman had sought her out.

"So the play is your project," said Candy.

The woman's smile didn't change. "I'm the producer. It's other people. I'm no writer. But you could call it my project."

The two women looked at one another a moment.

"Can I ask how you learned about the trial?" Candy said.

"It was a big story once. I've known about it."

"Do you know anything about how Anna was selected to audition?"

"You could say it's because she's a good actress. She has a promising career. She can act, and she's lucky, she inherited your good looks. I knew the role might be difficult for her. I saw her struggling with the personal aspect of it."

"I was there at rehearsal when she decided to go through with it."

"May I get your opinion about something? What d'you think is going to happen to your husband?"

Candy wondered if it was Neil Mrs. Farres wanted to talk about. There was a time she would have been protective of her husband and not discussed his business with anyone. But that was changing.

"There's some difficulties right now. He doesn't tell me much."

"He's in trouble?"

"I think he is."

"You think he might crash?"

"It's possible."

"Would you crash with him?"

Interesting that Mrs. Farres could see her separately from her husband. That had never happened much in her marriage.

"Yes, I would. But maybe not entirely."

CHAPTER TWENTY-SEVEN

Sam's phone dinged with a text from Melissa Merrill. Melissa was the paper's movie and drama reviewer. She wanted to talk to him. He texted back he would be at the Roanoke for a few hours if she wanted to meet him there. The Roanoke was a quiet vintage bar where some of the *News* staff unwound after a day in the newsroom. Sam sometimes spent the time between his day at the office and his custodial work there, nursing a beer.

When he first started with the paper, there had been a controversy about whether the paper should have a movie critic. Port Teresa had two theaters, the Avenue and the Cineplex. The owner of the Avenue, which had been in his family for ages, was threatening to pull his advertising from the paper if the films he was showing were panned. "I don't do blockbusters. I try to get interesting films. I'm happy to have your reviewer describe them. But if you say they're bad, people won't come. Why should I pay for advertising if you're hurting my business?"

The owner of the Cineplex, on the other hand, didn't care. His audience didn't read reviews. They saw trailers on TV with action heroes, hair cropped short unless they were Brad Pitt, leaping thirty feet in the air in the new fighting style firing trick weapons at huge robots, zombies, and bad guys, everything happening way too fast for anyone to get bogged down with plot issues. Just tell people what's showing, he said. In the end, Melissa was directed to use a light touch on the Avenue movies if she wanted to have a job.

Like Sam, Melissa had a second job to help keep the bills paid. She was a large woman with straight, graying hair who favored ponytails and striking, colorful scarves as her signature touch.

Sam offered to buy her a beer.

She thanked him and said, "Get me a Sprite. You know anything about this play that just started its run at the community theater?"

"Not really," he said.

"It's called *The Acquittal*. It's about a trial for rape. A girl claims she was raped by several boys after a prom. The boys are charged and tried. The defense claims the girl was a slut and the sex was consensual. There's testimony that she wasn't. But the father of one of the boys is a rich and important guy. The police detective has questions about the girl's character. So does the newspaper editor. The boys are acquitted. Play ends with a strong suggestion an injustice was done and there will be consequences. Any of this sound familiar?"

Sam rubbed his chin. "Is this a new play?"

"First time it's been performed. I went back and reread your story on the deaths and the old trial. It can't be a coincidence. How long did you know about all this? You been sitting on the trial story awhile?"

He shook his head. "I heard about the truck crashing and burning in the same place twenty-five years later. Until a couple weeks ago, I didn't know a thing about the trial."

"This play sure didn't get written and produced in ten days. But there's more that's weird, and you should know about it. The actress who plays the rape victim? A local actress, not bad, name's Anna Brenchlow."

Melissa took a swallow of Sprite and waited for Sam to react.

"As in Brenchlow," he said.

"His daughter by a second marriage. You see what's going on? Anna plays the role of the rape victim. That's Claire from the old trial. Anna's character gets accused of being a whore by the father character. Anna, the actress, is accused of being a slut by the character playing her real-life father."

She waited again for Sam to take this in. "Sam, somebody is fucking with us here."

"Who's the writer?"

"Yeah, who's the writer. I talked to Shelley, the director. She said she's been told it's the work of a veteran Hollywood screenwriter. Sam, I'm just a drama critic. I'm over my head here. You got to take this and run with it."

"Is the play any good?"

"They actually did a pretty decent job with it. But I don't even know how to do the review. Do I just ignore the real-life story around it? Some of the ads claim it's a story torn from the pages of Port Teresa's history. I'm even stuck for a straight review. Anna's performance was remarkable. You could feel her struggle to stay in character. But there's two brief scenes between her and the father. It's the most convincing anger I've ever seen on a stage, and now I realize she wasn't trying to generate anger, she was trying to contain it."

Melissa shook her head at the recollection. "Who wrote this? That's for you, Sam. Go talk to Shelley. Find the writer, find where he got the story, why the daughter got picked. Somebody knew about all this before you did. Somebody's trying to shove this old rape trial up our asses."

CHAPTER TWENTY-EIGHT

Sheryl, the receptionist, brought a printout to Sam's desk. It was an e-mail addressed to the paper's website from someone named Jackie Rimmlinger at jrimmlinger@bayviewhome.org. Jackie stated that she'd Googled Sam's name and found his byline on some sports reports at the *North Coast News*. She worked at an assisted-living facility in El Cerrito, California, where Walter Troshin was a resident, and said that in a lucid moment, Walter told her he had a son named Sam. Was Sam that son? Was Walter his father? If so, did he know where his father was? She encouraged him to visit.

Sam stared at the printout, then sent an e-mail to Jackie Rimmlinger saying yes, he was Walter's son, he would come immediately, and asked her for directions.

Two days later Sam was on a plane to Oakland. The assisted-living facility was a large single-level midcentury home on a grassy hillside looking west to Albany Hill and the bank of fog settled over San Francisco. His knock at the door was answered by a sturdy, smiling woman with a vigorous perm and lively eyebrows. He asked if Jackie was working.

"Hello, that's me," she said, and shook his hand warmly when he said who he was.

"I'm sure he'll recognize you, just maybe not at first. You want to be patient."

"Isn't he young for Alzheimer's?" Sam asked.

"Oh, it catches people in their forties," she said. "Nobody's sure how the genetics work. Here, he's on the back porch."

Sam drew a long breath and tried to prepare himself. When he and Jackie stepped through the doorway to the porch, he was relieved that his father was gazing off into the distance. The figure in the chair was recognizable as his father but transformed to look like someone thirty years older than the person in Sam's memory. His hair was graying around the edges and thinning. Time had drawn a slow, abrasive hand across his face, leaving folds, creases, roughness, and blotches of reddish-brown on the skin. He knew he himself wouldn't look much like the teenaged boy his father knew.

"Walter, look who's here," said Jackie. "It's Sam. It's your son Sam come to see you."

"Hi, Pop," said Sam, making no effort to smooth the nervousness out of his voice. "How are you?"

His father turned his head to look at Sam. "Who?" he asked.

"It's Sam. You know, me and Nolan. Your kids."

"Nolan?"

"Yeah. No, I'm Sam. Sam, remember?"

"Sam?"

"Yeah, yeah."

Walter smiled and nodded. "Sam."

A statement, not a question, thought Sam. That's good.

"They take good care of you here, Pop?"

"Oh yeah." The smile remained on his face. "This is Jackie. She's real nice. I haven't seen you for a while."

Sam nodded and smiled. "No, a long time. Pop, I'm sorry we didn't stay in touch."

"Stay in touch," his father repeated.

"Yeah. I wish we had. Seems nice here."

"It is nice."

Sam couldn't tell if the soft smile on his father's face was some kind of recognition or had evolved as a permanent feature that didn't express anything.

"I wish we could've talked all these years."

His father shook his head. "We didn't."

"What'd you do after you left us, Pop? I tried to keep in touch."

The smile remained on his father's face. He gave another shake of the head.

"I don't remember too well. I'm sorry."

"I messed up, Pop. Maybe you could have straightened me out."

His father smiled at him in silence. He didn't know how much comprehension was in the look. His father seemed to know who he was. But he was beyond any sense of how many years had passed since they had seen one another.

"I got married and had a kid. You're a grandfather. Were a grandfather. My girl, Ella, she's gone. I left her. Abandoned her. I don't know why. Why'd you abandon us, Pop?"

He hadn't meant to say that. He hadn't come to accuse his father. It had just come out.

Luckily his father didn't hear his words as an accusation. "How come?" he asked.

Jackie, seeing the conversation was moving along nicely, withdrew discreetly to the doorway.

"I was just chickenshit. I kept thinking when she got to be a grownup, you know, I could talk to her. But she didn't make it. She never …" Sam faltered and had to look away. "Wish she'd known how much I thought about her."

"I'm sorry," his father said.

"It's okay, Pop. The thing that makes it bad is I've got to know this girl. Same age as Ella. This girl's sixteen. They're more mature than you think. I could have talked to Ella. I shouldn't have waited."

"I'm sorry," his father repeated.

"Nolan, you know, he's okay. I don't see him much. I'll tell him you're here. He'll want to know."

"That's good. Nolan. The food's good here."

"Glad to hear that, Pop. It's good they take care of you. Maybe they'll let me stay for lunch."

"You'll like lunch," said his father, and turned toward Jackie. "What's for lunch?"

"Chowder and cornbread. You like Annabelle's cornbread. Your son is welcome to stay for lunch."

"Cornbread's good," said his father. "You'll like it."

Sam was aware that his heart began to beat faster. He could hear it in his ears. He didn't feel stressed, he didn't know why this was happening. He closed his eyes and let his awareness follow his breathing for two or three breaths. Opening his eyes again, he studied his father's face, the coarseness of age overlaying what was familiar, and succeeded in calming himself.

Jackie joined Sam and his father at the lunch table. Sam mostly listened as Jackie and his father carried on a conversation that was coherent in brief sequences of three or four sentences, mostly about what the other residents were doing. This is his world now, Sam thought, the people he lives with. He seems content. In the moments his father gazed at him, Sam wondered how much he remembered. His limited experience with Alzheimer's victims, the mother of a woman who lived in his apartment building, was that their thoughts circled around things, approaching but not quite reaching the words they needed. But if his father was content, it didn't matter.

When Jackie announced that Walter was getting tired, her signal the visit was over, Sam leaned over to embrace his father in his chair and said good-bye. As he drew back from the embrace, his father held his look with a bland and steady smile.

Waiting in the airport for his flight back to Seattle, Sam thought about his father. Memories he was surprised were there came back to him.

CHAPTER TWENTY-NINE

At what age did a boy begin to think about his affectionless parents as a couple that once had a romantic interest in one another? Sam must have been about fourteen, sleeping over at his buddy Jerry's before getting up early for a fishing trip. He'd been wakened not long after falling asleep by what sounded like a washing machine running in the house. What the hell's that? he asked Jerry.

"Shut up, Troshin!" Jerry had said in a hard whisper. "It's the old man."

It took Sam a moment to recognize the sound of bed springs working rhythmically. Jerry's parents were having sex. He lay in the bed listening and realizing why he hadn't recognized the sound. He had never heard it in his own home. He imagined, cautiously, his mother and father in bed together. They wouldn't be touching; they would be talking. His mother would be. Expressing with her dry, sarcastic wit her husband's inadequacy and her dissatisfaction with her life.

This happened a month after an experience that left Sam unsettled and confused. Their father's Plymouth was in the shop for the day. Nolan had just got his license and bought a beater Honda. The plan was for their father to take the bus home from work.

"Let's go pick him up," Nolan said. His car, and driving, was still a novelty. He looked for reasons to drive around town.

Their father worked in an office that sold insurance. He usually left the office at five thirty. Nolan parked near the building exit, and the two boys waited. At five forty-five their father hadn't appeared.

"Maybe he's working late," said Nolan. "We should go check."

They entered the Logan Associates Insurance office. The receptionist was gone. They could hear a loud voice coming through the opaque glass door.

"You fucked it up, Troshin. What were you doing, rubbing your dick while Caldwell closes? That's two this week. I mean, what the fuck!"

They heard their father's voice, too low to make out the words.

"You think I want to hear excuses? Be a man, for God's sake. What, does that wife of yours keep your balls in her handbag? Can you still get it up? We cannot lose any more of these. You're on the edge, Troshin. Get that Westland policy signed, or somebody else gets your leads."

"Listen to that fucker," said Nolan. "I'm going to kick his ass." He took a step toward the glass door.

"You can't!" Sam exclaimed. "They'll fire him." He wrapped his arms around Nolan to hold him. Nolan pushed him hard enough to send him sprawling on the carpet. Sam got back to his feet and held his hands toward his brother.

"What'll mom do if he gets fired? We gotta just wait."

A moment later their father came out of the office. He looked at his sons with surprise, then bowed his head and followed them to Nolan's car.

They drove in awkward silence.

"He gets really worked up," their father said. "You have to just let him vent."

"He's an asshole," said Nolan.

"Don't use that language. He's under a lot of pressure. It's just his style. You have to ignore it."

Sam, sitting in the back seat, saw Nolan glance at his father with a look of contempt.

A year later, Sam's father was gone.

"He just quit on us," Nolan said.

"She drove him away," said Sam.

"I will never badmouth your father to you," she told them. But she packed his possessions with her lips drawn back as if reacting to a bad odor and told Nolan to have the boxes shipped to wherever he'd gone. After a while an older man who drove a white Lincoln sedan appeared at the house. She dressed up when they went out, in clothes that struck Sam as fancier, in colors gaudier and less tasteful, than she had been accustomed to wearing.

"He treats me the way a woman should be. You could learn a few things from him."

But neither boy had much interest in conversation with the man, whose name was Gordon.

One day he came home after football practice and saw that Nolan had cleared out his room. His mother was sitting in the kitchen not hiding a martini glass. She was breathing hard, as if she had been running.

"He struck Gordon. I told him he didn't live here anymore."

Sam asked where he'd gone. His mother looked at him as if he'd asked a foolish question.

"I have no idea. I assume he's still going to school. Go ask him."

Sam missed his father. He was exasperated by his unwillingness to fight. But there was something to admire in his father's perseverance and acceptance of the contempt of his wife and older son. As a boy Sam had enjoyed conversations with his father. His father was always interested in whatever Sam was doing, and listened to Sam talk about his day as if he was narrating remarkable exploits. He made Sam feel he was an interesting person. He felt abandoned when his father left. Every few months he received a letter from his father that was something like their old conversations. His father wanted to know how school was going, what Sam was doing. Sam immediately wrote back long, detailed letters describing his activities. Later he would recognize the letters to his father as his apprenticeship as a reporter.

When he received the football scholarship and moved to a dorm at Central, he was welcomed by the coaches. He had no illusions; the coaches were friendly and supportive as long as he was a contributing member of the team. If he didn't make the tackles, if he didn't measure up to the standards that would enable the team to win games, they would cut him loose. But he was a good enough Division II safety. Sports teams could provide the family life he didn't have at home. That was probably why he had drifted into a life of writing about sports.

Later, when he was working at the *Review*, he made a trip to the city where his father lived. In a short, terse conversation, his mother, whose voice was developing the raspy grind of a lifetime smoker, though she wasn't one, told him the checks had stopped when he turned eighteen. She found the post office box number that had been the return address. She had no idea where he was.

The post office box had been closed years ago. There was nothing more he could think to do to find his father.

CHAPTER THIRTY

The Brenchlow estate was a lovely place, Zoey thought. The main house looked like a lodge, just visible through the trees beyond the gate. An attendant at the gatehouse called the house. The sliding gate drew to the side. The gate was high and substantial, not something a person could casually climb over. On either side of the gate, cyclone fencing reached into the tall juniper shrubs. You didn't notice it unless you looked closely, but a two-foot band of razor wire was cantilevered over the fencing. Some thought and money had been given to making the fencing attractive with nicely landscaped shrubbery, but the place was probably as secure as the prison where she had recently stayed.

Sam had told her that he and another reporter had tried to interview Brenchlow a few days earlier but hadn't been allowed in. The attendant gave them a phone number and told them to make an appointment. The number was a voice-mail box asking the caller to leave a message.

"I can get in," said Zoey. "His wife's a client. There's a couple pieces of French furniture she has me on the lookout for. She'll see me."

As she drove up the ascending approach to the house, she

could see the view would be exhilarating, encompassing the white snow mantling the Olympics, the strait, the sunsets out over the Pacific.

Candy met her at the door and led her to a spacious sitting area. High ceilings, rich, dark hardwood flooring, tan leather furniture, colorful rugs. When Zoey called she had more or less invited herself to Candy's home. "I'd love to look at those pieces I found for you in place," she said. "I have some suggestions about the French pieces you're looking for."

Candy had hesitated, sounding reluctant to have Zoey come to the house. "But there is something I'd like to talk about," she said finally, and agreed on a time for Zoey to visit.

I could live here, Zoey thought. But the décor was too much western, Bama and Remington prints, horseshoes, and a polished set of steer horns, a display of Winchesters and Colt pistols on the wall. The mission-style chairs and sofas were classy in their way but looked too stiff for comfortable sitting.

"Pretty nice, but where's the stuff I got for you?"

"The main floor's his. He wants cowboy, I get him cowboy. I get to do the upstairs."

"Does he wear the boots and spurs and all that?"

Candy laughed. "Spurs, no. Boots and hats, sometimes he does. It's a fantasy. This ain't exactly cattle country."

"So," Zoey said. "Haven't found that bombe chest you're looking for, but I can lay my hands on a couple of things you might be interested in. I have a few photos."

"We should talk about that. Come on upstairs."

The upstairs rooms were a different world, elegant and urban. The décor would have suited a Second Avenue penthouse in Seattle.

"You made a nice space up here," said Zoey.

"Yeah, thanks," said Candy. "I tried."

"Says city girl to me," said Zoey.

"No shit. Well, like the girl says in the book, reader, I married him."

"You want to see a few pieces?"

"That's what we have to talk about. Things are changing. I'm afraid I'm not in the market anymore."

"Really? So what's changing?"

"The money situation. I need to sell."

Zoey raised her eyebrows to form a questioning arc.

"This is just you and me. I think there's going to be difficulties. I'm going to need as much of my own cash as I can lay my hands on."

"Okay," said Zoey. "What exactly are we selling?"

"Anything I can."

"Wow. Okay, I'll get some shots of the good pieces. You talking all of it?"

"Anything you can get a decent price for."

Zoey began moving through the room, taking photos with her smartphone and entering notes. She had Candy help her move a few pieces to the center so they would photograph more distinctly. In twenty minutes she had created a catalog of furniture.

"None of my business, but second thoughts?"

"Aah. You make your bed. I don't get many friends willing to come out here. I make a nice space and spend the day sitting around in it. But I think it's ending."

"What do you mean?"

"I hear things. He," Candy said, nodding toward downstairs, "isn't saying much these days. He's in that office all day on the phone. Not so much in town at the bank as he used to be. Like bunker mentality."

"You'll land on your feet. Actually, I've got something I want to talk to him about. Could you point me to his office?"

"Really? You know him? I suppose from the bank."

"I don't actually know him. It's more I want to ask about some things he's involved in."

"Good luck. You may not find him very helpful."

She led Zoey back down the wide staircase.

"Straight down that hall. Door at the end. Just tap."

"Okay, thanks. You okay with me pricing the stuff?"

"Get what you can. You're welcome to come by and just visit. I don't have enough friends."

Zoey smiled and turned down the hall. She didn't say that she wouldn't be welcome here again.

"Hold on a second," Neil Brenchlow said into his phone when Zoey knocked and pushed open the door. "Excuse me, who are you?"

"I want to talk to you about what's going to happen to the bank."

"I'll get back to you," he said to the phone, and pushed the off button. "Who did you say you were?"

"I had some business with your wife. But it's you I need to see."

"Are you a reporter? You used my wife to get in here."

"Don't blame her. I'm not a reporter. What I really am is somebody who needs to know about the girl. I don't get it. Your setup with the Russians is showing some cracks. The story she was doing, that would just have just sped things up some. You had her killed just for that?"

"I have no idea what you're talking about. Since you invaded my home and I'm doing you the courtesy of listening, tell me who you are really."

"I'm a friend of hers, that's who I am."

"You should leave. You can walk out of here, or I'm going to get the police here and have you jailed for trespassing. If my wife invited you, it probably won't stick, but you should get a couple of days of hassle out of it."

"Would you get McCord out here?" said Zoey. "Aren't we outside his jurisdiction?"

Brenchlow gave her a long, flat stare.

"Here's what I think. I think you had the lieutenant do it. He's been your guy since your son's rape trial. I know about those sweetheart deals, the Cypress Street property in Port Townsend. I heard about another sketchy quitclaim deal on C Street in Sequim that somebody should look into. Forged papers, bet all those are still on file in Olympia."

"You should leave now," he said.

"I'm no lawyer, but I think forgery is different from fraud. I think it gets added on."

"Are you hearing me? Get the fuck out now."

"Go ahead, call McCord. He knows who I am. He really doesn't like me. He thinks I had something to do with his son getting killed."

"That's who you are," said Brenchlow. "You know, if this fantasy about me telling McCord to get rid of the tall girl was true, wouldn't you just be asking for trouble coming here and telling me?"

"You're right, I'm probably asking for trouble. I can't exactly go to the police with it, can I?"

"No, I can't see that would do you much good. You don't get why the girl was killed. I don't get why you care so much you're risking your ass."

"I cared about her a lot. You never should have killed her."

"You never should have come here."

"It's worth it just to hear you not denying you had McCord do it. You said the tall girl. You knew who I was talking about. You're right, I can't talk to the police. I'll go to the paper, but I'm not even sure about that. You're probably getting your money out as fast as you can."

"You're wasting my time," said Brenchlow.

"I think you're actually listening pretty carefully. Here's some more. My line of work, I do favors for people. Kind of like you do. Some of those people help me out. An example, somebody in the telecommunications industry I got some good deals for. I learned that the day Kirstin went to talk to Alexei about his construction loans, he made a call to you. Twenty minutes after that call you made a call to Detective McCord on a private line. Two days later Kirstin is killed. Prove anything? No, just another piece of circumstantial evidence. And it's totally illegal that I know about it. But if the AG's office or the FBI requested those phone files, they'd be there. You're in a net, Mr. Brenchlow, and it's tightening."

He rose, walked to her, and took her upper arm in a hard grip.

"Don't hurt me," she said.

"I'm just getting you out of my home." He pushed her ahead of him down the hall and toward the front door.

"Okay, okay, I'm going."

Candy was not in sight.

On the porch he gestured to a man working in a flower bed. "Get her to her car. Get the make and license."

CHAPTER THIRTY-ONE

A few days after her confrontation with Brenchlow, Zoey had a 6:00 a.m. phone message from a blocked number. "I hear you're looking for information about Neil Brenchlow and the Russian loans," said a woman's voice. "I can show you a couple documents you'll find interesting. I can meet you tonight." The woman gave the address of an auto repair shop fifteen minutes out of town and said to park there and wait.

Zoey thought about the message. The responses to her request for information about McCord and Brenchlow had been texts and an e-mail, communications that could be traced if she wanted. Someone calling at six in the morning would know she probably wouldn't answer her phone, just let the call go to voice mail, as she had done. The caller was being elusive. There could be good reasons for that. But the timing, two days after her meeting with Brenchlow. What if this was something he had arranged, and the purpose was to intimidate or even hurt her? Why the rush? Why a single specific time offered? She could drive earlier in the day to the address and scope the place out, but that wouldn't tell her much, other than that there probably wouldn't be many people around.

But if the call was legitimate and the information would help Sam complete his story about Brenchlow's fraudulent affairs?

She decided. She would follow up and go that evening. She would at least take the precaution of letting Sam know what she was doing.

"You want me to go with you?" he asked when she called.

"She might not show if I've got company," she said. "It's just if I'm not there in the morning, you know where to start looking."

There was barely enough light in the late summer sky for Sam to make out Zoey's truck as it drove past the parking lot where he had been waiting.

He'd listened to the recording she had forwarded to him of her confrontation with Brenchlow. He could tell from the banker's reaction that there was information he didn't want made public. Zoey was a real threat to him. It did seem possible that Brenchlow might become desperate enough send someone to prevent her from communicating what she knew. These were the people he was afraid might have killed Outside. He left a message for Horacio that he wouldn't be at the school until late.

Sam pulled out of the lot and followed Zoey's truck at a distance. It was probably just as well she didn't know he was there. His purpose was to find a place to watch inconspicuously and go to help her if something happened.

He stayed a third of a mile back. He knew more or less where she was going, so he wasn't worried about losing her.

He had driven a couple of miles when lights loomed behind him, and a big pickup passed him going well above the speed limit. He watched it close the gap to Zoey's truck.

The fast pickup didn't seem right. He accelerated in an effort to catch up. The pickup appeared to slow as it approached Zoey's truck instead of moving to the left to pass. As he came closer, he saw the pickup crowd the right shoulder of the road, then shoot forward into the rear of Zoe's vehicle. There was a sudden blur of thrashing movement as the pickup pushed to the left and spun Zoey's truck into the guardrail of the turn they were rounding. Her truck crashed through the guardrail and bounded like a huge toy down the embankment. The pickup fishtailed. The driver regained control and sped away.

Sam shoved hard on the brakes and got his car stopped about fifty feet from the ripped guardrail. He jumped out, scrambled over the rail, and looked for the best way down the embankment. One of the truck's headlights was aimed into the darkening sky. Thick dust swirled in its beam. He reached the truck and pulled on the door. Nothing moved. The door was jammed shut. He peered inside and could see Zoey bent over the steering wheel, unconscious. He scrambled around the back of the truck and tried the passenger-side door, which was also jammed but gave way as he strained against it and opened with a grinding sound. It took him several excruciatingly long seconds to climb onto the passenger seat and fumble to unlatch the seatbelt. He wrapped an arm around her and tried to pull her toward the passenger-side door. Her leg was caught. He bent himself down under the dashboard and tried to work her leg free from the twisted footwell. He pulled hard, aware he must be hurting her, but she was unconscious and didn't react. There was a frightening amount of blood around him. The foot came free. He wrapped an arm around her again, levered his other arm against the seatback, sending a shot of pain through his shoulder he was barely aware of, and pulled her out of the truck cab.

He could see the blood pulsing out of a gash in her upper arm. The flow of blood had to be staunched. He tore off his shirt, wrapped it around her arm just under the armpit, and twisted until the pulsing stopped. He was gasping from the exertion. Time now to catch his breath and think. With one hand he held the twist in the shirt; with the other he dug in his pocket for his phone. He pushed the nine key. When the emergency operator answered, he described as best he could where he was. Then he settled into a position where he could hold the shirt in one hand and slip the other under her head. All he could do after that was wait.

CHAPTER THIRTY-TWO

Sam wanted to follow the ambulance to the hospital, but the sheriff's deputy held him back to ask what he'd seen. He told the deputy a pickup going well over the speed limit had passed him a moment before the accident. It had driven into the rear of the crashed pickup, as far as he could judge not slowing before the impact. "You think deliberate, like road rage?" the deputy asked.

Sam said that was what it looked like. The road was clear, the truck should have been able to pass easily, but it was hard to judge from behind. He and the deputy walked to the back of the pickup and looked for signs of impact. The left side of the rear bumper had been damaged.

"Doesn't look like that happened when it went over," said the deputy. "We'll have them see if they can find paint traces. Lucky for her she didn't flip. You get any kind of a look at the truck?"

Sam said it was a large pickup, a long bed, not jacked up. Gray or black, not glossy, maybe an older model. That's all he could remember.

For a second time this summer, Sam found himself telling a policeman some of the truth but not all of it.

At the hospital he asked the receptionist in emergency how Zoey was.

"Unconscious," she said. "Vitals are okay, looks like a broken ankle. You family?

"A friend," said Sam. "I got her out of the truck. I was afraid it would catch fire."

"Lucky you were there," she said. "You want to wait in the waiting area, somebody will tell you more once they know."

"Thanks," he said. "I'll wait."

At eleven on a weekday evening, he was the only person waiting in the emergency waiting room. After about thirty minutes, a woman in scrubs put her head through the door, saw him, and approached.

"They said you got her out of the truck."

Sam nodded.

"And you did that tourniquet?"

Sam nodded again.

"Good job. She lost a lot of blood. You saved her life, my friend."

"Thank God I was there."

"So she's unconscious. Concussion certainly, whether there's brain damage we can't tell yet. Broken ankle, separated shoulder, gash in the arm, those things we can fix. The head injury, we just have to wait."

Sam called Horacio and said he was on his way. As he worked through his rooms at the college, pushing his mop broom and emptying the trashcans, he pondered what he should do. Zoey had been right to suspect the phone call was a trap. The guy in the pickup had been waiting for her. When he let Outside pursue her investigation of the unfinished houses, he should have realized that if something illegal and profitable was happening, the people making money might try to stop her. He wouldn't let that happen again. Zoey had initiative and a willful streak. He would plead with her to let him know what she was planning.

When he told Molly what had happened, she asked him how they should write it.

"There's no evidence it was an attempt to kill the girl, right? So it's just an accident. I'll call the sheriff's office and ask if they're investigating it as a road-rage incident."

"You have any idea how much the sheriff and city cops work together in this town?" Sam asked her.

"The sheriff is ex-military. He hasn't been here long. Maybe he's not it bed with McCord, if that's what you're wondering."

Later Sam had a text from Alison. "Zoey didn't come home last night. You know where she is?"

Sam texted back that Zoey had an accident and she should meet him at the hospital in an hour. He felt guilty that he hadn't thought to get in touch with her immediately.

Alison was standing just inside the entrance when Sam arrived.

"What happened?" she asked.

"Her truck crashed. Somebody ran her off the road. I was behind her. I saw it. Come on."

Sam asked at the desk where Zoey Franco was. He was directed to the critical care unit. When they entered the room, Sam thought it might be the bed where he had been lying not so long ago.

I saved her life, she saved mine. That was me under that sheet, IV drip in the arm, maybe oxygen. Don't remember it that well. Let her come out of it like I did.

Alison laid a hand on Zoey's shoulder and gazed at her face a long minute before turning to Sam.

"Somebody did it on purpose?"

"Somebody called and said they had information about the banker. She had her doubts but decided to meet them. She told me, and I followed her."

"Was it the policeman?"

"McCord? In the truck? Probably not. But if it's him, he could have had somebody do it."

"He's after her because she's trying to prove he killed Outside. He thinks she killed his son. He wants her dead."

"It's possible," said Sam.

"I'm going to stay and watch her."

"You want to protect her."

"Could you do me a favor? Could you stay here an hour while I'm gone?"

"Sure," he said. "What are you going to do?"

"Get some things."

Sam crossed the hall to the area signed "Family Waiting." He sat down in a comfortable living-room-style chair, placed there he was sure because the hospital knew that family members might sit in the room for long periods of time. He couldn't see Zoey through the room's window because the bed was below his line of sight, but he could see the entire room and the door.

He'd seen enough detective shows to know that finishing off victims in the hospital who had survived attempts to kill them elsewhere was a staple plot device. Did it happen in real hospitals in real life? What he remembered was that sometimes the victim was smothered with a pillow, sometimes a vital life support device was unplugged from the wall, once a nurse had added something, potassium chloride, to the IV flow. Unreal, and yet possible.

When Alison reappeared in the waiting room she was carrying a full daypack on her back.

"I'm going to stay awhile," she told him.

"All right," he said. "I'm late for work. Call or text if anything happens."

The next day, when he had done his work at the paper, he returned to the waiting room. Alison sat quietly in the big chair.

"She's still unconscious," she said. "They said stable."

"You've been here the whole time?"

The girl nodded.

"Look," he said, "you go get some sleep. I'll sit here until I have to go to the school at nine."

She sat a minute, deciding, then got up.

"I can come back around three in the morning and stay till six," he said. "You can get some sleep then."

"You have time?"

"For a few days, anyway."

CHAPTER THIRTY-THREE

Sam stood and walked around the waiting room to keep from falling asleep. He was tired. His life had never been as tightly structured as it was now. He was working at two jobs and giving Alison an afternoon and late-night break from her watch. But he was doing all right. His time in prison turned out to be useful training for keeping watch. He didn't let restlessness and impatience take over his mind. He was fully alert when, an hour and a half after he had resumed sitting, he noticed movement across the hall. He rose and walked into Zoey's room.

A man wearing scrubs and a gray hoodie stood near Zoey's bed. Wearing a hoodie while on duty? It was a red flag.

"Hi there," said Sam. "You checking up?"

The man turned and looked at him.

"Yeah, just checking."

"You mind if I have a look at your ID?"

Sam was looking hard at the badge hanging from a lanyard around the man's neck. The photo image was small, but Sam didn't think it looked like the man.

"Not really necessary," said the man. He stared at Sam, then walked out of the room. Sam stepped out into the hall and watched him. At the end of the hall the man turned, looked back at Sam, then left the building.

Sam hurried to the exit and went out into the parking area, but couldn't see anyone.

There was no one else in the lobby as he reentered the building. This was a small hospital, not like Harborview in Seattle, where there were people in the hallways all night. He went to the front desk.

"Do you know, was anybody scheduled to check up just now on Zoey Franco in the critical care unit?"

"Give me a minute," said the woman at the desk. She scrolled through a computer screen, then said that nothing was scheduled.

"Is there photo coverage of the halls here?"

"There is. What's happened?"

"There was someone in her room just now. Male, in scrubs, but wearing a hoodie. There's some reason to think there are people who might try to hurt the patient."

The woman looked at him with full attention.

"You think I could look at the film? I'm a reporter with the *News*."

"I don't have access. Come back in the morning and talk to security. You should contact the police."

"Right," said Sam. He thought about the value of doing that. What if the police were convinced to post a guard near Zoey's room? Would a policeman be selected who was one of McCord's people? Would he look the other way while the man in the hoodie returned? Or was he fantasizing a conspiracy that didn't exist?

If McCord was responsible for Outside's death, it was all possible.

When Alison appeared at six in the morning, he told her what happened. She did not seem to be surprised. And there was no need to make a decision about police protection. In the afternoon Alison sent him a text saying Zoey had woken up and seemed to be fine, no brain impairment. They would keep her twenty-four hours to monitor her and determine the right mix of pain meds, then release her.

CHAPTER THIRTY-FOUR

Sam threw a rock into the water, then tossed another, trying to hit the center of the expanding circle of ripples. This was the kind of thing he needed to be doing now. Maybe walking along the ocean shore was a stereotypical response to anxiety. Nothing wrong with that. You could just walk and be a small part of the physical world without thinking much about your route. Paralyzing anxiety, that was the expression the doctor had used. He needed to be in the open, away from anything that would close him in. A lingering effect he hadn't been aware of from the time he had spent in a cell.

The night before, as he was emptying a recycling bin into his cart, something hit Sam in the chest like a blow. He was sure he was having a heart attack. His pulse began racing. He started gasping, struggling to get air into his lungs. His face and hands began to tingle. He clutched at the cart to hold himself upright. Then he began walking with short, deliberate steps, leaning on the cart, down the hall. Get to Horacio was all he could think.

"Hey, wa's happnin'?" his workmate called in alarm.

"My heart, call nine one one," Sam managed to say. He dropped into a chair and sucked in air with loud, harsh gasps.

Only once, behind the Spruce, had he experienced an emergency that required an ambulance. All his life sirens had been part of the urban background. The sound would rise, then fade as the vehicle passed the point closest to where he was, or wind down as it arrived at its destination. He was aware now of the sound becoming louder and louder until it filled his head. When the EMT crew arrived, they strapped him to a collapsible gurney and began taking his blood pressure, that much he was aware of. In the emergency room, they gave him a shot that after a few minutes calmed his racing heart and slowed his breathing to a manageable rate. There had been times after Ella's death that he wouldn't have resisted if his life had begun to fade out. But now that he might be losing it, he just wanted to get through the night.

He didn't know whether to think of it as coincidence, irony, or some weird fate. Two days after Zoey was released, here he was in the hospital again.

After an indeterminate period of time had passed, the emergency doctor pulled open the curtain at the foot of Sam's bed and said, "It's not your heart. Your heart's fine."

Sam let out a long breath of relief.

"You had a panic attack. Ever happen before?"

"No."

But then he remembered the racing heartbeat he had experienced while talking to his father in El Cerrito. A precursor of what had happened last night.

"You're a little old for the first one. But not that unusual. You have anything really stressful going on just now?"

Sam nodded. The doctor, a young, short, energetic man moving quickly on his feet, nodded back.

"We gave you an anti-anxiety shot. The treatment is that plus some talk therapy. You want to say a little about what's causing the stress?"

Sam shook his head.

"That's all right. I'm no shrink. I can give you a couple names. But this kind of thing happens to some people when they don't talk enough. Best see a professional, but talk to somebody."

CHAPTER THIRTY-FIVE

His phone dinged with a text. "Are you coming to the book group" was the message. Alison. There was no question mark, as if she expected he would be there. But text messages tended not to have a lot of punctuation, even the ones he got from newspaper people who prided themselves on being wordsmiths.

"I'll be there," he texted back.

On Saturday morning Sam waited in the hall at the college until Alison walked toward the classroom.

"Want to talk after the meeting?" he asked.

In her manner she looked briefly at his face, then nodded and turned her eyes back to where she was going. Every time Alison looked at him was like that, a strobe-flash that made him blink. This was a girl living in a state of alertness. Every interaction with other people during a day could be a threat. Her dedication to Zoey during the watch he had shared with her left him a little in awe of her ability to stay focused. How did she find the energy to keep it up?

Sam started toward the cafeteria. He'd hang around until the book group was finished. Leah appeared. Instead of smiling a greeting and going into the classroom, she came toward him. She looked distraught.

"Alison wanted to talk," he said, to explain his presence.

"Please," she said, "can you join us? It's the final meeting for the group." Her voice was stressed. She wasn't offering a courtesy invitation. She was pleading with him to be part of the meeting.

"Okay, sure," he said, and followed her through the door.

Leah took her seat in the circle, now just Barrett, Denton, and Alison.

"You all know about Zoey," she began.

Barrett hadn't heard. His mouth fell open, and his eyes half closed in fear of what he was going to learn.

"She was in a car crash. She can't be here, but she's okay."

Zoey hadn't been somebody who went out of her way to be likeable. But her energy was contagious, and she had paid the other participants the compliment of listening attentively to what they had to say. It was obvious he had thought well of her.

"It's our last meeting," said Leah. "You all have to see your parole officer and set up a schedule. But you're free." She stopped, and her face tightened in an unconscious reflection of Barrett's. "Eight weeks, four of you made it."

"Yeah, what a thing," said Denton. "But you did good. I liked the books."

Denton reached into a large grocery bag and brought out a Safeway bouquet of flowers.

"I got this for you. You know, like, to say thanks."

He shuffled across the space between chairs and handed the bouquet to Leah. She stood, took the flowers, and put her arms around Denton.

"That's so sweet. No. I mean, thoughtful. Considerate. Oh God. Thank you, Denton."

"No problem," he said with a half-smile, and returned to his seat.

Leah wiped a hand at the corner of her eye.

"I'm sorry," she said. "I don't know if I can talk about books today."

Barrett held up a hand and fluttered it nervously. "I got some thoughts."

Leah looked at Barrett with surprise. "That's great. We'd like to hear your thoughts."

Leah had assigned Victor Frankl's *Man's Search for Meaning* as the final reading assignment. She wasn't sure how the group would react to a more philosophical work than the novels she had assigned. She wanted to see how they would respond to a book about prison life. Remarkably, Barrett appeared to have been caught up by Frankl's story of living in a Nazi concentration camp. He said that it sounded like prisons were different in different places but all alike too.

"No shit," said Denton. "Why you think so much life gets lived in jails? There that many bad people?"

"Sometimes the people putting you in jail are bad," said Leah.

"Yeah," said Denton. "I seen some of that."

Alison paid attention during the discussion but didn't say anything. "What do you think, Alison?" Leah asked her. "Did the book ring true for you?"

"He was a doctor," she said. "He had privileges. If he got out, he knew he could write about it."

Leah nodded. "I see what you mean. Knowing you can tell your story and somebody will listen."

"You're not alone if there's a reader who knows what happened to you," said Alison.

At the end of the session, Leah rose and smiled at the group. "Thank you so much," she said. "You made this a success for me. In a couple weeks, the court's letting me start another group. I hope they're as good as you guys."

"Can I keep coming?" Alison asked.

Leah raised her eyebrows in surprise. "Uh, if you really want to, sure. Absolutely. I'd love to have you continue. We'll read some of the same books, though."

"I can read them again."

Barrett had an awkward moment as they filed out of the room for the last time. He decided to offer his hand for Leah to shake. She gave him a wide smile and patted their clasped hands with her free hand. Alison followed Sam outside onto the grass.

Sam looked at her, trying to follow her thought process.

"Zoey told me you live in a hard situation. You really spend your nights in a cave?"

"I've been staying with her for a while."

"You okay there?"

"She made me feel welcome. It's safer with two of us."

"You still have the bow?"

She nodded.

"I think you should get rid of it. The cops could come looking for it."

"It's hid good."

"Oh man, it's asking for trouble. Alison, you're not Katniss. Even with what you did."

"I know she's just a character. But I'm more like her than you think."

Sam spread his hands in exasperation. "Okay. Okay. Maybe so."

He'd read in one of Melissa's film reviews that there was a whole series of movies coming out featuring warriorlike adolescent girls, building on the success of the *Hunger Games* films. Maybe he should see one of them sometime. As far as he knew, Alison didn't go to movies. Her idea of Katniss was formed by the book, not whatever the movie made of her. Zoey had told him about the girl's spartan life, hiding in the woods. Reading books with a headlamp in a cave must have invested the words with a hallucinatory vividness. Zoey said she had a fast-food job and came into town early to clean up before school. A lot of time at the laundromat. You couldn't tell by looking at her that she lived rough.

"Just keep, you know, what they call a low profile."

"I know."

"Is it at your cave?"

"It's more a lean-to. But it's not there. If somebody came looking for the shelter they could find it. But not the bow."

"Still ..."

"I know how to hide things."

The same feeling came over him he'd had the day they disposed of the body. She was a sixteen-year-old, not yet a grownup. A girl living with a girl's simplified view of the world. But everything she said told him she was thinking things through like an adult. Grounded in the real world of Port Teresa, the ugly part, probably better than he was.

"She's not afraid, you know."

"Yeah, I know. She saved my ass once from getting beat up, maybe killed."

To his surprise she stepped forward and put her arms around him, just as his daughter had once done. People hugged a lot now; it didn't mean that much, but he felt the tremor of a sob. He was moved by her impulsive act. He knew from things Zoey had said that Zoey was the girl's closest friend, closer to her than anyone in her useless family. The person she'd learned she could trust. He hoped she trusted him too. The shared watch in the hospital had formed a bond. He wasn't going to let either of them down, though he didn't know yet what that might require of him.

He watched her walk toward the street and the bus stop. He took half a step, but stopped when he realized Leah was standing beside him. She must have been waiting to talk.

"One of them killed, another almost dead in an accident. In eight weeks. It's hard not to think I did something."

He didn't know what he should say. "Nothing to do with you teaching this class."

"You know why I went to the judge and asked if I could do a book group for parolees? Because Zoey asked me to help Alison. I'd already been thinking about a reading group, but that's when I decided to actually do it. Is that who you were just talking about? Zoey?"

"Yeah," said Sam.

"You probably know things you're not telling me."

Sam didn't answer, but he could see from her expression that his own face was concealing his feelings about as well as if he was holding a poker hand of cards printed on Plexiglas.

"I know you're a reporter—you can't talk about everything. Can you tell me enough to understand what happened?"

"We can talk about it."

"We could have dinner. Any way you're free tonight?"

"Yeah, but don't you have to be home, do dinner …?"

"Scott's never home before nine. We don't do dinner together."

Something in her tone, not quite bitter, not quite sardonic, but still.

"Okay," he said. "Sure. Dinner tonight."

CHAPTER THIRTY-SIX

"I don't know much about wine," said Sam.

"Let's ask the waiter," said Leah.

He had picked one of the good restaurants in town, one tourists could read good reviews for on Yelp and the locals picked for anniversaries. He'd thought about his choice. Dinner at the Sundowner Café was casual, dinner at Chanterelle was more of an event. The quiet setting might help him figure out what he would tell her. He owed her a dinner for helping him do the story on the group. He liked what she had done with the book group. Those two, Barrett and Denton, most teachers wouldn't have been able to get a response from them.

"How long have you been here?" she asked. "In town, I mean."

"Three years," he said. "Had a sportswriting job at a metropolitan daily, but that went away. Found the sports job here, got a second job to pay the rent."

The waiter brought a bottle of wine to the table. They watched as he opened it and poured each a glass.

"At the college?" Leah asked.

"Right. About ten o'clock weeknights, I'm sweeping the room where you have the book group."

"Knowing that will make me careful not to make a mess."

"I'm on automatic pilot. I don't even notice."

"I wish I could be on automatic pilot sometimes. But it's not good for a teacher to do that."

"You always wanted to teach?"

"I try to think of myself as an idealist. I saw teaching as a way to live that."

"Do teachers stay idealistic?" Sam asked.

"I think most do. You have to fight settling into easy routines. Kids treating the process with contempt doesn't help. Wow," she said. "It's been a while since I talked education philosophy over dinner."

She drew a deep breath. "Starting this group meant a lot to me. How could it end this way?"

"I admire what you did," said Sam. "Life's hard for some of those people. More risks."

He did not feel at ease. She wanted his reassurance that Gary's death and Zoey's accident had nothing to do with the book group. They did, of course, but not in a way she had any responsibility for. He poured another glass from the bottle of wine the waiter had brought and drank down half of it. Then he set the glass on the tablecloth and stared at it in embarrassment.

"Sorry, I'm guzzling like it was beer. I don't drink a lot of wine."

"Drink it any way you like. You seem kind of nervous, Sam. It's me. I'm pushing you to tell me it's not my fault."

"No way it's your fault. But yeah, I'm probably a little wound up. It's this story about the old rape trial. I do sports. I'm out of place writing about it."

"What a story," she said. "You think the girl who was the victim has come back on a vendetta?"

"Nobody knows anything about her. But it's hard to believe it's all coincidence."

He couldn't tell her the real reason he was unsettled. He wanted to tell her about Alison and Gary, but he didn't know how she'd react. The best way to keep Alison safe was to keep his mouth shut. But he wanted to tell her.

"Okay." He made a decision. "Let me put a what-if question to you. Like we're talking about one of your novels. What if a woman was being raped by a man who had some leverage on her and she killed him to defend herself. How would you feel about that?"

Leah didn't hesitate. "A woman has a right to defend herself," she said. She looked at him. "What are you telling me?"

"Would you feel that a person should go to the police, or tell somebody official if they knew about something like that?"

"If it was a case like you say, no, I would just try to help the woman. Good God, Sam, what is this?"

"If you knew something it could eat at you until you had to do something about it."

"That's never happened to me. Can I keep things in confidence? Yeah, I think so."

"I don't know how much to tell you," said Sam.

She ran both hands through her hair. "Would it help if I promised no matter what you tell me, I'll say nothing? You want to tell me something, but you're afraid I can't keep it to myself. I can. I'll do nothing without your okay. But I'm not trying to get you to tell me something you don't want to. We can change the subject."

"Gary," he said. "After book group. He made Alison go up behind the school. Maybe you know his dad's a cop. He said he'd have her busted for selling drugs if she didn't keep going with him. She learned to use a bow, and she shot him."

Leah's hands went to her face. "How do you know this?"

"Zoey. I helped them move the body."

She looked down at the table for a moment. "Thank you for trusting me."

He nodded. "I figured you deserved to know."

"Would you go to jail if this got out?"

"Probably," said Sam.

"Well I'm glad you helped."

"I had a kid about Alison's age."

"You had a kid? Don't you still?"

"My daughter was killed when she was sixteen."

"Oh," said Leah. "I am so sorry. I have no kids. I can't imagine that. You're not married now?"

"Not for a long time."

Talk, the doctor had said. He had been thinking about that. He didn't want to talk about the past because the past consisted of things he should have done but didn't. And the thing he never should have done. So he had just talked, a little. A start. This woman, wearing her heart on her sleeve for her parolee book group but hurting for them without blubbering about it, she was the first person he'd met he thought he might be able to talk to. Here he was, talking intimately with someone he'd decided to trust though he didn't know her that well. Maybe this was the right distance apart from someone he needed if he was going to talk.

"Look," he said. "I'm a felon. I did eighteen months in prison for assault. You should know that."

She looked like she wanted to ask more questions, but she stopped herself.

"Thank you for telling me that."

"Doesn't make me somebody to be afraid of."

"If you assaulted someone, I'm sure you had a good reason," she said.

He looked away. "I thought I did, but I didn't."

She took a breath and changed the subject.

"What are you working on now?"

"They want me to write about this search for Carl Tillis. Judging from e-mails and phone calls at the paper, there's a lot of interest. His daughter, Kelsey, you know her?"

"She was in my class."

"She and Kirstin asked me to help find him."

"What is happening here, Sam? Outside, is her death connected to this?"

"I don't know. It's maybe this cop. Gary's dad. I think he

might do the dirty work for the banker, Brenchlow. There's stuff coming out. Somebody needs to investigate him."

"You think the police department is corrupt?"

"In a town this size, I think the city government and the police have a lot of power. There's nobody to check on them."

"Except the newspaper."

"Which is me, my editor, and the business writer."

"What was your daughter's name?"

"Ella."

"I thought studying literature would help me understand life. That was naive. Why do such bad things happen to these young women? It's hard for me to understand why life is like this."

"At least one of them, Alison, learned how to defend herself."

"Is it going to come out?"

Sam's forehead creased. "I don't think they're looking at her."

"What's going to happen to her?"

"I think she's doing okay. She seems to be able to manage her life without a family. Zoey's being a real friend to her. I couldn't have done what she's doing."

"You have a girlfriend, Sam?"

"No."

"You'd probably go back and do parts of your life over if you could, wouldn't you?"

"Yeah," he said. "I would. How about you? You probably made good enough choices."

"Not really. No disasters. You just wish you had more experience when you made some of those decisions."

"But no re-dos."

"I think about it," she said.

CHAPTER THIRTY-SEVEN

The name of the woman Sam spilled his beer over when he jumped up from his seat with too much enthusiasm at a Mariners' game was Megan. She had a wide, attractive smile, knew a slider from a fastball, and during the seventh inning stretch told him to stop apologizing and gave him her number.

After six months of spending their weekends together, he decided he was more comfortable with her than he had been in any of his previous relationships. Her baggage was light, and there were no hints about expectations and commitment. Their lives seemed to fit together without any great effort. Megan said she'd like kids someday, but there was plenty of time. She had years, she said, before she would hear her biological clock ticking.

He didn't really propose. They had just finished the New Year's Day Resolution Run 5K that included a dunk in the frigid water of Lake Washington and were waiting in the hot chili line, knowing they had about five more minutes of residual warmth from the run before they began shivering, and decided their resolution would be to get married.

He loved her because he trusted her. He trusted her because

she trusted him and never questioned anything he said. They had a daughter they named Ella after Megan's grandmother.

He relaxed into a family nest. He hadn't expected he would settle so easily into family life. There was no nest for him growing up. His father had found no nest for himself in marriage and couldn't provide one for his sons.

So he was stunned when he learned that after six years of marriage, Megan had an affair.

She had always taken short trips to trade shows as part of her job repping a line of sportswear. After the last of those trips, something, he could not have said what, started him wondering. No words, no behavior he could have identified. No way he would have asked her questions. He would never risk fracturing the bond of trust.

But she knew he had a question, and one evening after Ella was in bed, she broke down and confessed. She had spent two nights with the guy and loathed herself afterward and never wanted to see him again. A few glasses of wine, the energy and excitement and a loss of judgment that frightened her every time she thought about it. He sat numbly as she sobbed out her story. His instinct told him not to interrupt, even if he had been capable of speaking. When she was done, she sat for a moment with her eyes shut, then looked at him, waiting for his reaction.

"I trusted you," he said.

"I know," she answered. "I fucked up."

He couldn't speak. She sat, and later he would give her credit for not giving in to the urge he could see in her face to throw her arms around him and beg to be forgiven.

"Just one thing I'll say and then not say it again," her voice coming in teary, scratchy jerks. "You always said you can't predict the future. You're right. I remember the moment I felt the first twinge of whatever stupidity you want to call it, temptation. I am so filled with anger and shame and horror at myself that if ever, ever in my life I feel even the first second of that twinge, I'll fall on the floor and start vomiting. I'll buy a gun and put it in my mouth."

"Don't talk about shooting yourself," he said.

"I'll quit my job. Stay at home with Ella."

"You like your job. You shouldn't quit."

"What are you going to do?"

"I don't know," he said. "Right now I need to leave."

When Sam played football, his job as a defensive back was to react. The offensive team on the field were the planners. They came to the line of scrimmage with a plan, and the question was how well they carried it out. Sam's task was to grasp the plan as quickly as possible and prevent it from happening. When a receiver ran downfield to catch a pass, he had to decide whether the receiver was going to break left, break right, or run a go route. A defensive back developed reflexes, quicker than any conscious thought process, that read clues in the receiver's movement and let him close on the receiver in time to disrupt the pass.

Though he wasn't aware of it, the habits of the defensive back had shaped Sam's way of living in the world. He wasn't very good at planning. He let his reflexes react.

That's what he did now. He rented a mother-in-law room with its own entrance from an acquaintance and e-mailed Megan to box up his clothes and have them delivered. He went to a lawyer and told him to give his wife anything she asked for.

"What about visitation rights?" the lawyer inquired.

He said he didn't want any. When the lawyer raised an eyebrow, he said it would be more painful to see his daughter occasionally than not to see her at all.

"You don't think she wants a father, even part-time?"

He could see what the lawyer was thinking, that he was putting his own feelings ahead of his daughter's welfare.

"I couldn't handle seeing her," he said.

"Your call. But let me write in some language that you can review the arrangement if you change your mind."

"Fine," he said. "Can't predict the future."

After the divorce Sam began putting in longer hours at work. He volunteered to cover any kind of high-school sports during the week. He began stopping off at a bar after work for a few beers. The beers helped him unwind and put a little distance between memories of his failed family life and the present moment. Not too many, though. If he let himself get drunk, he would wake abruptly at three in the morning, and images of Megan, Ella, and the house he had been remodeling would overwhelm him with a sense of his uselessness. A year ago he had felt useful, doing a decent enough job of retiling the kitchen with the Home Depot instructions. He was doing nothing useful now. There were days he was tempted to stop off near the school and see if he could spot Ella. But he didn't. He risked being busted as a pervert, and he had made his choice. He wondered what Megan had told Ella about why he wasn't there. He was sure Megan would have taken the blame. But at some point it would come out that her dad didn't want to see her. He did, just not yet. When his thoughts went there, he had another beer and tried to immerse himself in conversations about coaching changes and upcoming games with anybody he could get to hang out with him into the late evening.

Then he had a DUI. Not long after his hours at the paper were cut. There were budget cuts at the paper; he was last in and first out at the sports desk. He was overtaken by apathy. He walked or took the bus home from his drinking spots now. He got into a couple of barfights and beat a guy up, shattering his jaw, luckily a big guy with a reputation for fighting who wasn't going to sue for damages.

He waited for the right opportunity to see his daughter. It would be easier, he could handle it, when she'd become a young adult and they'd be able to talk. Though how that conversation would go exactly, he couldn't work out the details in his imagination.

She probably was that young adult when he got a phone call from his brother Nolan, who told him in a clipped and angry voice that his daughter had been raped and murdered, and he could read about it the next day in his own paper.

He didn't remember how he passed the night, or anything that happened until the next morning when he found the reporter who was covering the story. "Oh Jesus," she said, when he told her the girl was his daughter.

There are anesthetic drugs that can be given to a patient undergoing a painful procedure who needs to be kept conscious during the procedure. The function of the drug is not to suppress the pain, but to suppress the memory of the pain. If the patient doesn't remember pain, was there any? Sam was never able to remember the first weeks after learning about Ella's death.

The funeral service would be a miserable experience, but he couldn't think about not being there. He wished he could be by himself and not have to talk to anybody. But he was guided to a seat next to his ex-wife. His eyes were so blurred with tears he could barely see where he was going. He vaguely remembered reaching across Megan to shake the hand of her husband, whose name didn't register. But other than the introduction, she didn't say anything to him, and he couldn't say a word to her.

He made his way out of the church, aware of people tentatively approaching him, but no one actually spoke. There would be a time he would be ashamed of how he was behaving, but not now.

On the sidewalk leading to the parking lot, he saw Nolan waiting for him.

"You absolute fucking asshole," he said to Sam.

Lucidity returned some days later while he was waiting in his car near a South Seattle apartment where the man the police were investigating as the rapist lived. Time had passed and events had occurred that led to this moment, but he would have had a hard time reconstructing them if anyone had asked. He had a photo of the man, a level-three sex offender, convicted and sentenced for a previous rape. In the middle of the night the man appeared. Sam approached him, told him who he was, and beat the man viciously.

Sam was arrested. While he was in jail he learned the police had identified another man who confessed to killing his daughter. The man he had beaten lost some brain function, could not speak clearly, and would spend his life in a wheelchair. At his trial Sam said nothing in his defense. His court-appointed attorney argued that between guilt and grief, Sam was being punished enough. He was sentenced to eighteen months for assault, a light sentence that probably reflected the court's understanding of his state of grief and the criminal history of the man he had beaten.

The time at the Monroe correctional facility was, like everything that had happened since his brother's call, a clouded memory. Occasionally he engaged in conversation with other inmates. He tried reading novels, lifting weights, and a few times took part in activities organized by the staff as ways to distract himself from his memories. He only really succeeded for the odd hour when he became engrossed in a football or basketball game on the rec area TV. Since his divorce he had felt he was living a useless life. He had no respect for useless lives. And with the mistaken beating he had carried out, his life was worse than useless. There was no reason for him to continue his existence. Sometimes the things going on in his mind that he couldn't shut up exhausted him to the point he wished he could just go to sleep and not have to wake up. There were ways to do that involving self-strangulation, but he never reached the point of taking the step.

The time for his release came. He had made no plans about what he would do. A friend from the sports department told him about the position open for a sportswriter at the paper in Port Teresa, on the Washington coast. Sam made an appointment to meet with the editor. During the interview he told the editor, an older man with a flushed complexion who looked at him over the top of his glasses, that he was a recently released felon. He had let a couple of inmates know what he'd been sentenced for because the inmate population didn't like not knowing why somebody was there, but after his release there had been no occasion to make a simple statement of what he had done and why. The editor looked through the portfolio of sports articles Sam had given him and said, "So you're probably not going to do anything like that again."

"No," said Sam. "I'm not."

The editor said he could have the job if he wanted it, told him about how many column inches he expected every week, and said he would probably need a second job to have enough to live on. While he was scanning recent back issues the editor had given him to get a sense of the paper's style, he found a job posting for a part-time custodian at the community college. He scheduled an interview. He told the personnel department interviewer about his record. He said the evening hours of the job would fit with his newspaper work. The interviewer, reflecting the liberal values of institutions of higher education, told him he could start the following week.

He moved what he had to Port Teresa. The custodial job started at nine, as the last of the evening classes were finishing. He and Horacio were responsible for the buildings on the east half of the campus. They usually finished about two. When he began he had to clock in, but after a few months the supervisor said he didn't have to bother. The supervisor went through the buildings at seven in the morning. If everything was done to the standard, he was happy. X amount of payroll dollars for X amount of cleaning was what he wanted, and he didn't care how fast or slowly his crew did it.

Sam wrote sports reports in the morning, cleaned rooms in the evening, found a pickup basketball game that let him burn off energy, and held on to a vague hope that if enough time passed, things would get better.

CHAPTER THIRTY-EIGHT

When he arrived at the paper in the morning, he was greeted by the sight of two huge white six-wheelers, green and blue CMT logos on the sides, taking up half the newspaper's parking lot. Generators thrummed, a run of cabling covered with rubber-lined squares of maroon carpeting to prevent people from tripping led through the door to the office. For God sakes, he muttered. It's gone national.

The receptionist raised her hands in a gesture of helplessness and said, "Get ready."

His desk had become a stage set. Hot-looking lights and seven or eight people clustered around his workspace. Molly and his workmates hovered outside the circle of light. A man in a tie stepped toward him.

"You must be Sam," he said.

He gave Molly a questioning look. She grimaced and said, "I tried to give you a heads-up but couldn't reach you this morning. They've been running me around since I got here."

He waited for the man in the tie to say something.

"I'm Steve Kane," he said. "I'm the director."

Steve Kane gave Sam's hand a quick single shake and

pointed to his chair. "Just go ahead and sit, we'll mike you up and get started."

"Get started with what?" Sam asked.

"You know the show? *Hunters and Fugitives*?"

"Not really. What kind of show?"

"We're reality TV, the Truth channel. We're not *Duck Dynasty*, but we got nearly two million viewers. You don't watch cable?"

"Yeah, sports," said Sam.

"We're here to help you find Carl Tillis."

Someone clipped a mic to his shirt. A woman gave his face a critical appraisal from fifteen inches away and began brushing powder on his forehead.

A striking blonde with carefully sculpted hair who'd already had the full makeup treatment smiled a tooth-glittering smile at him, stepped into the circle of hot light, and said, "Hi, Sam, I'm Sarah Craft. I'm the star," wiggling air quotes at him. "I'll be asking you some questions. The way we like to do this is we don't rehearse, I just talk with you and you say what comes to mind. We don't try to take advantage, if there's anything you're uncomfortable with when we're done we can reshoot a specific question. We're after spontaneity. Any feelings you want to express, it's all good. Just relax. Maybe count to ten out loud a couple times, get the vocal chords warmed up. Okay?"

"One, two, three, four ..." What the fuck? Was he really doing this? They didn't care if he thought it was okay. They were going to roll right through, and if he dragged his heels, they'd grab Molly and stick her in his chair. Serve her right, not warning him. Yeah, but he had his phone off. Okay. It should be him.

An assistant adjusted his position as if he were a grade-schooler having his posture corrected for the class picture. After watching someone move a light stand to one place then another, Sarah said with a touch of impatience, "We about ready here?"

"Ten seconds," said Steve Kane. "Sound. Camera. Okay, action."

Sarah beamed at a camera and said, "We're in the newsroom of the *North Coast News* in Port Teresa, in the state of Washington, where reporter Sam Troshin first uncovered the link between two recent deaths, one here in Port Teresa, and a thirty-year-old rape trial. Sam, thanks for meeting with us."

He forced a smile and nodded. His camera smile had always been self-conscious and phony.

"So what was it, Sam, that led you to make the connection?"

"The truck," he said. "I learned it was the same truck that belonged to the victim. It crashed and burned at the same spot thirty years ago."

"That's right, a Ford F-100 pickup. As a sidenote, we've learned that pickup is now being restored at a shop in California. We understand Barrett-Jackson wants to put it up for auction as a collector vehicle with a unique history. They're calling it the Twice-Torched Truck from Port Teresa. There's a hot market out there for crime-scene memorabilia. They think six figures. Now, you have been looking for Carl Tillis, the third of the alleged rapists?"

"We asked everybody we could find if they know where he is."

"And you've had no luck."

"It seems he didn't tell anybody where he was going."

"According to your story in the *News*, Carl Tillis left his daughter Kelsey a note, so we can be pretty sure he wasn't abducted."

"He probably was scared. He might have gone into hiding."

"That's what I think too, Sam."

She had several more simplistic questions that were easy enough to answer. It sounded like an investigation, but they already knew the answers to their questions. He tried to imagine anyone finding this entertaining. There had to be an audience for this crap or they wouldn't be here. There probably really were people interested in things like twice-torched trucks. For a hundred grand? There were people with too much money. She ended by urging any viewers with information to call the tip line, which he assumed was flashing across the bottom of the screen out in the trucks.

"We good?" Sarah asked Steve.

"Need to redo?"

"Nah, that's about what we can get here."

"Wrap it up."

Like bees released from a hive, the crew swarmed over Sam, Sarah, and the desk. Not quite a three-second Ferrari pitstop, but they were fast. Lights were switched off, cord rolled up on reels, telescoping stands folded up and packed into foam-lined cases. Sarah gave him a wide but very brief smile and thanked him.

"Watch the show and see if we find him," she said.

The TV crew needed only ten minutes to pack their gear into the trucks and pull out of the parking lot. They were good at leaving in a hurry. Molly dropped into the chair next to Sam's desk. With Preedy's frequent absences from the office, she had become the *de facto* managing editor.

"What do you think?" she asked. "Is this a story?"

"You mean reality TV comes to Port Teresa? Aren't we supposed to report the news, not be it?"

"You're right," she said. "Even if this circus is the most exciting thing going on in town today. But this could sell some papers. I had the photographer get some shots of you on camera. They use us, we use them."

"It's crap," said Sam. Molly's job was to sell newspapers, but still.

Fifteen minutes later Sam, still trying to settle himself and review the sports he'd missed on his weekend in California, had a call from Matt Moore at the police station.

"Hey, help me out here, man," said Matt in a voice near panic. "What am I supposed to tell these TV people? Can you come over here?"

"The TV people there?" Sam asked. "How much time before they film?"

"God knows. Do I just tell them we haven't done shit to look for Tillis?"

"Why are the cops even letting them in the station?"

"The captain thinks any publicity is good publicity. He's a politician."

"Circus is right," he said to Molly, with a shake of his head as he left the newspaper office and drove to the police station.

The white trucks were now parked on Fifth in front of the city hall. In the station the techs were lining up the lights. Matt waved Sam to his desk. He was sweating profusely. Sam's impression was that Matt didn't mind being the focus of the local news cameras, but the attention of the national media and a roomful of professionals he didn't know was overwhelming him.

"What do I say?" he pleaded.

"What we already said, right? There's no crime been committed. Tillis left a note saying he's going, and his daughter says it's genuine. Tell them you made inquiries into his whereabouts, but nobody in town's been able to help."

"Shit, we didn't even to that."

"They won't know that."

"I've seen these shows," said Matt. "They like to make the police look incompetent. I don't know what the captain was thinking. Makes their fucking bounty hunter look like she's the real deal. A blonde with boobs and a Sig strapped on her leg, for fuck sake."

"Smile, don't apologize. Say you sympathize with the family and are ready to help."

"Okay. Okay. I can do this. Thanks, Sam."

"That blonde will keep herself the focus. Let her. You know, be supportive. Do not apologize."

"Do not apologize." Matt suddenly reached out and shook Sam's hand with some warmth. "Thanks, Sam. You're better at this than I am."

Am I? Sam thought. If that's true you're in the wrong business.

He watched the crew wire Matt up and daub on the makeup,

what he'd just been through. Except just as the director said "action" the makeup woman waved a hand and wiped Matt's perspiring brow a last time. Matt looked up at Sam halfway through the interview. Sam gave him an encouraging thumbs-up.

CHAPTER THIRTY-NINE

Candy had never in twenty years snooped in her husband's office. She dusted and cleaned because he didn't want the hired help in the room. But she'd never paid attention to whatever level of security might be in place. Maybe the estate's perimeter security—expensive, she was sure, and well maintained—was all he felt he needed. Maybe he'd once set little booby-traps in the drawers to see if she was opening them, but after two decades she must surely have passed that test. The morning she knew Neil would be gone for a couple of days, she stood at his desk and nervously gave each drawer a gentle tug to see if it was locked. None of them were. She decided when she was done she would give the place a thorough cleaning and tell Neil it was the spring cleaning she'd been putting off.

She had thought hard about what Helen, his ex-wife, had told her. Serious financial problems on the horizon. Not just bad judgment, some kind of illegal activity. Chickens coming home to roost. She was too old to start over. She didn't want to be disloyal to Neil, but he'd made his bed, and if it turned out to have spikes instead of springs for a mattress, she wasn't going to be lying down beside him. She had listened carefully to the

IT person who worked with Helen, taken notes. The opportunity had come. Wiping the perspiration from her fingers on her blouse, she turned on the computer. Then she phoned the IT woman. Slowly, answering all the woman's questions, she pushed the buttons and described what came up.

Forty-five minutes later she was sweating profusely and wiping her hands every few minutes. The woman told her they had probably learned what they could. Some of Neil's programs were password protected, others not. She asked Candy if Neil was particularly computer savvy. She said as far as she knew he wasn't.

He probably keeps the most important information, anything sensitive, written down in notebooks, she said. Look for anything that could be an account name, and any numbers associated with it. Bring what she could find to Helen.

She took her time going through the papers. She was looking for financial information, and found some, but also for anything else that might be interesting. The name and number of a little chickadee or two. She would have been surprised but not shocked. When she was done, she let out a long breath of relief and began the coverup housecleaning.

"This is good," Helen told her later. "This gets me updated on some things I already knew about."

"Is there anything here if things go bad with Neil?" she asked.

"Yeah, I think so. A lot's going to disappear, worst-case scenario, but not all of it."

A few times she was tempted to ask Neil about his financial situation, but after what she'd done, she knew it was better to be ignorant of any looming problems. And after all, he was her husband, her daughter's father, a distant but generous enough provider. She did not like the feeling of being disloyal.

That was until she read the newspaper article her daughter had brought waving in her hand into the theater. After the rehearsal she sat down and read the article more carefully. The three boys were named. The reporter referred to "the father of one of the accused rapists" paying for an out-of-town lawyer.

The play depicted the father as paying for an expensive lawyer and for perjured testimony as well. She drove downtown to the newspaper office.

"Sam Troshin, that's the name on this story on the old rape trial," she said to the receptionist. "Is he here?"

"He'll be in tomorrow morning. You want to leave a note or a voice mail?"

She said if she could leave a note, that would be fine.

At ten the next morning, the reporter called.

"Thanks," she said. "My name is Candy Brenchlow. Ronnie Brenchlow was my stepson. Neil is my husband. Your story, that is all news to me. Kind of a shock. You mention in the story you found your information about the old trial in the newspaper files. What I'm wondering is if I'd be allowed to read through those files."

Sam Troshin asked her to give him a minute.

"The old newspaper files aren't really open to the public," he said when he returned. "But they said okay. If you want to set a time, I'll show you how to use the microfiche."

She asked if an hour from now would be all right.

The receptionist opened the door to the editorial room and pointed toward Sam. Candy walked to his desk and introduced herself. A sportswriter, as she remembered. He looked like a sportswriter, a retired jock, not gone to seed.

"It's in the back," he said, and led her down a hall past a door with rippled opaque glass and "Editor" in old-fashioned lettering to the room at the end. Sam took out a key, unlocked it, and turned on a light. She'd seen larger walk-in closets. He switched on the microfiche light and showed her how to thread the film.

"Each reel's got six months," he said. "This is the one you want. Look away from it a lot. It gets to your eyes."

Candy smiled at Sam and thanked him again for letting her do this.

"It's still an active story," he said. "We're trying to locate Carl Tillis. You might find something here important I didn't recognize. Would you let me know?"

She said she would.

Two hours later she stood and stretched her back. She hadn't been aware how stiff she'd become. The reporter had been right. If she hadn't unfocused her eyes and shut them periodically, she'd have a wrenching headache by now. When she walked back through the editorial room, the reporter was gone. She thanked the receptionist and said she could relock the library.

That evening she called Helen.

"You see the story?" she asked.

"Chickens coming home big-time," said Helen.

"You remember much about it?"

"Some. It was ugly."

"You think the girl was innocent?"

"Probably. They made her look bad."

"There's a reference to a witness. Testified she was a party girl. The way I read the story, that's what pretty much turned it against her. Remember anything about that?"

"Oh yeah. That was a guy named Warren Bunty. Neil gave him a good job at the bank. I'm sure there was a cash payment. He still works at the bank."

"Are we all right?"

"To a degree. There's a couple offshore accounts so convoluted I don't think Neil could sort them out if he tried."

When she hung up, Candy called the number the reporter had given her and left a voice mail. The witness not named in the old accounts who wrecked the girl's reputation was Warren Bunty, and Helen thought he'd been given cash. He still worked at the bank. She thanked Sam for letting her look through the newspaper's files and said Warren Bunty was somebody Sam might want to talk to.

CHAPTER FORTY

Sam watched the Volvo wagon pull into the driveway. When the man he assumed was Warren Bunty got out, Sam walked toward him.

"Warren," he called out. The man turned and looked at him with apprehension.

"Warren," Sam repeated, walking not too fast, smiling, and giving what he hoped was a nonthreatening wave.

"My name's Sam. Would you mind talking for just a minute?"

"Who are you?"

"I could use your help. I'm trying to get some information together."

"What are you talking about?"

"That trial business in Port Teresa. You probably didn't see the play they had there about the trial."

Bunty stared at Sam and began shaking his head.

"I don't know you," he said.

"Okay," said Sam. "I don't want to bother you. But you could really help me out."

"What are you, police? You a reporter?"

"I'm with the *North Coast News.* I wrote about Brenchlow for the paper. I need you to straighten me out."

"I can't help you," he said, and went into the house, closing the door behind him with a bang.

When Sam told Molly he should see the play everyone was talking about, she offered to have the paper buy a couple of tickets and go with him. The remaining performances in the small community theater were sold out. She had to use the paper's leverage to move to the top of the waiting list.

Sam never had much interest in the theater. The English-major girlfriend had dragged him to a couple of college productions, classic plays, Ibsen and something else that hadn't inspired him with a desire to see more. But he was immediately absorbed in *The Acquittal.* Someone had turned the events he had written about into a performance. The names were different, but it was his story. Some of the speeches in the trial scenes went beyond the old newspaper coverage and were very convincing. He thought about what Melissa had said. The author might have talked to people who had been there.

One of the scenes was set in an office rather than the courtroom. The father of one of the accused rapists was persuading a younger man to testify that the victim was a loose woman. He offered cash and a job in his bank. The man wavered, revealing some moral scruples, but let himself be convinced by the father's argument that shading the truth was justified by preventing a miscarriage of justice.

Here was the man who had taken the bank job and may have had a debate with himself similar to the dialogue in the play. He had just told Sam he didn't want to talk to him.

Finding Bunty had been easier than Sam expected. When he had knocked on the door of the family home just before dinnertime and introduced himself to Bunty's wife, she said there wasn't anything she could tell him. She said her husband was afraid he was in danger because a madwoman was trying to kill the witnesses from an old trial and had left the area. Sam said he was the reporter covering the story and had information that might help Bunty. The moment came that Sam was learning to recognize, when the person he was questioning decided the reporter was either someone to be trusted or not to be trusted.

The woman must have decided to trust him. She gave him an address in a Portland suburb.

After Bunty's refusal to talk, Sam drove to a bar not far from the motel where he'd taken a room and tried to think about how you got somebody to talk to you who didn't want to. He'd been around newspapers long enough to know reporters tried to make themselves likeable as a way to get people to talk, but the good reporters he'd seen at work had no need to actually be liked. They could quickly become antagonistic if they thought that goading someone was the best tactic to get the person to respond to questions. They knew an implied accusation could elicit a reaction.

A little after five, the bar began filling up with blue-collar workmen having a beer before going home. Sam struck up a conversation with a couple of men who had given him a nod as they took seats at the bar. When Sam said he was a sportswriter, they began talking about who the Trailblazers should trade for and the chances of Portland or Seattle getting an NHL hockey team. Two others overhearing the animated conversation joined in. Sports, the lingua franca among males in bars everywhere.

"Another story I'm working on," said Sam. "Any of you heard about the guy in Port Teresa who disappeared because he thinks the victim of an old rape is hunting down the guys who did it? Some reality TV bounty hunters are looking for him."

"Hey, I saw that show," said one of the men. "*Hunters and Fugitives*, right? I recognize you now. That was you they talked to, wasn't it?"

"Yeah, they did. They interviewed me. Anyone else see that?"

Heads shook. One out of four, Sam thought. He was probably lucky to find even one. The number of people in the Northwest who know about Carl Tillis was not going to be one in four.

In the morning he sat in his car up the street from the house where Bunty was staying. Someone, probably the homeowner, maybe a cousin, maybe an old friend, came out at eight and drove away. Bunty emerged an hour later. Hard to know how long he's planning to stay here, Sam thought. A frightened man, trying to keep out of sight and let time pass. He followed Bunty to a mall where the banker parked his car and walked to a coffee shop.

Once Bunty had his coffee and pastry, picked up a paper, and found a table, Sam slid into the chair across from him. Bunty looked up and recognized Sam. Sam saw dismay in his face as he jerked his chair back from the table and jumped up.

"Get away from me, or I'm calling the police," he cried out, loud enough that several of the customers in the coffee shop looked up from their phones and computers at the two men.

"What would you expect the police to do?" Sam asked. "I'll tell them I'm a reporter who wants to talk to you. They know the press is allowed to do that."

Bunty stared at Sam, uncertain. Sam was bluffing, but Bunty couldn't be sure.

"Look," said Sam, "I don't like hassling you. But I need to get your side of things. So I'm just going to stay around awhile until we can talk."

This was the tactic Sam had decided on. He wondered if investigative reporters used it much. Don't threaten your subject, don't intimidate him, don't cajole. Exasperate him. Let him see you have nothing better to do with your time. Make him realize the only way to get rid of you is to talk and get it over with.

After letting a brief silence pass, Sam said, "I don't know if you saw that play I mentioned. *The Acquittal*? There's an actor who plays you. Your character doesn't come off very good. My guess is it's an unfair portrait. Probably didn't really happen like the play."

"I didn't see any play," said Bunty.

"So what actually did happen?"

"You're going to write about me."

"Only if I can get the truth."

"You're the one who wrote the story in the paper?"

"Yeah."

Bunty sucked in a breath. "Look. That was a long time ago. I was just a kid. Just trying to get a job with the bank. I really needed the job. The banking job I had before, I cut a corner. Being young and stupid. Then this whole thing happened."

"It was Neil Brenchlow you were dealing with?"

"Neil told me the girl was a schemer who'd probably been put up to it. Have his son sent to jail for years, and then come after him with a lawsuit for a lot of money. He asked if I could help by testifying against the girl. There was no deal. He wasn't offering me a job for testifying. I just wanted to get into his good graces. He had me talk with the cop about Claire's background."

"McCord."

"Was that his name? Yeah, probably. He gave me the names of a couple of lowlifes and said talk about them as known associates. Christ. Claire Draghici. You think she's insane?"

"Nobody knows anything about her," said Sam. "It's possible."

"I didn't plan to say what I did. But while I was on the stand, she looked at me. I remember it. Utter, utter contempt. Like I was some kind of insect that deserved squashing. Really pissed me off. So I looked back and said we'd had casual sex a few times."

"Is it true, what the play presented, you got a cush job and a bribe?"

"No," said Bunty. "Not exactly. Yeah, I got the job. He said I'd showed my loyalty. I was the kind of person he wanted working with him. There was no cash payment. A couple years later, I did get a loan on good terms from Neil to help buy a house. But it was a loan."

"What do you know about the bank's construction loan business with the Russians?"

"I was never involved in that."

"But you knew there was something going on."

"Yeah. Russian named Alexei was in there a lot. But he only dealt with Neil."

"You think there's going to be problems?"

"Now? There already are. I think Neil got in over his head. I heard about a young woman reporter who was trying to talk with the Russians about it. Neil got really pissed. I know something happened to her."

Sam lost his train of thought for a moment. He sat still while Bunty waited for the next question.

"What are you going to do now?"

Bunty shook his head. "I don't know. It scares the shit out of me you found me so easy."

"I had your wife's help. I told her I was trying to help you. I told her she shouldn't tell anyone else."

Bunty stared into the cup of coffee he hadn't touched. "What are you going to write?"

"Up to the editor whether we use your name. I won't say where you are."

"Christ." He glared at Sam as if he wanted to hit him. But the moment passed, and he continued staring at the cup is his hands.

"I don't know what to do. You think she's coming after me?"

"It's probably just the rapists she wants. If that's what's really happening here."

"Oh," said Bunty. "It's really happening."

CHAPTER FORTY-ONE

Candy expected that the next meeting of her monthly book group would be an interesting hour.

Three years earlier Shelley had invited her to join. The five members rotated hosting the meetings in their homes. Except Candy. After the first meeting at her home, Shelley said the others loved the space, spectacular house and view, but the security at the entrance had made a couple of the ladies uncomfortable. "Fortress Brenchlow," one of them called it. At Candy's request Neil had taken the step of hiring a female guard at the gatehouse for the day, but the feedback was she reeked of tobacco. Candy now rented the banquet room at the Chanterelle when it was her turn to host.

"Is anybody going to feel put down that I pay for a nice lunch?" she had asked.

"Honey, nobody minds a little of Neil's money spent on us," Shelley assured her.

The length of the actual book discussions varied. If no one said they liked the book when they first went around the room for opinions, the person who'd recommended it shrugged and apologized, and they moved on to general conversation that was always good for an hour or more.

What was going on with the bank, and her husband, that would be the question in everybody's look today, even if no one asked. She thought someone probably would.

Luckily the group really liked the book they were discussing, Kate Atkinson's *When Will There Be Good News?*

"Love that Jackson Brodie," said one of them. "He's one of those heroes that comes across as socially inept and keeps making mistakes in his personal relationships. But supercompetent at some key things."

"What about that girl Reggie? Isn't she way too capable for a sixteen-year-old?"

"I was more capable at sixteen than I got credit for," another responded. "I just never had a chance to show it."

That turned out to be a topic of interest, the capabilities of sixteen-year-old girls. They all agreed they had known more about life and men at sixteen than their mothers had at the same age.

"Right," someone said. "Our daughters are saying exactly the same thing."

"We must be the first generation that doesn't dare interfere with our teenage daughters' sex lives."

Sex and parenting, good stimulating topics for the book group. No questions about Neil as it turned out. Maybe next time. At the end of the session, one of the women gripped Candy by the hand and said, "You'll get through this okay."

Candy thanked her and said she hoped she was right.

"Did you see this?" Shelley asked her as they were gathering themselves to leave. She unfolded the morning's issue of the *News*.

Candy looked at a full-page movie ad. "Did Hollywood Know the Port Teresa Story before We Did?" was printed like a banner headline across the top of the page. The ad announced a special one-week run of a film titled *I Spit on Your Grave*. The story line, the ad read, followed events in Port Teresa with uncanny accuracy. It looked as though someone with a good memory had dug up an old film on the rape-and-revenge theme.

"I don't remember ever seeing a full-page movie ad," said Shelley.

After saying her good-byes to the book group, Candy walked through town to pick up a few things on her shopping list. She sat down in a coffee shop to rest for a few minutes and bought a paper so she could take another look at the big movie ad. As she was scanning the paper, the letters to the editor section caught her eye. All the letters were responses to a review of *The Acquittal* that must have run a few days earlier, though she hadn't seen it.

Dear Editor,

I enjoyed the play and found it as good as anything the municipal theater has done since their excellent Waiting for Godot three years ago. Is this play really about something that happened in Port Teresa back in the eighties? Seems like too many coincidences for it not to be. A suggestion: please invite the author to come to Port Teresa and talk about the genesis of the play. Many of us would be interested in knowing more.

Morgan Ternan
Port Teresa

Dear Editor,

It's hard to avoid the conclusion that The Acquittal is an attempt at justification of Claire Draghici's accusation of rape following her high-school prom. According to your drama critic, the play's author couldn't be reached for comment. The play seems to be a message to all of us that the jury got it wrong back in the eighties. Maybe they did. Wonder if there's anybody left around from that jury who could talk about it. Are the lawyer, the cop, and the reporter in the play still in town? Have somebody go talk to them.

Raymond Abernathy
Port Teresa

Dear Editor,

My question is, have the police made a thorough investigation of the deaths of two men accused of being rapists, both dying in fires in the past two months? The news stories haven't said much about what they are doing to learn more. Is anyone out there arguing this is a coincidence? We are seeing a killer at work who also happens to be a playwright. Imagine Robert Blake, who played the killer in the film In Cold Blood, writing a screenplay justifying his murder of his wife. Well-acted, but I squirmed through the whole play.

Stanley Renquist
Port Townsend

Dear Editor,

Does your drama critic live with her head in the sand? I agree with Melissa Merrill's assessment of the staging and acting of The Acquittal. But the highlight moment of the play, Cassie's speech accusing the rapist's father of adding to the humiliation of rape by paying a witness to claim she's a slut? I was electrified by the power of Anna Brenchlow's emotion. This play is part of an ongoing real-life drama in this town. Your reviewer played it way too safe by ignoring that. This isn't just a play, folks, this is living theater. Get tickets if you can and see it!

Clark Henebill
Port Teresa

She wished she'd seen the review. Maybe she could dig it up. I guess I'm going to have to see this movie, she decided. She stopped at the theater to buy a ticket for the movie opening that evening. Next to the box office a pair of large glass-covered gold frames for displaying movie posters were mounted on the wall. Instead of a printed poster, she saw an artist's rendering of an athletic big-busted woman in a black leotard with a weapons belt around her waist. Lettering over her head read "Black Widow, the Avenger," and a Marvel Comics logo. In smaller but clear lettering on the emblem on the Black Widow's front she could read "Claire."

Black Widow would be starting next week, after the *I Spit* run. The theater operators must be digging up all the avenging-women films they could find. What have we unleashed here? she wondered after looking at the poster.

When she returned to the theater in the evening, people were lined up along the sidewalk. She didn't go to many movies and wasn't sure who the movie crowd was. There were older couples with beards and full-length skirts, the people who had bought seats for *The Acquittal*. Also, the twentysomethings you'd expect to see queuing up for the next zombie and bridesmaids-getting-raunchy flick. Two women she recognized as checkers at the Safeway. Kids from the college laughing and pushing one another. Everybody really. She waved to a couple of women she knew who were headed around the corner looking for the end of the line. Enough people must still read the paper. That big ad, there'd probably been radio ads as well.

"A third-rate sexploitation classic," somebody said behind her. "I saw it in the nineties. A piece of shit. You'll love it."

It looked like every seat was taken. The trailers began ten minutes after the scheduled start. When did previews become trailers? An example of the changes that happen you never notice until ages later.

The feature began with a young woman writer renting a cabin in the woods to work on a novel. At a gas station, she inadvertently offends four young men. After a few days, they appear at the cabin and harass her. It's clear that one of the four, Matthew, is a naïve and somewhat simple youth, and the others decide this is an opportunity for him to lose his virginity. Matthew resists but is forced to mount the girl while the others hold her down. The camera stays on Matthew, recording his gasps and the girl's screams until he comes.

She escapes and runs into the woods, where she is found by

the sheriff. At first it seems that he will help, but the audience gradually sees that the sheriff and the boys are buddies. They converge on her on a puddled roadway, where they nearly drown her facedown in a puddle. The sheriff announces he's an ass man and penetrates her as she lies in the puddle. It is a scene in which the filmmaker seems to be saying to each male in the audience that I know there's a rapist in each of you, however buried under a veneer of morality, and I'll prove it by making you feel a little aroused by what you are watching here. At least that was Candy's guess at the male response around her. She broke her focus from the screen and looked across the theater to see how the audience was reacting. A woman a few seats further in her row sat with her head turned half sideways and her lips drawn back in disgust. Male voices, some deep, younger ones shrill, hooted and cried, "Yeah!" as the rape proceeded.

The five men try to drown the young woman in the river, but she escapes.

Then the revenge begins. First the girl takes Matthew captive. He is wracked with guilt and doesn't offer much resistance. Then she catches Stanley, a heavyset youth obsessed with videographing her, in a beartrap.

The third youth wakes to find himself bound and lying facedown over a bathtub filling with water and lye. She pulls out the board supporting his chest, leaving him to use his trembling core muscles to hold himself above the lye, which he can do for a gasping minute or two before collapsing into the burning water and drowning.

Johnny is the last of the youths, a good-looking guy who took offense at the gas station and pushed his buddies to rape her. She uses a pair of hedge clippers to snip off his genitals and stuffs them in his mouth.

The sheriff is the nastiest of the rapists and earns the climactic act of vengeance. He is bound facedown in a cabin. His shotgun has been stuck up his ass. A blast of buckshot rips through the sheriff's guts and face. In the closing shot, the girl stares into space a moment; then a barely perceptible smile begins to form.

With each graphic stage of the vengeance, the same hoots, howls, yeahs, and laughter fill the theater. The same laughter that rang in Candy's ears during the rape scenes. When Stanley is caught in the beartrap, when the vigorous snip of the hedge clippers is heard, when the trembling abs of the man suspended over the lye give way and he falls into the water, the theater erupted with the audience's reaction. What is this? she wondered. Is there some kind of pleasure we get out of watching the torment and death of someone who is deserving but isn't us?

No one seemed to have much interest in watching the credits roll. At the exit she overheard people talking about what would happen when they caught Tillis. "She'll toast him," someone asserted with confidence. "He'll end up fried like the others."

She was a little surprised she'd been able to sit through the whole thing. She felt greasy, as if she'd been lingering around the exhaust vents at a KFC on a muggy summer afternoon.

As the crowd dispersed, people moving briskly toward cafes and cars, she noticed one person walking more slowly than the others. Candy recognized her as the woman she'd talked to at the cast party, the woman who'd helped produce the play. Mrs. Farres. Candy lengthened her stride and caught up with her.

"That was pornography," she said. "Worse. I don't know how I sat through it."

"You did, though," said the woman.

"Curiosity, but that's no excuse. Wish I wasn't the kind of person who could be fascinated by something like that. You're Mrs. Farres. From the *Acquittal* cast party."

"Mrs. Brenchlow."

"Candy. I thought that play was really good. Were you happy with it?"

"Happy? I don't know what I expected. The theater was full for every performance."

"Listen, would you like to sit down and have a glass of wine?"

Mrs. Farres looked at her, then said, "Yes, why don't we do that." Candy stepped toward the curb and saw a cab trolling for customers among the movie crowd. She waved. Lucky, usually you had to call for a cab if you wanted one in Port Teresa. Mrs. Farres told the driver to take them to the Olympic Hotel. At the entrance to the hotel, Candy took her arm and led her to a table in the hotel bar.

"The movie wasn't that close," said Mrs. Farres. "Just the coincidence of vengeance for a rape."

"Enough to fill the theater."

"Do you think the filmmaker was showing the girl as insane at the end?"

Candy thought about the ending. "I think he left it unclear. Just that slight trace of a smile in the last frame."

"Did you come away with an idea what her life would be like afterward?"

"Now that's a good question," said Candy. "No idea at all. It's like there was nothing left that could happen."

Mrs. Farres looked at Candy with disconcerting directness.

"Has all this, the play, the news stories, the film, made you wonder what your life would be like if something like that happened to you?"

"By now every woman in Port Teresa has asked herself that." Candy picked her next words carefully. "I think if something like what happened in the movie, or the play for that matter, if something like that happened to a person, it would difficult to lead a normal life. Probably impossible."

"Would you have to be insane to do what she did?"

"You'd have to be really capable and smart to do what she did."

"But sane?"

She let the waiter set the glasses of Rioja Mrs. Farres had ordered on the table.

"The newspaper stories, the play, the movie." Candy shook her head. "It's getting harder to tell the reality from fantasy. That's a definition of insanity, isn't it?"

"What would you do?"

"I don't know. The way Anna's character reacted in the play, what the girl did in the film, I don't know, I just can't wholly put myself in that place."

Mrs. Farres nodded. "What did Anna really think about the play?"

"Maybe you're asking what she thinks about her father. If that's the reason she was cast in that role. She's upset with him. Really upset. She confronted him last week. I suppose she always loved her father, the way a girl does. She always had his support. Now I don't know. It's like a lifetime relationship ripped up in a week."

Mrs. Farres waited for her to continue.

"I didn't know whether to stay in the room with them or leave when she started yelling at him. When I did leave, he was making excuses, and she knew that's what they were. Telling your daughter you spent a lot of money, paid people to lie, maybe wrecked a young woman's life, all to give your son a chance is not a good argument to use on a kid. Especially the way the son turned out."

"Were Anna and Ronnie close?"

"No," said Candy. "They hardly knew one another."

Candy sipped the Rioja. She enjoyed a good wine, and this was delicious. She decided to ask the question she really wanted to ask.

"Would you guess that … the rape victim would be satisfied with how it's worked out?"

"I think she waited too long." Her eyes glinted in the low bar lighting. Her words were neither loud nor shrill but gave Candy a shiver. She listened carefully and caught the steel-blade ferocity of a peregrine falcon sliding down through the air currents toward a bird in flight. "I thought the play would generate some compassion. Maybe a remembrance for the older people in the audience. But people want entertainment. Do they care about some old injustice? You heard the laughter. Thank you for inviting me to sit. I'm tired. I'm going upstairs. Good night."

"Do you think anything is going to happen to Neil?"

"Neil has shaped his own fate."

"He probably has," said Candy. "Good night."

CHAPTER FORTY-TWO

When Claire Farres rose from the table and walked through the bar to the elevator, he followed. The woman she'd been talking to was Neil Brenchlow's wife. He let the elevator take Claire to her floor, then pressed the up button. When thirty seconds had passed, he tapped on her door.

He saw the viewer open. Then the door opened the five inches the safety catch allowed.

"What is it?" came her voice from behind the door.

"I apologize for the lateness of the hour. I was hoping we could talk for a moment."

"Who are you?"

"I think you know."

"The only person I can think of would never meet with me."

"A client, you mean. You're right. I never have. I am now."

"There must be an unusual reason."

"Yes. I want to ask you something."

He waited. She looked at him with a single eye around the door's edge. Then she closed the door enough to release the catch, opened to let him in.

"Can I offer you a glass of cognac?"

"That'd be fine, thanks for offering."

The suite was spacious and comfortable in the dark-wooded craftsman style of a hundred years earlier. Probably the nicest space the town had to offer, left over from the turn of the last century when wealthy tourists from the East Coast came on the trains from Chicago to experience the pristine wilderness of the Northwest. She poured two glasses from a bottle with a faded label, offered one to him, gestured for him to sit, and took a seat herself.

"Give it a minute in the glass," she said.

He saw she was waiting for him to begin. So he asked his question.

"Are you satisfied with what's happened?"

"Yes," she said. "You've done good work. You fully met expectations. The truck situation was very well managed."

"I wasn't asking about my work. I'm asking if it was worth it."

"I could afford your fee and more, if that's what you're asking."

"That's not what I'm asking. I have an idea what your resources are. I mean, have you found the satisfaction you were looking for?"

"I was just asked that question. Vengeance. That's what you're asking about. I will think about how to answer you. But you can tell me something. Is that usually what clients hire you for?"

"Sometimes."

"Have you ever learned from them whether their revenge was satisfying to them?"

"I never asked. Sometimes I could deduce what they felt. Usually there's not such a lapse of time between what I do and the situation that led to wanting revenge."

"There's a saying, revenge is a dish best served cold. I don't think I believe that."

"Emily Dickinson didn't either. 'If any would avenge, let him be quick, the viand flits.'"

"Emily Dickinson? Really!"

"Sorry, I guess that's showing off."

"I did have a sense you would be more than an efficient thug."

"My dad taught philosophy at Berkeley. I grew up in that world."

"A Berkeley boy. I went to Stanford."

He smiled. "Maybe we watched the Big Game together, opposite sides of the stadium. You want me to complete the contract?"

"That's what you're here to ask me about, isn't it?"

"It is."

"Are you having qualms of conscience?"

"Maybe I am. I don't know how much you learned about these men before you brought me in. The first two, Westingale and Brenchlow, not much to be said for them. Brenchlow, keeping the old truck, he shouldn't have done that. Flaunting something he was probably proud of."

"I think you're right. I never cared for people who flaunt themselves."

"There's revenge where you just want somebody gone, and revenge where you want somebody to suffer. Your instructions were to simply terminate these individuals, not to make them suffer or to make them aware of why they were dying."

"Would you have made them suffer?"

"Didn't Montaigne ask what the point of revenge was if the subject didn't know it's you getting back at them? As someone paid to do the work, it doesn't matter to me."

"Maybe I'm content with that."

"I'm here to check in with you. Make sure with two of them gone the last one's going to satisfy your desire for revenge."

"Are you suggesting I should forgive him?"

"I have no suggestions. I just know from experience these situations aren't static. So I'm checking."

"You'll go through with it if I decide not to forgive him."

"We have an agreement. I'll complete the contract."

"Montaigne and Emily Dickinson. I'm pleased we had a chance to meet."

"This cognac is excellent."

"A hundred and fifty years old. I would think someone doing what you do would never give any personal information. You told me your father taught philosophy at Berkeley."

"I did, didn't I?"

"Are you retiring?"

He looked at her a moment. "That's perceptive," he said.

"We're both perceptive people."

"Then here's another question. Why did you wait this long? You've had the resources for years."

"I wasn't sure. But I've learned I don't have much time."

He nodded.

"You retiring," she said. "Is it moral issues, or are you also running out of time?"

He looked at her, expressionless, not saying anything.

"I see. You look healthy enough. This seems to be about what they call closure."

"Do you know what the neuropeptide Y is?"

She shook her head.

"It's a hormone related to appetite management. For people with high levels in their system, there's an unusual side effect. When there's a sudden life-threatening situation, most people pump adrenaline, go to fight or flight mode, their reactions fall to reptile level. The neuropeptide Y people are different. Their heartbeat remains steady. They think as clearly as if there were no crisis. It's called a metronome heart. Military special forces recruiters try to screen for it. But there's a downside. These people start having heart issues in their fifties. I had a heart event a couple of days ago. I went to a clinic in Seattle for an exam. If there'd been a critical action scheduled when it hit me, I would have failed. I can never let that happen."

"So you're not like an athlete who can continue playing for a time while his skills fade."

"No. If I keep doing this with fading skills, I'll be dead. I'm going to ask you to do something. I'm going to leave you a single-use phone. Two days, a couple of hours earlier than this, I'll call. If you tell me to go ahead, I will."

She looked at him a moment before speaking.

"I haven't decided if you've offended me. But, in fact, you're right. Situations aren't static. I'll expect your call."

CHAPTER FORTY-THREE

What a circus it had turned into. Word came from the editor through Molly that he was supposed to return all the calls that came in with ideas where Tillis was. Every caller was a newspaper reader, and answering their calls was good customer service. Rack sales had spiked with the Tillis story, and rack sales statistics would increase ad sales. It turned out that not that many people actually knew Tillis. People called to say they'd seen somebody at the Walgreens that looked like the photo the paper had run. No one actually knew anything useful. Most of the callers, he realized after several conversations, just wanted to be participants in a newsworthy event. He suggested to a few that they contact the police department, but he suspected most wouldn't. He wondered how much fun Matt Moore was having returning calls.

Sam asked himself if there was anything he wasn't doing in the search for Claire Draghici. The story would never be complete until someone talked to her. But apparently that wouldn't happen until she wanted it to. Earlier, a few days after Sam's story about the trial broke, Molly had asked Charles, the paper's computer wizard, to find out what he could about Claire Draghici.

Charles hunkered over his computer for two days before he sat down with Sam and Molly to report what he'd learned.

"Interesting project you gave me," he said. "Here's what I know. There's photos and records at the hospital here of her burns, but no head shot. I'm guessing that means her face wasn't burned. Back, upper legs pretty bad. Then Stanford. She graduated with a degree in electrical engineering, good grades, here's the graduation photo."

He handed them a print showing a woman with a high turtleneck, severe, high cheekbones, the barest trace of a smile, hair pulled low across the forehead.

"After graduating she married Douglas Galvant, fellow Stanford grad. Probably don't recognize the name now, but he was big in the early go-go dotcom days. Made way too much money, let it go to his head. There's a wrecked Ferrari, dismissed charges for cocaine possession, and time with the beautiful people in Hollywood. Rumors of flings with a couple of those babes famous for being famous. She divorced him and took a nest egg in the fifty million range. Worked at the VP level at a couple of tech startups. She made smart choices. Both did well, got sold, and she got richer. Then she married a man named Farres, Lebanese businessman, another very rich guy. She probably lived in Europe with him. He died six years ago."

Charles dropped his file folder with a dramatic flourish on the table between them.

"And that would be it." He tapped the folder with a finger. "Haven't seen anything quite like this. Some very astute computer people have gone deep into the Internet and deleted her. It's possible to be a billionaire and reclusive. There's several examples. But not like this. My guess is that not only are Internet records gone, somebody got into the various places she worked, medical facilities she used, and physically removed photos and everything except basic name, rank, and serial number-type stuff."

"You're saying she's done a lot of work to hide," said Molly.

"Let's say this: I sailed pretty close to the wind in FBI files I will never acknowledge I know how to look at, and she is nowhere on their radar. Disappearance this thorough doesn't happen in a week. Somebody's probably worked on this for years. My prediction is she will not be found by anyone till she wants to be."

"No photos at all?"

"She probably decided there were enough of the graduation photos in Stanford yearbooks to leave them be. That shot is the last one I could find. She's twenty-two, and even then half-concealing herself. I'd guess somebody who's got a lot of burn scarring would do that as second nature."

Sam held up the photo and asked Molly, "If she's here and you saw her on the street, think you'd recognize her?"

Molly studied the photo. "You could look at every middle-aged woman wearing a turtleneck and not be sure. I think all we do is wait for the day she decides to tell her story."

Later word reached the newsroom that Sarah Craft's bounty hunting crew had located Carl Tillis in northern Idaho.

"Is that something we run?" Sam asked Molly.

"We have to," she said. "We can't make the circus go away by ignoring it."

Hunters and Fugitives aired on Wednesday evenings. Sam let Horacio know he would be coming in a couple of hours late. Most of the *North Coast News* staff had come back to the office to watch the show in the newsroom.

The program opened with a panning shot of a doublewide in a forest and a voiceover summary of the search for Carl Tillis. Then a shot of Sarah Craft, Stetson on the table in front of her.

"We're here at an undisclosed location in northern Idaho," said Sarah to the camera. "With the help of tips from you, our viewers, *Hunters and Fugitives* has found its man."

The camera drew back enough to reveal a figure sitting at the table next to Sarah. He'd grown a beard and had his hair cut short, but Sam recognized Carl Tillis from the photo Kelsey had shown him.

"Carl," said Sarah, turning her smile on him, "a lot of people have been looking for you. Do you think your life is in danger?"

"Yes," said Carl. His voice was weak and scratchy, as though he was forcing just enough air through his vocal chords to be audible.

"Why are you afraid?"

"This mess when we were kids," he said. "The other two been killed. It's just me left."

"The three of you were accused by a classmate named Claire Draghici of raping her after the high-school prom. Carl, the night of the prom, June tenth, nineteen eighty-five. Take us back. What happened?"

Carl had been looking at Sarah. Now he brushed a hand across his mouth, looked at the table and shook his head.

"I tried to remember, but I can't. I got drunk at the prom. Everybody was."

"Then what happened?"

"There was this party after. I got worse drunk. I just can't remember."

"Is it possible that you and the other two did what Claire accused you of? Is it possible you raped her?"

He began shaking his head, slow, from side to side, still staring at the table.

"It's possible, yeah. I remember the trial, sitting there. I was scared. I was scared because I didn't know if I did it."

"Is it possible that you not only raped her but pushed her truck off the road and set it on fire?"

"God. Any of it's possible." Carl's voice broke with a flutter as he said this.

Sarah placed a hand on Carl's arm and asked in a sympathetic solicitous voice, "Carl, if you did what Claire accused you of, is she justified in seeking revenge?"

Carl resumed shaking his head before answering. "I guess, yeah. We were just stupid, stupid drunk kids, but still. Can't blame her. I just want her to know if I did it, I'm really sorry."

"Carl, we can't know this for sure, but there's some chance that Claire Draghici is watching us now. Why don't you take this opportunity and tell her you're sorry?"

The shaking of the head became a nod. "Yeah. Yeah, if she's listening …"

"Look into the camera, Carl. She's there. You're talking to her."

He couldn't do it. He spoke to the table.

"I am so sorry. If I did it, I don't remember. But you would know. I'm sorry. If you could forgive me."

Carl had begun shaking his head and sobbing. The camera held on him. He dropped his head into his arms on the table.

"That's the wrap they're looking for," said Molly, breaking Sam's concentration on the monitor. The camera drew closer again, only Sarah Craft's professionally bemused, nodding face on the screen.

"What happens now?" she asked. "Will Claire accept Carl's obviously heartfelt apology? Carl, what are you going to do now? Stay in hiding, or go home?"

A switch to the camera focused on Carl. "I'm sick of this."

And back to Sarah, solemn expression yielding to the signature smile. "The bounty hunter doesn't control the future. All we know is that we got our man. And now let's look a little more closely at how *Hunters and Fugitives* did it."

In the next segment, Sarah interviewed an eager-beaver type with a ponytail and sideways grin who talked in rapid spurts about how he'd spotted a man in the Leonard Paul store in Coolin that looked like the fellow they were tracking on *Hunters and Fugitives,* except with a beard. What a bozo, thought Sam. Eating up his twenty seconds of national TV fame and making a leering reference to the tip fee he'd been paid. Carl Tillis didn't deserve to be spotted by such a dumbshit *Hunters and Fugitives* fan.

"What are they going to do with him, do you think?" Sam asked.

"I'd bring him back here and set up a shoot with Kelsey," said Molly. "They'd get the kind of emotion they like out of that."

CHAPTER FORTY-FOUR

His call came at the time he had stated.

"I'd like to meet with you again. Is that possible?"

"Not at the hotel," he said.

"Where then?" she said.

He gave her the address of a place that would be secure. "Take a cab," he instructed her.

She waited at the place the cab had brought her for fifteen minutes before he appeared.

"You really are retiring, aren't you?"

"I think the time has come."

"Yes, the health issues. For both of us it seems. You said you haven't thought much about your future. What are you going to do?"

"Italy always appealed to me. Sunshine, warm water to swim in. Got tired of swimming in cold water years ago. Though I worry a sunny climate will make me soft. There are people who'd like to find me. I don't believe you have children."

"No."

"Never wanted to?"

"It's more that my first husband was too busy making

money, and my second husband already had his children. You, I assume family life doesn't suit your work."

"You're right."

They looked at one another a moment, the man with the sinewy neck and graying hair, the woman holding her head upright and her mouth tightly drawn as if concealing pain.

"I want to check with you this last time. Do you want me to complete the contract?"

She looked down, touching her cheek with her hand.

"I can see you're reluctant. I will make you an offer."

"I'm listening."

"I want you to arrange to have the daughter raped. I'm sure you're capable of finding people to do something like that. Not injured. Raped. Then let me talk to her. I will tell her I know who the rapists are and can have them brought to justice. If she will forgive them and not have them punished, I will not pursue her father."

"You see her guilty because her dad's guilty?"

"It's not a matter of her guilt. I want her to understand what she's asking when she asks to have her father forgiven."

"You want a little time to think this through?"

"You haven't insulted me till now. The daughter's rape, or finish your contract. I leave it to you."

CHAPTER FORTY-FIVE

A damp wind moved the leaves overhead and made spheres of light visible around the streetlights. A Jake brake blatted in the distance, a big rig slowing to turn off the highway. A man in a hoodie crossed a parking lot, looked around, and walked to a bench at a bus stop. He sat upright on the bench, looking ahead. He shifted his weight uncomfortably on the hard, enameled wood.

After a minute someone behind him said, "Don't turn around."

The hooded head nodded.

"There's an envelope with instructions taped under the bench. Reach under and take it."

The man did as instructed. "The woman's name, the address, the time. She'll be alone. The place where you take her. Be sure you understand, no more force than necessary. No beating. The money is in the envelope. The second payment will be here in the same place tomorrow night, after it's done. Do you have any questions?"

The voice giving the instructions was low and uninflected. Clear, but not a normal conversational voice. The hooded man said, "Sure nobody's going to be there?"

"I'm sure. Anything else?"

"No."

"Sit there one minute, then walk away."

The man paced the living room of his apartment. The room was really too small for thinking, so he drove to a waterfront park where he could walk undisturbed. He was facing a dilemma. Usually when he had a decision to make it was about the best method to do something. He wondered if he had faced moral decisions in the past and simply hadn't recognized them. Now he had to weigh the interests of people who wanted different things. A girl, a wealthy older woman, a man who had committed a crime in his youth. Was there something he could do that would satisfy everyone involved? These were questions that had probably been there in the past, but he had never asked them. There was only one person to be satisfied, the client. Now he was thinking of compromising the client. How had that happened? Too much time on site, he said to himself. I've let myself form attachments. He lived, he survived through his objectivity.

It was the lovely tall girl, he realized, the volleyball player. She'd awakened something in him he had never been aware of. How could a girl you'd known for half an hour grow in your imagination into a surrogate daughter? Was this the aging process, or had the template been there all along, waiting for the one young woman who fitted it? Maybe he had been looking for her for years without knowing it. A daughter would represent a vulnerability, that was probably why he had never let himself think about it. Now he was.

But he was an efficient decision-maker, and after ten minutes of brisk walking, he knew what he was going to do. He looked at his watch. There was time. He returned to his apartment and dressed in apparel suitable for the situation.

Forty minutes later he was crouched at the edge of a thick grove of pines in a campground that had been closed by the forest service for habitat restoration.

Kelsey Tillis, known as Setter to her friends and classmates, didn't like taking Ambien. She knew the side effects could include depression and confusion. But she found herself so tense at night she would be holding her breath and have to force her abdominal muscles to relax. Her best friend had been killed in a brutal, incomprehensible murder. Her father had apparently been involved in a rape when he was young and had disappeared. The drug allowed a fitful unconsciousness for parts of the night. She was weak and wracked with headaches from loss of sleep. The volleyball workout that morning had been miserable. With Outside's death, though, the game hardly seemed important anymore. She struggled to find the motivation to continue to play.

This night she woke from an uneasy sleep of troubling dreams to a real nightmare. For several seconds she thought her dream was continuing. But powerful arms had seized her from behind in her bed, covered her mouth with tape and pulled a sack over her head. She was strong, and in her panic she tried to strike out with her fists and elbows. But her arms were pinned to her sides. Her cries were too muffled to reach beyond her bedroom.

She was carried by strong men to a vehicle that started and accelerated away. She breathed hard and forced her panic to calm. She prepared herself for whatever horror awaited. She would try to stay alive.

The vehicle left the smooth roadway and bounced hard over some kind of rough surface. The girl knew that they were going someplace remote where whatever was going to happen would happen. I will survive, she told herself. The vehicle stopped, and the engine was switched off. She was pulled out and laid on her back on the ground, the sack taken off her head. A low light came from somewhere, a lantern or cellphone maybe. There were men, maybe four, but she couldn't think to count. She knew what would happen next. A man on either side grasped her arms. They pulled her sleeping T-shirt over her head, fingernails dug into her hips to yank her panties down.

Then something changed in an instant. She heard surprised, angry grunts. The hands released her. There was chaotic movement, fighting. Two of the men fell to the ground. A flashlight switched on. One man was holding another by the arm. A low growling voice. The man with the flashlight slapped something, a manila envelope, into the other man's chest. Then he stepped back and held the light on the fallen men. The two standing—there seemed to be four, not counting the man with the light—half-carried the other two to the van she must have been brought here in. In a moment the van engine fired, the transmission clunked into gear, and with its engine revving high, the van bounced away.

She heard the man holding the flashlight tell her in a low, hoarse voice to put the sack back over her head. "You're safe now," he said. "I don't want you to see me, but I'm taking you home."

CHAPTER FORTY-SIX

"You didn't do it."

"No."

"Did you never intend to follow through?"

"I arranged it."

"And?"

"I've been places where rape is used as a political tool. I've seen soldiers ordered to rape wives, sisters, children with all the violence they wanted while the husbands and fathers watched. Decent women taught in fifteen minutes to loathe themselves."

"I don't need details."

"It's not an abstraction when it's done. It's all details."

"And ...?"

"It's an evil I don't want to be part of. So I cancelled the arrangement."

"You've become a sentimentalist."

"If that's what you want to call it."

"You met with me, and you've never met with a client, you said. You've refused a task a client asked you to do. You just used the word 'evil.' I can see the time has come to leave this work."

"The time has come."

"You didn't let them hurt Kelsey. So many years without a family. Ever think you might have liked having a daughter?"

"Funny you should say that. There was a girl here. I met her briefly. She was killed last month. Friend of Kelsey's, in fact. I had a reaction to her I never experienced. I see how parents can be proud of a child that turns out well."

"Here we both are calling Kelsey by her name. Not Tillis's daughter."

"Does make her more of a person, doesn't it? I will carry out the Tillis part of the contract if that's what you want."

Her chin dropped to her breasts. The small tremor that pulled at her lower lip expressed profound sadness.

"How could I let this happen to me?" she asked.

He was silent, knowing it wasn't him she was asking.

"I let it control me. You know the line from Auden, the one about school children?"

"Remind me," he said.

"'Those to whom evil is done do evil in return.' I should have acted then. I let it ferment in me like wine going bad. Now I'm ashamed of what I've done."

He nodded.

"I'm glad you turned out to be somebody I could talk to. I never talked to anybody. Maybe it would be different if I had."

Claire Draghici closed her eyes a moment, then raised her head.

"Leave Carl Tillis be. There's something I want you do instead. I'm going to arrange a meeting with Neil Brenchlow. I want you to find a place and make some arrangements. Of a kind you do well."

"What kind of arrangements?" he asked.

CHAPTER FORTY-SEVEN

"You wanted to talk about Anna?" said Candy.

"I do," said Mrs. Farres. "Thank you for meeting with me."

"Sure," said Candy. "And congratulations. I read the Seattle Rep is adding *The Acquittal* to its program for next year."

"Thank you. It will have more life than I thought."

"I know a lot of people in town saw the play because of the old trial publicity. But it's a good play."

"And your daughter rose to the occasion."

"She put so much emotion into it, she scared me."

"She matured in a week as an actress. That's what I want to talk to you about. Assuming Anna agrees, I've contracted with an agent in Los Angeles. He'll take her on as a client. I showed him clips from the play. He thinks she could be the next Hilary Swank, an actress I'm not familiar with but who apparently came from this area."

"Why do you want to help her like this?"

"It's quite satisfying to be successful as a talent spotter."

"Okay," said Candy. "I'm sure she'll thank you."

"I'd like to ask a favor."

"Sure, ask."

"I'd like to meet your husband. To talk about Anna and tell him what I'm doing."

"You want to meet Neil?"

Mrs. Farres nodded.

"To talk about Anna."

"I'd like to tell him in my own way about her prospects. Let him know his daughter is talented."

Candy looked at Mrs. Farres and considered. If Mrs. Farres wanted to meet Neil, she could probably arrange it without her help.

"I don't see a lot of Neil these days," she said. "I don't have much influence on his schedule."

It was true. Things changed after Zoey Franco's visit. Neil had told her not to invite anyone to the house. He didn't appear to be angry at her, though he was so preoccupied she couldn't guess what he was thinking. She stayed out of his way and watched him. The question of whether his angry meeting with Zoey had anything to do with the road-rage accident she'd had a few days later nagged at her.

"You and I talked about the problems Neil is likely to be having," said Mrs. Farres. "I want to reassure him. Let's call it that, reassuring him. No matter what happens to him, his daughter will have support. Yours, of course. But mine too."

"I can try," said Candy. "You want to come to our place?"

"I'd prefer not. I will be at the Haven Bluff cabins. Five miles east. My last few days in the area, that's where I'll be. Sunday evening. I've written the information on a card."

"I'll tell him. That's all I can do."

"When we talked I asked if Neil had major financial problems, whether you'd be left without resources."

"I remember. His former wife and I have taken some steps. I think I'll land on my feet."

"Good. I'm glad of that. Would you tell him it's Mrs. Farres who wants to meet him? The producer of the play to talk about Anna's career."

Mrs. Farres rose from her chair, which Candy could see took some effort. She appeared to be weaker than she had been during the production. Maybe the intensity of the play production had stimulated a temporary energy she couldn't sustain. The natural lighting here wasn't kind to her. Her mouth sagged more than Candy remembered.

Smiling wanly, Mrs. Farres took Candy's hand in both of hers.

"I'm so glad I was able to get to know you a little. I'm counting on you to persuade Neil to visit Sunday."

"Anna having a sponsor, that'll be important to him," she said.

Mrs. Farres's desire to meet with Neil had to be about more than Anna's career. But it was Candy's opinion that the woman deserved a chance to talk to Neil. She would do what she could to make it happen.

CHAPTER FORTY-EIGHT

The first thing Teddy Tsalevets was aware of as consciousness came to him was that he couldn't see anything and couldn't move. Comprehension of his situation came gradually. He couldn't see anything because it was dark. His inability to move was like one of those dreams where you had to get away from something but couldn't move your limbs. As he slowly came awake, he could tell he really was immobilized. Like lying on an arm and it goes to sleep so you can't move it for a minute. Only this was his whole body. He could turn his head, but that was all.

The next thing he was aware of was rhythmic motion. He was in some kind of conveyance. Someone was sitting in front of him. He could make out the shape because of a weak light source behind and just to the side of the figure. There was a soft sloshing sound matching the steady surges of movement. He was sitting in a boat. A small open boat. It was night. When he looked down, there was enough light for him to see he was wrapped in duct tape. His arms were taped across his stomach. He could kick his feet back and forth a small distance, but something stopped the swing. He saw a thick nylon tie strapped painfully tight around one ankle and through the handle of a kettlebell. He recognized it immediately as a seventy-four pounder. He used kettlebells to work out and was familiar with the sizes.

"*Shto eta*?" he asked in a voice thick from whatever had made him unconscious. "*Kto vui*?"

"We have about ten minutes to where we stop," said the man in a deliberate, rusty Russian. "That's where the current goes out into the Pacific. Not back to land."

"Why are we here? What are you doing to me?" Teddy strained against his binding, but it didn't take him long to realize no amount of effort was going to provide any movement or slack at all.

"You killed the girl. The girl was my friend."

"I didn't kill any girl. What are you talking about?"

"I think you did. Alexei told you to do it. The tall girl."

"No. I don't know anything about a girl."

"You were just doing what you were told. Alexei is responsible for killing her."

"Please listen. This is a mistake. I do not know about a girl."

He sat facing to the rear as the man steered the boat. He tried to get a sense of where he was. Behind them he could see the rigging lights of a freighter a mile or more in the distance. A sprinkle of lights from a distant shore.

The man killed the motor. The boat came to a stop and began to rock lightly in the gentle nighttime chop. The man stepped behind Teddy and hoisted him to a position sitting on the gunwale. He was strong.

"No, please!" Teddy cried out.

But the man didn't push him over. He sat and looked at Teddy for a moment in silence.

"Please! Tell me why you think I killed a girl," he said. "Ask me questions. I'll tell you anything I know. Maybe that helps you learn who killed this girl."

"You work for Alexei."

"Yes. Six years since I come from Russia."

"What do you to for him?"

Who was this man? He couldn't be a policeman. In America policemen didn't do things like this. Was this someone from a rival gang? But the only gangs he knew of in the area dealt with drugs, and he and his friends didn't have anything to do with drugs.

The man prodded his shoulder, not hard, and repeated the question.

"What do you do?"

"I make sure the men who come here and get money from the bank start building their houses. Foundation, framing, some walls. House has to look like it's being finished."

"What happens if they don't?"

"I put pressure on them. Threat, even sometimes hit them some. Once a man didn't even start. Took the money and went back to Novosibirsk. I went there and found him. Convinced him to return to US and start building."

"How did you convince him?"

"I made some unpleasantness for his family."

"Do these construction loans all come from the same place?"

Teddy had fought to keep himself calm, but the complete immobilization from his neck down threatened to overwhelm him with terror. He shuddered, closed his eyes, and struggled for control. Who was doing this to him? These were the questions a police investigator would ask. But this man would kill him if he didn't tell what he knew.

"All through Alexei," he said. "He works with a bank. I'm not sure, but Peninsula Bank is the name I see on paper."

"How does Alexei make money on these loans?"

"I wonder that myself. The loans are easy to get, that's a thing I don't understand. The men who come here from Russia have no good credit or wealth, but they all get loans. Some money from the loan goes back to Alexei. Some goes back to the bank. Somewhere a lot of money is lost. Houses never have the value of the loan. I don't understand American banking system."

"Neil Brenchlow. He's the president of Peninsula Bank. You know the name?"

"Yes, bank president. I think he and Alexei are good friends."

"Did Konstantin Stivits kill the girl?"

"I don't know anything about the girl. But Kostya, no, not possible. He's soft, like a poet. Wouldn't hurt anyone."

"Why did he suddenly fly back to Novosibirsk?"

"That's a strange thing. He wasn't happy here, wanted to go back to the motherland. Suddenly Alexei tells him to get ready in two hours, buys him airline ticket, drives him to the Seattle airport himself, and puts him on a plane. Tells him never come back."

"Does Alexei ever have you do work for Neil Brenchlow?"

"You mean like hard persuasion, that kind of work? No. If the bank president needs that kind of work done, he must have his own people. It was never us."

The man watched Teddy in silence. In the dim running light, Teddy could just make out the silhouette of a man wearing a hooded jacket and some kind of wind mask on his face.

"Okay," said the man. "This is the place. You go to the bottom. Two hundred meters, like two blocks down. There's no sharks here or anything like that. I think what happens is the bottom fish chew away your flesh. Little mouthfuls till it's just the bones. Tell me who killed the girl." He leaned forward and gave Teddy a gentle push in the chest.

"I don't know! I don't know about a girl!" Teddy cried. He was close to panic. He'd been trying to be hard and fight it off, but he was losing. His brain was filled with the image of himself tilting over the side and diving down, down, down, pulled by the kettlebell into thick, black water.

The man waited another minute, then stood and pushed a hypodermic needle through the duct tape into Teddy's trembling shoulder.

CHAPTER FORTY-NINE

"I hear we're even," said Zoey.

"I think we are," said Sam. "You remember much about it?"

"No," she said. "I think I heard a huge bang, but maybe that's what I think I should have heard. They said I would have bled out."

"Christ, you were a fountain. You scared the crap out of me."

"Good thing you didn't panic."

"I may have made your ankle worse. You were stuck in the footwell. I was afraid it'd catch fire. I had to haul on your leg."

"Well, don't apologize. You got me out, and here I am."

"Here you are. How are you feeling?"

"Not that bad. I'm contributing a little to the opioid epidemic. You saw it?"

"Pickup went hauling ass past me. I didn't really get a good look. He pulled in behind your truck and plowed into you."

"They told me they're calling it road rage. That means they'll investigate, sort of. Guy's probably hidden the truck or got rid of it. I see anything on Craigslist, I'll show you, see if you recognize it. But they probably wouldn't be that stupid."

"No, I wouldn't expect to find the truck."

"So I want you to listen to this. I recorded my talk with Brenchlow. Tell me what conclusions you draw from it."

She put her phone on the table and pressed the play button.

When the recording was done, she gave Sam an inquiring look.

"You sent this to me earlier," said Sam. "That's a good job. He doesn't deny anything. You'd think he would."

"Exactly," said Zoey. "He was afraid Kirstin would learn too much, so he told McCord to stop her. You find out anything else?"

"McCord seems to have disappeared. Our business writer is trying to get the paperwork on a couple of Brenchlow's properties. One of them is a house in Port Townsend he sold or gave to McCord. The one you told me about. Looks like an illegal transfer."

"You have the address for that place?"

"What are you thinking?"

"I was thinking I might like to go meet McCord's wife."

The house was a large, handsome older home located on a spacious lot on a hill in Port Townsend with an unobstructed view of the strait and Whidbey Island, probably one of the houses built by the ship captains when they retired a century ago. Likely on the historical register. An extensive, well-maintained lawn bordered by a six-foot hedge kept the neighboring homes at a distance. She heard a motor running, and saw a man in coveralls and a wide-brimmed straw hat riding a big John Deere mower. She knew that McCord's personal vehicle was a Ford SUV. It was nowhere in sight. She didn't want to meet McCord here.

The woman who answered the door gazed at Zoey with the inquiring look of someone who didn't have many visitors knocking at her front door. She was middle-aged, black, carefully shaped hair, jawline a little fleshier than it had been when she was younger but still attractive.

"Mrs. McCord?" Zoey said. "I'm Jane. I'm doing a story

for the *North Coast News.*" She flashed a laminated ID she had made after borrowing Sam's ID long enough to make a photocopy and paste in a photo of herself. Nothing Sam needed to know about.

"I want to write about some of the great old houses in the area. Would you mind if I asked you a few questions?"

The woman smiled and invited her in. "You have an accident?" she asked, referring to Zoey's cast and crutch.

"Yeah, car accident. I'm going to be gimping around for a while."

The room they entered was thick with furniture. Zoey's professional judgment made a quick evaluation. Calling this a blend of styles would be generous. There was almost no wall space not covered with colorful landscapes and paintings of flowers.

"How long have you lived here?" Zoey asked.

"Going on fifteen years."

"Have you made many changes since you bought it?"

"We took down a few walls in the kitchen area. In the old days, they liked a lot of small rooms."

"You've made it very cozy for such a large place."

"Thank you."

"With a home like this, you must entertain a lot."

"We used to. Not so much now. My husband likes his quiet time."

"Yeah, reflecting on his life and things like that."

"Well, I suppose."

"Did you ever meet the person you bought it from?"

"No, as I remember we only dealt with the realtor. The realtor was a friend of my husband."

"The reason I ask is that while they were looking at the paperwork on the history of the house, I hear they found some peculiarities."

"Peculiarities? What do you mean?"

"It turns out the title for this place may not actually be clear. Have you had any recent communications from the tax people or the attorney general's office?"

"I have no idea what you're talking about."

"From what I've pieced together, the person you bought the house from wasn't actually the owner."

McCord's wife shook her head in bewilderment. "This is some kind of mistake. My husband stays in Port Teresa during the week. I'll ask him about all this when I call him tonight."

"I'm surprised you haven't heard anything. Probably it's because those big bureaucracies like the attorney general's office can be pretty slow. I hope it all works out. It would be awful to lose such a beautiful home."

Zoey could see anger drawing the woman's lips tight across her mouth.

"This is some mistake. My husband will get to the bottom of it."

"I'm sure he will," said Zoey, who rose from her chair and held out her hand. "Thank you so much for talking to me."

"Don't you want to see the house?"

"I just wanted to ask a few questions. I'll be back later with a photographer if that's all right with you. Have a pleasant afternoon."

Let's see if that doesn't rattle your cage, Mr. McCord, she thought as she hobbled toward the classic whitewashed gate at the end of the walkway.

At the Port Teresa police station, the woman at the desk said Detective McCord was out of the office. Matt Moore was on patrol.

"Could the dispatcher give Matt a call and tell him Sam Troshin from the paper wants to talk to him? I think he'll want to meet with me."

She gave him the jaundiced glance people associated with police departments give citizens trying to involve themselves in police business but stepped away from her desk. When she returned she said Matt would meet him at the park in fifteen minutes.

"What's up?" Matt asked when his patrol car pulled up alongside the bench where Sam was waiting.

"I'm trying to talk to Mac McCord. They said he wasn't around but wouldn't tell me anything else."

"He's taking a leave of absence. Could be at his place in Port Townsend, but I don't think he told anybody where he'd be."

"So do you know, is he just dropping the Kirstin Kelly case?"

"That's in the DA's hands now. They'll decide whether they've got enough on the Russian guy to file for extradition."

"That amounts to a suspended investigation. Does this seem like an odd time to you for McCord to take off?"

"Gotta allow a guy space for his personal life. But yeah, maybe so. Did you see that play they did here a couple weeks ago? My girlfriend made me take her. Your story about the old rape trial and that play, there's a cop character that has to be him. Doesn't put him in a real good light. Enough people in this town know who he is. There's things I hope he comes out and explains."

"That's what I think. That's why I want to talk to him, hear his side."

"Well, good luck. People he doesn't want to talk to he doesn't talk to."

His phone binged with a text. Alison. She wanted to see him.

The message gave him an unexpected feeling of gratification. Except for being there to help Zoey, he couldn't feel good about much right now, but the girl's desire to stay in touch, even if it was just to get information from him, meant she trusted him. He knew from Zoey she liked to hang out at libraries, the city library or at the college. "How about the college library?" he texted back. If he met her, he'd just stay on campus till his shift started.

He found her and stood next to her at a library computer before she looked up from the screen. She gazed steadily at Sam. It was disconcerting how she could look at someone without taking her eyes off them. Wouldn't a girl with her history try to make herself small, avoid being noticed? Surviving rape had not crushed her spirit.

"Was it the policeman?"

"It's looking more and more like maybe so. Could be the banker, Brenchlow, had him do it. Zoey went out and accused him of having Kirstin killed."

"You know where he is?"

The girl should be the reporter. The way she looked right at you and asked questions you had no choice. You answered.

"I've been looking for Officer McCord for a couple days. They said he took a leave."

"What did Mr. Brenchlow say?"

"I'm trying to find him too. I called his bank. They said he hasn't been in for a couple days."

"If you find the policeman, will you tell me?"

"All right," he said. "There's no evidence, though. We don't know the policeman did anything. It's possible the Russians are responsible. We just know Zoey thinks he's the killer."

"He's the one trying to kill her, isn't he? He had somebody run her off the road, and he sent somebody to the hospital to kill her, the one you saw."

"I need to be with her as much as I can. You too."

She nodded. "He'll keep trying."

"I need to find him and ask him about all this."

"We should tell him it's me, not her, that was hanging out with his son."

"No!" Sam exclaimed. "You know how pissed she would be if you did that? We can protect her until I find the guy."

"I'm trying to stay with her, but she went somewhere this morning without me. Had her phone off."

"If there's two of you, she'll be safer. Have her stay where there's people around. For God's sake be careful."

CHAPTER FIFTY

At five thirty Candy stood in front of her husband's closed office door, hand raised to knock. But she hesitated. He hadn't been home for days. He had slipped into the house a few hours earlier and gone directly to his office. They were either going to sit across the table from one another at the dinner table in a heavy silence, or they were going to talk. She realized she was a little afraid.

When they had issues in the past, his style was to say what he wanted in a strained but level voice and finish by saying they would talk about whatever it was after taking some time to think about it. Only once had she gotten into his face and yelled that he avoided problems and had no feelings. But it wasn't true. They would talk later, and the conversations probably went better because the temperature between the two of them had gone down. She accommodated herself to her husband's style. She would make her case and let it go without pushing, knowing that within a day or two, they would have a discussion.

But their issues had never involved anything like rape, bankruptcy, embezzlement, and murder.

She tapped on the door, pushed it open enough to put her head in, and said dinner was ready if he was hungry.

He said he'd be there in a minute.

She'd taken a steak out of the freezer and grilled it with care, exactly the way he liked them. However this conversation would go, she would get in a point or two for a nice dinner, a wifely concern about her husband's welfare.

He cut a couple of thin slices from the steak before looking up.

"It seems you're acquainted with my ex-wife," he said.

"I met her at Ronnie's funeral," she said. "It was nice of her to introduce herself."

"Have you talked to her since?"

"She invited me to have a glass of wine with her."

"Mind if I ask what you talked about?"

"She told me some about her chamber of commerce work. We talked a little about Ronnie."

Silence hung over the table.

"She asked how you were. Nothing negative, just curious, I guess."

"And you told her …"

"That you were fine."

"There are some things around here that aren't going so well right now. You've probably picked up on that."

"You've been pretty preoccupied. I noticed that."

"Preoccupied. Yeah, you could say. Construction loans to some Russians. You know anything about that?"

"What I read in the paper. They say the bank is involved in some kind of fraud. Is that right? Is that you?"

"The bank is me. I made a couple bad judgment calls a while ago. Now it's going to bite me. Why did you invite that woman here?"

"You mean Zoey? She's an antiques scout. Someone told me about her a year or so ago. She's found me a couple of nice things I was looking for. I wanted to see her about trading out a few things."

"She used you to get in here and accuse me of some bad shit."

"I had no idea. I'm sorry."

"It's being dealt with. You're not inviting anyone else here?"

"I said I won't. What's going to happen?"

"To me, do you mean, or to us?"

"To us."

"I'm very fond of you, Candy. I've always tried to give you what you wanted."

"You have. You always provided for me."

"You would never have reason to undermine me, would you?"

"Of course not. What do you mean?"

"There has been some financial information about me coming out recently. Very private information that is hurting me. You know anything about that?"

"Why would I do anything like that? How would I know anything?"

"I'm just asking you, as the wife I trust. Have you been a party to giving anyone information about me?"

"Like I said. How would I know anything even if I wanted to?"

"I don't know. So it's a simple question: Did you or didn't you provide someone with financial information about me?"

"No. Of course not. I want you to beat whatever this is."

"I probably won't beat it. Well, I trust you. So we'll let it go. You were involved in this play Anna was in, weren't you?"

"I helped Shelley, same as I've done with all her plays."

"I hear people talking about the play. What did you think of it?"

"As a play it's good. The town history part, I don't know what to think of that. You never talked to me about any of that."

"Somebody wanted me and Mac McCord to look like fools."

"As fools? I didn't see that at all. They did want to show that you and he didn't treat that girl very well."

"Does it count for anything that I was trying to support my son? The play didn't show much of that."

"Of course it counts. The play showed everything from the girl's point of view."

Neil had sat with his forearms resting on the edge of the table during their conversation. He took the time now to chew meditatively a small piece of steak.

"When a father takes steps to defend a son who turns out to be somebody they admire, everybody respects the father. If the son doesn't turn out so well, they feel contempt for the father. You think I'm responsible for the way Ronnie turned out?"

"No," said Candy. "Kids just turn out however. Look at what a good job we did raising Anna."

"Yes," he said. "We did."

"Are we going to go broke? Are we going to lose this place?"

He shook his head. "It's mostly out of my control. You should be ready for anything."

"Would you go to jail?"

Neil shrugged.

"Jesus. I do want to talk to you about Anna."

He raised an eyebrow, inviting her to say more.

"The woman who produced the play. She wants to meet with you. She thinks Anna has real talent as an actress. She wants to help sponsor her. She has a Hollywood agent lined up. You and she can coordinate support."

"The producer of that play wants to talk to me?"

"About Anna. That's what she wants to talk about. If we're going to have money problems, this could be really good for Anna. The woman's leaving town in a couple days and she's not very mobile. She set a time and place to talk with you."

"Now's not a good time for social visits."

"But this isn't a social visit. Don't you owe this much to Anna?"

Neil looked at the card Candy had passed across the table to him, a time and place in Mrs. Farres's frail but neat lettering.

"All right, you're right." He rose from the table. "Steak's good. I'm not that hungry. Put it in the fridge, and I'll warm it up later."

He looked directly at her. "You didn't go through my office recently, did you?"

"Yes, I did. I vacuumed the carpet, dusted the shelves, emptied your waste basket in the recycling. I know you don't want the regular housecleaners in there."

He gave his wife a long look.

"So this Mrs. Farres wants to talk about Anna's career."

"Yes."

"She's the one who produced the play."

"Yes."

He held his look at his wife, a questioning, meditative look, then turned and left the kitchen.

She sat unable to move. Jesus. What had she done? She had never lied outright to her husband. Never told him no when the answer was yes. She had betrayed him. Their wealth was about to be taken away, and she had conspired with his ex-wife to save some of it. And she had persuaded him to visit Mrs. Farres. The woman's intense, carefully worded rationale for the visit, Anna's career, had a subtext, Candy was certain. Mrs. Farres wanted to see her husband about more than Anna.

Her train of thought led her back into her past. She had been twenty-two when she married her first husband, a stunningly handsome actor named Cory. Things were great for the first year, except that they didn't really have enough money. Candy had innate good taste and a growing appreciation for good things. After four years she became too frustrated with Cory's lack of ambition and lack of money to continue, and divorced him.

She began dating and met several men who treated her in a style she could appreciate. A few were ready to marry her. But as she gained experience, she realized that Hollywood, with its culture of magnificently enhanced egos, was not a good place to find a loyal and selfless husband. She fled on an impulse to Seattle, where she met Neil Brenchlow, a successful banker who introduced her to the relaxed attractions of boating in the San Juan Islands. She was aware that her good looks wouldn't last forever, made a judgment based on substantial experience that Neil was well enough off and looking to settle rather than continue a life of roving romance, and accepted his proposal. Yes, there was an element of a transaction to their marriage. He provided a handsome cruising boat almost large enough to be called a yacht and a splendid home, and on her side, if people made jokes about her being arm candy, she was fine with that.

And now she was sitting there, in a house she would apparently soon lose, feeling her resentment of her husband growing. She resented him for what the play showed he had done years ago, humiliating an innocent young woman. She resented the imminent loss of the nice things in her life. She resented being forced to take actions that made her feel unclean. She resented being made to not like herself for what she was doing. But she wasn't going to turn around now. She would take whatever steps she had to. She was haunted by the idea of herself living an impoverished life as her looks faded.

CHAPTER FIFTY-ONE

"You're Sam Troshin, aren't you?" said the man who took a seat next to Sam at the Roanoke. "Reporter with the North Coast News."

"I am." Sam nodded.

"I'm John."

Sam shook the hand the man extended. A firm, slow handshake that said, "I'm strong but I'm not trying to intimidate you."

"I read your story about Kirstin. It was a really good story. I could tell you thought a lot of her."

"I did," said Sam, looking at the man and wondering what he wanted. "I think I admired her more than any athlete I ever wrote about."

"I had a chance to meet her, just briefly. It's surprising how much of an impression some people can make in a short time. You couldn't help liking her."

"How'd you meet her?"

"I helped her with a car emergency. I know you're still working on the search for the killer. I think I might be able to help you a little."

Sam raised an eyebrow. The man was his height or taller,

hard to tell sitting, dark-rimmed glasses, solid looking without being heavy, something serious in his demeanor.

"I'm an insurance investigator," he said. "In town dealing with some banking issues. The reason I wanted to talk to you is from what I read in your stories, the police and you too are looking at the Russians, the one who went back in particular. So my work has me checking into these Russians pretty closely. I speak some Russian, one of the reasons I got the assignment. I am almost certain Konstantin Stivits, that's the guy, had nothing to do with Kirstin's death."

"Can you give me anything specific?" Sam asked.

"Wish I could, but at this stage everything I'm doing has to stay confidential. So I can't give you anything you can use in a story. My reason for talking to you is to encourage you to stay focused on the banker. Kirstin's death makes me angry. Right now you're doing a better job than the police of looking for the killer. I hope you can nail the person."

"It's true, the police aren't doing much. They could even be involved."

The man gave Sam a long look. "I think you're right. Be careful how you go about it."

"When your investigation is done, would you be willing to talk to me about it?"

"When it's done I might." He rose from the stool and laid his hand for a second on Sam's arm. "Keep after the policeman. Good luck to you."

CHAPTER FIFTY-TWO

Maybe Candy Brenchlow could help more than she had, Sam decided. She'd helped him with the Bunty lead. Maybe if he pressed her, she could help him find her husband, or McCord. He texted and asked if she would meet him at her convenience. She replied she would and named a time and coffee shop in town.

"Thanks for coming," he said when she sat down across from him.

"I appreciate that you let me look at those files."

"Your tip about that banker. That was good. I found him. Maybe you read the interview I did with him?"

"I saw that."

"Did your husband see the story?"

"I have no idea. He wouldn't have been very happy about it."

"All this coming out about your husband, I'm sorry …"

"Don't be. He's probably not going to be accused of anything he didn't do."

"I hope I can talk to him. Though the person I really wish I could talk to is this detective, McCord. He's kind of an associate of your husband's?"

"You have a chance to see the play?"

Sam nodded.

"The father and the cop. Neil and McCord. In cahoots. I'm sure they were, and I think they still are."

"Even now?"

"I think they work together."

"There's evidence, not conclusive, that McCord might be responsible for the volleyball player's death."

Candy pressed her lips together. "He's not somebody I talk to."

A moment passed.

"Since you wrote the story about the old trial and Claire," she said, "you probably know some of what Neil's involved in."

Sam thought about what he should say. Another lesson he was learning about investigative reporting—figuring out the motive of someone who was talking to you. Was she going to try to get him to lay off her husband? From her tone he didn't think that was where she was going.

"I don't know much more than what you read. The business reporter is working on this Russian construction loan business. He thinks there may be criminal charges coming up."

"There'll be more than the Russian loans if they really start investigating. Neil could be in deep shit."

Sam made a small shrug and nodded.

"So you think it's possible McCord killed the girl?" she asked.

Sam stalled for a moment to think. He was losing his judgment of how much to tell people. Mrs. Brenchlow was angry, he could hear that, though she was keeping her voice and face calm. But the anger was not directed at him and the questions he was asking. She wasn't trying to get him to lay off Neil. That wasn't where she was going at all.

"There's some reasons to think it's possible."

"More than what's been in the paper so far."

"There have been a couple of attempts to kill Zoey Franco. Since she talked to your husband."

"More than the road rage?"

"Somebody came after her in the hospital. Luckily they were spotted."

"Shit. Neil told that son-of-a-bitch to do it. I'm really afraid he did."

"One thing I know is Zoey is sure McCord killed Kirstin Kelly. Zoey was close to the girl."

"That's the girl who started asking questions about the Russian loans, isn't it? She could be right. I heard a conversation Neil was having with someone about her, that she was talking to the Russians. He was really pissed about what she was doing."

Sam was sure Candy Brenchlow's husband didn't know she and Sam were having this conversation. She didn't trust him anymore. Trust between a husband and wife. What a fragile thing it was. What do you do if your spouse is cheating? What do you do if your spouse is a crook? What do you do if your comfortable lifestyle has been made possible by criminal activities? What do you do if you think your husband is trying to kill a friend of yours?

"I went over to the station to talk to McCord," he said. "They said he's taken a leave. Nobody's sure where he is."

"My husband seems to have done the same thing. Hasn't been home for a couple of days and no message. Maybe they've gone to ground."

"I don't think they're covering for McCord at the station. I think they really don't know where he is."

"Your story about Bunty, the banker. All that stuff about bribing him to lie about the girl, so it really happened like in the play."

"Pretty much."

"How'd you get him to admit all that?"

"I said if he'd talk to me I wouldn't write about where he was. The guy is scared."

She took a long breath and exhaled with a soft whistle.

"I was pretty naïve when I got married."

"We all were," he replied.

"The first time and the second time too. Right now I'm not sure what to do. I was glad you contacted me, actually. I wanted to ask what you think is going to happen now."

"I won't know until I talk to them."

"What would you do if you found them?"

"Ask some questions. Ask your husband about the Russians. See what he says about the attempts to kill Zoey. The cops think the Russians killed the girl, but I don't think so. I want to give McCord a chance to explain."

"He won't talk to you. He's not a man you can mess around with."

"You have any guesses where?"

"Probably more than a guess," she said.

Sam lifted his eyebrow and waited.

"Neil owns a big piece of property down around Shelton. He doesn't know I know. Thick timber country, uninhabited. Except somewhere in the middle there's a meth lab. I'm not supposed to know about it. So sometimes I snoop. Neil's got some dodgy friends, but those guys are the scary ones. McCord has something to do with security. Nobody goes there. It's a bad place, and those are bad people. There's a lot of wilderness in this state. If they're in there, you'd need an army to find them."

"Could you draw me a map or something?"

"You want to go there? When I put together things I've heard over the years, I think there are people who've gone there and never come back."

"I'm a reporter. All they can do is kick me out."

As he watched her sketch a map, on a sheet of paper borrowed from the waitress, that might lead him to Brenchlow and McCord, he thought to himself, sometimes you don't need to be a good reporter to learn things, you just need to be the reporter.

CHAPTER FIFTY-THREE

The Haven Bluff cabins were spaced far enough apart along the wooded bluff overlooking the strait that guests could feel a sense of privacy and comfortable solitude. The cabins were log structures, rustic but with modern furniture and enough kitchenware in the cupboards above the tall burner grids of the Wolf stoves that guests could prepare a cassoulet, drink their Oregon pinots on the deck, and watch the sun set over the Pacific at the mouth of the strait, if that was how they chose to enjoy a few upscale vacation days.

Neil saw there was no car in the covered parking space. He'd noticed a Ford Explorer parked at the first cabin, but he hadn't seen any sign that the cabins beyond the first one were inhabited. Surprising, since this was an attractive, well-maintained resort that probably had good ratings on the travel sites and it was still high tourist season. He knocked at the door. He wasn't sure whether he heard a voice respond or not, so he slowly pushed the door open.

A woman, slightly hunched, with a pale, thin face and glittering eyes that bore into his, was waiting for him on the sofa.

"Please come in and sit," she said. She spoke slowly, as if

speaking above a whisper and articulating clearly was an effort. She gestured for him to sit across from her. There were two brandy snifters on the coffee table between them.

"I'm Neil Brenchlow. My wife said you wanted to meet and talk about Anna."

"Thank you for coming. I am Mrs. Farres. I produced the play."

"I'm not sure what that means. Producing."

"Your wife asked the same question. You're a banker. A play is a business event. Somebody has to rent spaces, get the programs printed. Write paychecks. Four carpenters did four twelve-hour days to build the sets."

"I see what you're saying. You don't think about that when you're in the audience."

"You see eight actors, but forty people make it happen."

"This play. Can I ask who wrote it?"

"A screenwriter in Los Angeles."

"His idea?"

"I helped."

She leaned forward and raised a glass. "A toast," she said. "To Anna."

"All right," said Brenchlow. "To Anna."

"She gave a very good performance at every show. Actors can't usually do that."

"I saw some of it. I'm no judge, but I thought she was really good."

"You didn't see it all?"

"No. The play was offensive."

"You should have. She's good enough to have a career as an actor. What most aspiring actors dream about."

"That's great. I'm glad you think so."

"I've hired an agent to work with her. A good one. I wanted to tell you about that. I hope that's all right with you."

"Of course," he said.

"She'll have to relocate to Los Angeles."

"Fine."

"I wish you'd seen the whole play. Even if it was offensive. I'd like to know what you think."

Brenchlow looked at her a moment without speaking.

"I heard enough. I heard lines somebody had to be at the trial to know."

"Words you remember yourself."

"You think I don't remember what happened?"

Brenchlow stood and walked behind the sofa, looking over her head.

"Your play made everything black and white. If you think it was an easy decision, it wasn't. I had to figure out what to do about Ronnie. The stupid kid. Playing football was the only thing he was ever good at. If he got convicted, his life was done. Never be anything but an ex-con bum."

He looked at her, his eyes narrowing to a frown.

"I thought, the dumb shit. If he did this thing, he should pay for it. He deserved it. But he's my kid. My only son. All I could do for him was give him a decent start. They said she was a party girl, and I let them convince me."

"Detective McCord told you that."

"Yeah, he was one."

"And he was rewarded."

There was a hesitation. "Yes."

"You had no idea what she was going through."

"I probably did, actually. I felt like crap about the whole thing."

He came around the sofa and sat again, exhaling with resignation.

"I take it you're her."

She gathered herself and rose from her chair. She unfolded the front of her blouse, which had been unbuttoned in preparation for her gesture. Raising the hem of the blouse to her shoulders, she turned away from him. Her back and thin neck to the hairline was a delicate, flowery tissue of pink and amber scarring.

"I'm sorry," said Brenchlow.

She lowered her blouse, turned, and sat again, looking at him without speaking.

After a minute she said, "Now you see me as a person."

"I thought you were probably here. What are you going to do?"

"I wasn't going to do anything more than what's been done. But I've learned things since I came back to Port Teresa."

Brenchlow waited.

"There was a tall girl, the volleyball player. She was going to write something about bank loans you were making for the Russians. She seems to have been a remarkable young woman. People are very upset about what happened to her."

"One of them came to my home and accused me of killing her."

"Did you? That young woman was one who cared about the volleyball player. Since she visited you, they've been trying to kill her. What you did at the trial, defending your son, I can understand that. Maybe it was the bribing you had to do that turned you. What I see now is a man who has turned evil defending a crumbling financial empire."

"You had people killed. My son. You call me evil. Are we that different?"

"Maybe we are. I was raped and burned. Those are physical events that can be endured, assuming you survive. What is not to be endured is being humiliated in front of everyone you know. When you had your lawyer convince people I was a slut who deserved what she got, you tied your destiny to mine."

"Destiny. That's too metaphysical for me. What, are you seeing this conversation as a theatrical production?"

"I hadn't thought of that, but maybe so, maybe I do. If this were a play, the ending I've prepared will have the symmetry a critic would admire."

"I know your people are good. I don't know how they worked that with Ronnie's truck. You killed my son. You made my daughter curse me with disgust. I thought maybe you'd be satisfied with that."

"I might have been. It's what I learned since coming home about the murder of the young woman that changed my mind. The trial was just the beginning of your corruption."

"I should have gone to Argentina. I've thought about it for a while now. Extradition from there is tough. I've spent time there. They have these estancias. American dollars would go a long way toward buying a nice one. Raise a herd of that lean, tasty Argentine cattle, maybe sheep. Condors with ten-foot wingspans coasting over your head, block out the sun for a few seconds in their shadow. The land in Patagonia goes on forever."

"But you didn't go."

"Waited too long, didn't I? The bank regulators are about to come down on me. Like wolves on the fucking fold. I do ask myself sometimes what I was thinking. You're right, you know. I didn't have to do those things. It was going to come out. I panicked. I guess I'm glad we talked. I'm leaving now, and you can do whatever you're going to do."

Brenchlow stood and took several long strides toward the door. Claire picked up one of the two small black boxes, each the size of a pack of cigarettes, that lay next to her on the sofa.

"The green button," she murmured, and pushed the green button on the box. The startling clang of steel on steel resonated from several locations in the cabin. By the time Brenchlow reached the door, an array of horizontal steel bars had slotted into receptacles fitted into the heavy timber doorframe. He stared frozen for a second, then ran quickly for someone his age and condition to the window in the kitchen area and ripped back the curtain. Steel mesh had been securely bolted to the window frame.

"Fuck!" he yelled, jumping away from the window.

"Please sit," said Claire, watching him without moving herself. "You'll never have Cognac like this again."

Brenchlow stood, not moving anymore except to tilt his head up as if he was staring into the ceiling. His fists tightened, then relaxed. She read rage fading to resignation in the gesture.

"I'm going to have another sip. There are certain things you come to appreciate as you get older. This Cognac is one of them."

"You're taking us both," he said.

"You tied our destinies together thirty years ago. This is the closure."

"I take it that was all bullshit about Anna, just to get me here."

"Not in the slightest. Contract's signed, the agent's been paid in advance. I think better of you for thinking of her instead of yourself at this moment. I wish I had a daughter. Maybe it all would have been different."

"I thought you'd resent her."

"Because she's your flesh and blood? Far from it. Your children aren't responsible for what you do. As I told your wife, she's a lively, outgoing, likeable young woman. The opposite of me at her age. Maybe that's what draws me to her."

"Please just fucking get on with it," he said.

She picked up the second box. "The red button," she said in a meditative tone. "He said it would be very quick."

She pushed the red button.

CHAPTER FIFTY-FOUR

Everyone except the receptionist was gathered around Molly's desk when Sam came in the door of the newsroom. That usually meant a major news story.

"What?" he said.

The staff turned to him.

"They identified a body at the Haven Bluff fire," said Molly. "It's Neil Brenchlow."

Sam sat down in the nearest chair. Only a couple of days earlier, he had been talking with Brenchlow's wife. For all he knew, the fire had burned while they talked.

"The other was a female," Molly said. "Not identified yet."

"Maybe he was having an affair," Sam said.

"That's possible. But they're saying the fire was arson."

"Who's the woman?"

"She hasn't been identified. Keep checking with the sheriff's department to see if they learn anything."

"I have to go tell somebody about this," said Sam. "I'll be back."

He texted Zoey he had news and was on his way to her apartment.

Zoey sat at her kitchen table with a hand on her computer mouse, scrolling through the wanted categories on Craigslist.

"They just identified the male in that resort fire," said Sam when he got there. "It's Neil Brenchlow."

She took in what Sam was telling her. She knew she wasn't processing things as quickly as she normally did. She'd never spent any time on serious pain meds. When she looked at her surroundings, it was as though she was seeing through glasses that slightly magnified everything. Her feet, one in a massive cast and black ski-boot thing, appeared to be far below her. Sound seemed to come through a length of pipe. She had been able to stay focused and sharp when she talked to McCord's wife in Port Townsend, but afterward she had recognized what an effort of will and even physical strength that had taken. On the return drive, she had miscalculated a turn and just caught her insurance loaner as she was about to drive off the highway. She couldn't let herself do any more driving for a while.

"Are you sure?"

Sam nodded. "The other body's female, not identified yet."

"Why do you think they could identify him but not her?"

"Maybe there's no records for her."

"This day and age? Isn't that what you told me about the woman from the old rape trial? No records anyone can find?"

"Something like that."

"You think it could be her?"

"Unless he was having an affair, yeah, it could be."

"You never can be sure, but he didn't strike me as somebody having an affair."

"Sheriff's department is investigating. They say arson."

"So that's it," said Zoey. "We'll never have proof he sent McCord to kill Kirstin."

"No."

"The cops will bullshit about the Russians. The investigation of her death will just peter out till it's a cold case."

"I'll find McCord and talk to him. We'll get something."

"You're an optimist, Sam. You can try to investigate him.

I'm going to go kill him. There aren't going to be any trials and big-time lawyers and plea bargain shit."

"You can't let yourself do that," said Sam. "We've been flat-out lucky about Gary."

"We have, you're right, and maybe we won't stay lucky. McCord will keep working it. He might figure it out."

"Maybe there's evidence somewhere tying McCord to Kirstin. I hear the sheriff's not one of his old buddies."

"I went to see his wife in Port Townsend."

"You did?"

"I told her what I learned from the guy in the retirement home. About the forged papers. When she tells McCord, he'll guess it's me. That'll give him something to think about."

"Jesus," said Sam. "You really want to be taunting him?"

"I appreciate your help, Sam. But I'm going to go kill the fucker. You have any idea where he is?"

Sam hoped a half-second's hesitation didn't give him away. He was not going to let her get herself killed. He wasn't going to tell her about Shelton and the map.

"I'm working on it," he said.

When he returned to the news office Molly waved him to her desk.

"We just heard from *Hunters and Fugitives,*" she said. "They're bringing Carl back. They're doing a shoot at his house in the morning with his daughter there. They want you too."

"Not to be on camera again, I hope."

"That's what they want. You're one of the players."

"They're going to do it without me," said Sam.

"It's the best story we can get out of it. You should be there for the meeting."

Sam paced the length of the newsroom and came back to the editor's desk.

"I'll go. But I won't play along with that woman again."

Molly looked at Sam with exasperation, then flipped her hand in a dismissive gesture. "All right. You don't have to go on camera. But get an interview."

When Sam arrived at Carl Tillis's address in the morning, he saw that the white trucks had rolled again into Port Teresa with their traveling circus. He slipped through a crowd of people milling in front of the house and showed his ID to someone at the open door trying to keep the neighborhood from pushing into the living room. He stood at the side of the room with three or four other observers with cameras and journalist IDs looped around their necks.

Carl sat on a sofa next to Kelsey. He stared down, showing no awareness of the preparations of lighting and microphones taking place in front of him. Kelsey looked ahead, holding her father's arm with a firm grip, as if holding him upright. She was as tall as he was.

The interview began. Sarah asked Carl how it felt to be home with his daughter. The questions that followed came in a voice oozing with sympathy, but Carl had less to say than he had in Idaho. He said in phrases of two or three monotone words he was glad to be home and was still afraid. Kelsey answered the questions directed to her with a flat voice, looking straight ahead without smiling. Yes, she was relieved her father was home and safe. She thanked the crew for finding him. Sarah couldn't entirely keep the exasperation out of her voice as she coaxed Kelsey to be more emotional and expressive in her responses. Kelsey appeared to Sam to be distant and preoccupied.

Sarah did most of the talking and wrapped the interview with a comment about how usually a fugitive doesn't want to be found but sometimes they do. As the TV people were hauling gear out the door, Sam went to where Kelsey was sitting and asked if he could ask her and her dad a few questions once things had quieted down. Kelsey nodded.

Sam pulled a chair to the sofa.

"I'm glad you got back safe," he said to Carl. "Now that they're gone, I want to tell you something. Something they don't know." He gestured toward the street. "There was a fire at a resort near here few days ago. They found two bodies. One was just identified as Neil Brenchlow."

Carl grimaced and appeared to shrink where he sat.

"She got him too," he said.

"It's possible," said Sam. "But here's the thing. The other body was a woman. Hasn't been identified. But we're thinking it's possible it's Claire Draghici. If it is, that means she ended it with a murder-suicide."

"Does that mean all this is over?" Kelsey asked.

Sam nodded. "We don't know for sure, so we can't say anything. But the fact that the woman can't be identified … Claire Draghici is one of the few people who there's no information about that could be used to identify her."

"Whoever it is setting the fires," said Carl. "He's still coming for me."

Carl made a sound, something between a curse and a sob, and bent his face forward into his hands.

"Can we talk to you another time, Sam?" Kelsey asked.

"Another time," he said. "I'll call later. Are you okay?"

"I had a bad experience," she said, and didn't say more.

"Okay," said Sam. "We'll talk later."

Sam returned to the office and wrote a quick story about the reality TV interview.

"This is the end of the revenge story," said Molly when she had scanned the copy he handed her. "It feels anticlimactic."

Sam would try to interview Carl and his daughter again in a few days. He felt contempt for the man's fearfulness. But he caught himself. This was fear fueled by guilt. How much time would pass before the man stopped fearing he'd die in a fire? If Claire Draghici could see him eaten away by a guilt that may not have diminished in thirty years, she might decide the punishment was sufficient. Carl's like me, he thought. Vengeance is self-inflicted.

"What now?" Molly asked.

Sam returned to the moment. "Kirstin Kelly."

"You're right. That's our story. The detective, McCord. Are we going to be able to find him?"

"That's my job now," said Sam.

"Doyle says the AG is finding stuff about his Port Townsend house."

"They're working on it," said Doyle, who was listening to their conversation. "As we speak."

"You okay, Doyle?" Molly asked.

"Yeah, yeah," he responded.

But Sam could see that Doyle had something on his mind.

CHAPTER FIFTY-FIVE

Sam made his usual stop at the Roanoke after reviewing the Carl interview story and filing it with Molly.

He found Doyle Shafter sitting at a table by himself, clutching a schooner of beer with both hands. He was surprised. Doyle was a family man who didn't hang out at bars after work.

"Joyce left me," he said to Sam.

So that was what had Doyle sweating and pacing in the newsroom. He knew Sam often passed the time between jobs at the Roanoke. Sam realized he had come here to talk.

"Man, sorry to hear that," said Sam.

"How could I not see it coming?" Doyle began cursing himself for not being aware of what was happening to his marriage. Doyle was a talker. Sam occasionally overheard him working his sources on the phone. You gave information; you got information. Doyle was good at it. One of his techniques was to keep himself informed about his sources' kids. Names, ages, what they were majoring in at college. Now he was telling Sam about his own daughter, Julie, graduating from Pullman next year.

Sam listened, nodded, and felt a surge of envy. He decided to tell Doyle he had a daughter who had died in her teens.

"Jesus," said Doyle. "I didn't know that. I'm really sorry to hear."

Sam knew he should talk about his daughter. He'd been able to say a little with Leah and his father. His girlfriend from college had been right. Try to talk about what you feel. Don't squeeze it in like it was a grenade with the pin pulled that would blow your guts apart if you let loose.

But right now he couldn't. He turned the conversation back to Doyle's marriage. He listened, then got up to go to the toilet for a piss. Whoa. He steadied himself. He'd been soaking up beer as if he was hydrating with Gatorade on a hot day at the basketball court. He brushed a knuckle along the wall as he walked down the dimly lit hallway to the restroom to make sure he was moving in a straight line. Doyle's lament had forced up images of Ella from the box of photos his brother had sent a month after his daughter died, photos sorted for him, he knew, by his wife. He had a catalog in his head, he realized, of every photo in the collection, each as clear as if he was holding it in his hand. His beautiful daughter.

When he had made his way back to the table, he sat and let Doyle continue voicing his grievances.

"What's she gonna tell Julie?" he asked Sam. "Is Julie gonna blame me? What do I say to her?"

"Kids, they're more grown-up than you think. She'll handle it."

"You're a bachelor. What's it gonna be like? I don't even know what to do."

"Get an apartment," said Sam. "Focus on work. You got a big story to work on with this real-estate fraud. Keep in touch with your daughter. Keep asking her how she's doing. Let her know you care."

Later, when he tried to order one more pitcher, the bartender said, "Sorry, Sam, can't let you get yourself into trouble here." He almost opened his mouth to tell the bartender to fuck off, but shut his eyes instead for a long second and nodded. Man was right. Doyle put an arm around Sam's shoulder as they left the table, and with the profuse friendliness of someone not used to being drunk thanked Sam for letting him bend his ear. At the bar Doyle asked the bartender to call a cab for him.

"C'mon," he said. "Give ya a ride."

"S'okay," said Sam. "Need the walk."

He had walked a few blurry blocks away from the Roanoke when someone stepped in front of him. A policeman who had just pulled up beside him in a cruiser.

"Got some ID, sir?"

Sam fumbled for his wallet. "Anything wrong?" he asked.

"Sir, you're intoxicated. Are you driving somewhere?"

"No, no, jus' walking."

"I want you to get in the car, Mr. Troshin. You're in danger of hurting yourself."

Sam looked at the officer in confusion. He wasn't driving. Weren't you allowed to take a walk even if you were wasted? An irrational fear told him McCord had sent this policeman to find him. Heard he was asking questions about the detective and sent his men to find him.

"Sir, please?"

The officer gripped Sam's upper arm and began forcing him down through the back-seat door of the cruiser.

"Excuse me," said someone, a woman's voice. "Can we help with Sam?"

"This man is intoxicated. I'll take him to the station for the night."

"We're his designated driver," said the woman. "We're here to take him home."

"You have a car?" said the policeman.

"Next block," said the woman, giving the officer a friendly smile and taking Sam by the arm not held by the policeman. Her smile widened. The policeman released his grip.

Sam let himself be guided along the sidewalk. He realized it was Leah who was helping him. And Alison? He felt a surge of relief that he was out of the hands of the police. He made a drunk's effort to be mindful and deliberate in his movements. He wanted to ask Leah where she'd come from, but his tongue had become thick and inflexible. Anything he tried to say would come out stupid. He decided to wait till later to talk. Right now it was one foot in front of the other, straight line. Keep yourself balanced, priority numero uno.

When Sam woke he felt like a large radiator hose clamp had been tightened one too many notches around his head. Christ! What was he doing? Becoming a binge drinker was what he was doing. Waking up woke his bladder. He needed to urinate right now. He stood and didn't know where he was.

"Don't move so fast," said Leah.

Where had she come from? "Bathroom," he mumbled.

She took his arm and directed him to the toilet. When he was done, he looked at himself in the mirror. The face he saw looked like crap, his mouth hanging stupidly open, his eyelids drooping slackly beneath his eyes. He returned to the sofa, where he had apparently spent the night. Leah and Alison sat in the chairs facing the sofa.

"Where's this?" he asked.

"A friend's. Shelley's. I'm looking after her cats while she's gone."

He sunk back in the sofa and squeezed his temples with his hands.

"Christ. Not a good night." The memory came back in pieces. "How'd you find me?" he asked.

"A friend of yours called. He said you might need some help getting home."

"A friend?"

"From the bar. Can you get down some coffee?"

Sam clutched at the mug of coffee she handed him and began sipping. Later he would wonder what friend at the bar knew who Leah was. But no complicated thoughts now. He looked at Alison. Why was she here? he wondered.

"She told me what happened," said Leah, following his gaze.

The girl looked steadily at Sam. She could just look at you. Then a shot of pain lanced through his forehead, and he stopped thinking about Alison.

When he opened his eyes again, the girl was still looking at him.

"You know where he is?" she asked.

He took another swallow of coffee. The taste was harsh, but he could feel the caffeine digging into the fog in his head. The girl should be the reporter.

"The policeman, you mean? I don't know. I looked for him. They said he took a leave."

He stood, felt the blood drain from his head, sat back down.

"Be careful," he heard Leah say. He closed his eyes with shame. Didn't want either one of them seeing him this way. He hated being something pathetic.

"Are you writing about all this, Sam?" Leah asked, after letting him compose himself.

"It's part of the rape story. Brenchlow's wife, you know who she is?"

"I never met her."

"I talked to her. She told me about a place around Shelton Brenchlow owns. Said there's something illegal going on there, maybe a meth lab. She thought it's where Brenchlow and McCord would go to hide. She drew me a map."

"You should get the police to look for him."

"McCord's one of them."

Speaking of the map, did he still have it? He patted his pockets, found it, pulled it out, and unfolded it.

"What are you going to do?" Leah asked.

He looked at Alison, answering her as much as Leah.

"I'll try to find him."

"Maybe he won't talk to you."

"Only thing I can think of doing. The whole police department could be his people. Maybe there's no real investigation of Kirstin's death going on at all."

"Isn't there a district attorney here? I don't think they work for the police. At least on *Law and Order* they don't."

"Maybe so," said Sam. "Zoey recorded a conversation with Brenchlow. It's incriminating. It wouldn't be evidence, though."

He slumped back in the sofa. "I think I need to close my eyes for a while."

"We're asking too many questions. Just lie down and sleep."

When he was stretched out, she pulled the blanket she'd covered him with the night before back over him. He was out in a minute.

When Sam woke he lay still and, for the second time, stared at an unfamiliar ceiling, working out where he was. A friend's, the drama teacher. Right, there were the cats watching him. He was stark naked. For Christ sakes. Look at something else, he thought to the cats. His clothes, underpants on top, were neatly stacked on the coffee table. Washed. He pulled on his shorts and pants as quickly as he could, but there was nobody in the apartment. He moved his head. Neck stiff, but at least the head moved.

He raised himself into a standing position. The clock on the microwave in the kitchen said eight. That had to be morning. Had they washed his clothes in the middle of the night? Or had he been here a day plus? The chronology was more than he could sort out at the moment. He flexed his neck, not too quickly. He ran his tongue around a dry mouth. Orange juice would be really good about now. He opened the refrigerator and thankfully found a carton. "Hello?" he called out.

He was alone in the apartment. He remembered drinking at the bar. Doyle Shafter drunkenly grappling with his failure as a husband. But Doyle had succeeded as a father. The daughter graduating at WSU. His compulsion to confess his own miserable failure as a father. Had he said something about turning his back on his daughter as a way of getting back at his wife? That couldn't be true. Could it? No, that line of thinking was intolerable.

He had a cloudy recollection of wandering the street like some drunken bum wallowing in self-pity, a cop ready to haul him in, and being gathered up by a woman and a girl, two people whose respect he wanted. Well, so much for anyone respecting Samuel Troshin, aspiring journalist, failed father, ex-con, tragically thoughtless coach of a newspaper intern, dealing with his problems, apparently, by working on establishing himself as another town drunk.

Fuck this wallowing. He needed to be doing something. He saw Candy's map on the coffee table, looked at for a few minutes, thought about it. He let himself out of the apartment, locking the door behind him. Once he'd figured out where Shelley's house was located, he started the long walk to where he'd left his car. He considered stopping at Starbucks but decided to find a café instead, where he persuaded the staff to fix a tuna melt from the lunch menu. He ate that, then a piece of cherry pie. It must have been a long time since he'd had a meal. The walk and the food cleared his head. As he ate, he considered his choices.

How do you investigate the police in a small town? There wouldn't be an internal affairs department. Could he talk to the chief? Or could he talk with someone in the state patrol? There was a chance anyone he talked to would know McCord, maybe be an old friend. The detective had decades of connections in the law enforcement world. If he succeeded in finding a neutral law enforcement officer, the sheriff possibly, what evidence did he have to offer? The recording didn't prove anything. The best he could hope for was that someone would agree to look into the situation. He would sit and wait, and every few days Alison and Zoey would ask him if he had learned anything more.

Or he could go looking for the people he wanted to talk to. He could take advantage of the small amount of leverage he was learning how to use as a newspaper reporter and persuade people to talk to him. He could find a Russian interpreter to help him press Alexei and the Russians for information about their connections with Brenchlow. But the helpful insurance investigator told him not to waste his time there. He could drive to Olympia and begin the process of finding someone official to talk to about Brenchlow and McCord's real-estate documents.

Or he could fill the Toyota's gas tank and set off for the woods.

CHAPTER FIFTY-SIX

After the gas stop, he drove back to his apartment, put on a sturdy pair of shoes, and headed south toward 101. He compared Candy's map with a road map of the state. It looked like Brenchlow's property lay somewhere south of the Skykomish reservation, north of Dayton. It would be heavily forested hills rising to mountains.

His route took him through Quilcene to Hoodsport. A rain shower had come through in the morning, but the sun was out and evaporating water shimmered over patches of road that were still wet. He took the 102 exit west.

There was almost no traffic, only a couple of vehicles going the other way, and no one visible driving in his direction. He saw an unmarked dirt road on the left. Was it the road he was looking for? He continued a couple of miles further to be sure there wasn't another road in the area. He turned back and pulled off onto the road. A few puddles were left in the deeper holes. His Toyota didn't have much clearance. He had to edge up onto the side of the road to get around the biggest puddles. He came to a fence with a gate and stopped.

The gate was a heavy structure, six feet high, built from

steel tubing. There was no gap between the gate and the cyclone fencing on either side. No rust on the sturdy, painted hinges. A sign in the middle of the gate read "Do Not Trespass." He couldn't find a button or intercom connection.

He held his press ID over his head, turning from one side of the fence to the other. He couldn't see any cameras, but they might be there. He didn't want anyone to have the impression he was sneaking in.

He loosened his shirt, made sure everything in his pockets was secure, and looked for footholds in the gate. His left arm wasn't much use, but he pulled himself up, squirmed over the top, and dropped to the ground.

The road from here was two well-worn ruts. Short-cropped grass grew on the ridge in the center, but the ridge was flat. They must use pickups here or four-wheel drives. You couldn't drive a passenger car on the road without high-centering. The road bent through the trees. The trees didn't tower overhead like the Douglas firs and cedars around Port Teresa, but the spaces between trees were dense with undergrowth. He couldn't see much except brush and the road fifty yards ahead. He walked for what seemed like a mile. He wished he'd thought to bring a water bottle.

He heard a motor, then saw a pickup truck ahead driving toward him. He stepped to the driver's side of the road and waited. The truck stopped at Sam's side.

"You're trespassing," said the driver. "This is posted property."

"I know," said Sam. "I didn't see a way to make contact. I need to talk to Mac McCord."

"That's somebody I'm supposed to know?" asked the driver.

"Brenchlow owns the place. McCord works security for him. I'm pretty sure he'll want to talk to me. Tell them Sam Troshin from the *North Coast News*."

The driver looked at him a moment, then skillfully backed the truck up the road. Sam saw him make a cell call. Or a larger device, maybe a walkie-talkie. Could be off the cellular grid.

He signaled Sam to walk forward to the truck.

"Get in," he said.

The man continued backing until he found a space to turn the truck around. He was big, carrying a paunch but with the thick, calloused fingers and sinewy forearms of someone who lifted things. A tattoo of an Iron Cross or something Germanic on his neck. The thick black beard Sam associated with middle-aged bikers and off-the-grid places like this. He knew the man wouldn't answer any questions, so he didn't ask any.

The road led to a cluster of low buildings. Two more pickups and a pair of Suzuki ATVs were parked in a space between the buildings. Some of the buildings were old wood structures, two were newer, galvanized metal siding, corrugated zinc roofing. The trees had not been cleared from between the buildings. It would have been hard to see the structures from overhead. He didn't see any people.

"In there," said the man, pointing to one of the buildings. It was the only one that didn't have a pull-down garage door. It must be the residence, he thought. But there was nothing to suggest a house.

He tapped a couple of times and pushed the door open.

An older man with a full gray beard and thinning hair pulled back in a ponytail turned from a computer screen and looked at him. The room contained several desks and office chairs. Along the far wall, a half-dozen monitors sat three on top of three on a table. The monitors showed images of trees, a road. The gate he had climbed.

"Who are you?" he said.

"Sam Troshin. I'm a reporter with the *North Coast News* in Port Teresa. I'm doing a story on a murder case and wanted to talk to Mac McCord. He might have information that would be helpful."

"What murder is that?" the man asked.

"A girl, Kirstin Kelly, killed in Port Teresa about a month ago. I think he can tell me something about what happened. He works for Brenchlow, who owned this place, right? I'm pretty sure there's things he could tell me. I don't want to write the story without getting my facts straight."

"Troshin" came a voice from behind him. "You're the one dug up the files on the old trial."

"Yessir."

"And now you want to see me."

He turned and saw McCord standing in a doorway. He wore a billed cap, tan windbreaker, jeans, and his duty belt.

"Yeah, I've got some questions. Sorry to come invading the property, but like I said, I'm doing a story. I don't want to write it without hearing from you. Getting your take on what happened."

"What's the story?"

"The woman who was killed. Kirstin Kelly. She was trying to talk to the Russians about the loan scams."

"The Russians killed her," said McCord.

"It doesn't look like it. A woman, Zoey Franco, learned about some real-estate documents, forged signatures. A place on Cypress in Port Townsend. She went out to Brenchlow's place to talk to him."

"Zoey Franco is under investigation for the murder of Gary McCord. My son, you know that. She's holding back information."

"I have a recording. You should listen to it."

"Recording of what?" said McCord.

"Her talk with Brenchlow. She recorded it on her phone."

He fumbled with his phone a few seconds to get the sound utility up.

"Don't bother. I doubt you have anything there that would stand up in court, right?"

"That's true. I can tell you what struck her most when she talked to him. He never denied sending you after Kirstin."

"You're going to write a news story based on that?"

"Not till I hear your view."

"You mean the police view? The Russians killed the volleyball player because she was asking too many questions about their business. I really don't understand why you came here."

"Like I said. Get your side of the story. Maybe some parts

of the story aren't what they look like. Anything you want to say, I'll print. Or anything about the forged documents for the Port Townsend house."

"Is that my place you're talking about?"

"A fine old house, I hear. You've got good taste."

"I haven't been able to get in touch with Brenchlow. You have an idea where he is?"

"You haven't heard?"

"What?"

"He's dead. Killed in a fire at a resort."

McCord stood a moment looking at Sam without saying anything. "A fire."

"Yeah," said Sam. "There was a female with him, not identified. We think it might be the rape victim from the old case. The one you were involved in."

"Did Preedy send you here?"

"He doesn't know anything about it."

"You're telling me the fucker can't keep control of his staff?"

"I don't know about that," said Sam.

"He's too old. He should get out."

"Was he ever in cahoots with you guys? I get a sense he was, and now he's having second thoughts. So go ahead, tell me what you'd like me to write."

"How'd you find this place?"

"Asked a lot of questions."

"People at the paper know you're here?"

"I just decided this morning to drive down."

McCord sat down. Then he gave an audible sigh and stood again.

"You know, I don't get you. Somehow you find this place. You come here alone, you say you haven't even told anybody where you're going. You think I've killed people, and you come here to accuse me. If all this is true, doesn't it seem reasonable we'd just make sure you don't say anything?"

"You can give me your side. I'll write up whatever you tell me. Your chance to be heard."

"I guess I see your thinking. You think I want my story told, and I'll let you go back safely and tell it."

"Got pen and paper. Or I can record it on my phone."

"But what if it's basically true? What if I have nothing to say?"

"You're telling me you killed her?"

"I'm telling you you're a fool for coming here."

"You must have a story. I'm ready to write."

"I think this is what they call being in denial. Aren't you hearing me? There isn't going to be any writing."

Sam puckered his lips. He realized he should have thought out this conversation ahead of time. Maybe he had depended on his reflexes one too many times.

"Let's take a walk. You came all this way. I'll show you around."

McCord walked to the door and waited for Sam.

"I don't really need a tour," said Sam. "What do you want me to say?"

"I don't think you're hearing me. Come on."

"Really, no need," said Sam.

"No, I insist."

The man with the ponytail remained where he was, watching Sam and not moving.

"Okay," said Sam. "Okay. Show me the place."

They stepped outside and crossed the open space between the buildings. Sam noticed a gray long-bed pickup parked next to the last outbuilding.

"Excuse me just a second," he said, and walked around the front of the truck.

"You looking for something?" McCord asked.

"Just wanted to check the bumper. I'm looking for a truck involved in a rear-end collision. This one's got some dings in the right place."

"Would be hard to tell, though, wouldn't it?"

"Yes, it would."

"What we got here you could call a light industrial operation," said McCord as Sam returned to the walkway. "Marijuana grow over there."

"Going to be legalized one of these days."

"Then we'll plant more. Soil and climate here pretty good for it. Terroir they're calling it. Stuff grades out very well."

"What else?"

"Some very marketable chemical products."

They entered the forest. Sam walked along a wide path, McCord followed a few steps behind. Sam gestured for McCord to lead, but McCord said, "No, no, you go ahead," and waved him forward. After several hundred feet, the path came to a *Y*.

"Bear right," said McCord.

After ten minutes of following the path under the canopy of pines and firs, McCord said, "We're just getting a tour of the place, right, Sam? You uncomfortable with that?"

"A little," said Sam.

"Just take it easy."

"No worries."

"You're an athletic-looking guy, Sam. Maybe even a tough guy. I'm remembering your record, couple of assaults. I can see you're kind of nervous. I'm a little concerned you'll panic and do something stupid. Maybe think you'd be more comfortable if you had my Glock. Keep in mind I've been a cop thirty years. I deal with violent assholes all the time. Kind of a specialty even."

"I'd really like to hear your side of the story," said Sam.

"Don't have a side," said McCord.

Sam's heart began beating faster. Oh no, not a panic attack now, he thought. "Focus on the breathing if you feel it coming," the doc had said. Visualize the air flowing in and out. He tried to do that now. Had he really thought McCord would see him as an envoy sent to the enemy camp to bring back the enemy's message? He'd deceived himself with the reporter rationale. He wanted to find McCord and accuse him of killing Kirstin and hadn't thought it out beyond that. He should have. By coming here he'd made himself a threat, and McCord probably had experience dealing with threats.

"People know where I am," he said. "If I don't get back, there'll be a big mess."

"Yeah, we're at the point I don't see how we can avoid a big mess," said McCord. "But I'll tell you this: they'll have one fuck of a time finding you."

The soil underfoot became damp. Brackish water began smooshing up around his shoes.

"Keep going," said McCord. "We're going to get our feet a little wet."

By the time he'd walked a hundred yards further, Sam was up to his knees in a bog. He stopped.

"No, keep going," said McCord. Tall grass grew in clumps. The place was mucky with a sheen of rotting ferns. An odor of rot and mildew. There were cattails and pale big-leaved marsh flowers, yellow skunk cabbage thriving in the gloomy, sunless mire. Birds, a multitude of species, chirped, whistled, and twittered. He had just read the account of the massacre of the Polish officer corps by the Soviets in the Katyn Forest in the World War II history Molly had given him. The story had seized his imagination, grisly as it was. Why he thought of that now he didn't know. Maybe because he wondered if it had been like this in the forest, birds hunting for nest materials, males glowing in their summer colors and strutting for the females, red-winged blackbirds whistling their melodious tune in the cattails, swallows scooping bugs out of the air, indifferent to the soldiers among them pushing carts of men shot in the back of the head to be dumped in pits dug in the forest floor.

Sam was afraid. He had walked into the trees half-believing McCord would let him leave after providing some kind of justification for what happened or just lying about it. No, he couldn't really have believed that would happen. It was odd. He was afraid of being shot, of being hurt. But not so afraid of dying. How could that be? His death, or his disappearance, since nobody was going to find him out here, would be one more confirmation of McCord's and Brenchlow's guilt. Justice was coming. If his drive to Shelton turned out to be a sacrificial act, his life had served a purpose. Crap, what was he thinking, seeing himself as a martyr? He was not martyr material.

So why had he let himself come here? He knew. He'd driven to Shelton because of all the women he'd let down in his life. Megan. Ella. Kirstin. Alison. If he'd been smarter, if he'd learned more about investigative reporting, if he'd had more patience, he would have found a way to finesse the information he needed. All he'd known how to do was to go forward and turn himself into a blunt instrument, clambering over the fence and bearding the lion on his turf.

As a defensive back, he relied on his reflexes. Now he'd come to the crisis in the game, where his reflexes were not enough. There was a point you needed to be part of a team. He didn't have one.

Maybe he should try to save himself by rushing McCord. He'd probably fail. Nobody could move fast in water up to his knees. He was sure McCord was telling the truth about being used to situations like this. But the attempt would be a kind of gesture, something almost expected of an ex-football player still halfway quick on his feet. He just didn't feel up to it.

"Okay, stop here," said McCord. "Go ahead, take a look around. Could you guess there's five bodies out here? The business they do in this place has its touchy moments. Four guys, one bad-tempered woman. All parted out into the ecosystem now."

"Meth business," said Sam.

"Very lucrative if you can get a stable operation going. Which is not easy. Want a tip? Get a crew of bikers involved. They won't be the sharpest tools in the tool chest. You wouldn't want 'em making decisions. But they have this thing about loyalty. Number-one virtue. Beat the shit out of them, throw them in jail for years, fuck, offer them big bribes. They won't snitch on a brother. Their whole self-image is you never snitch. Great work force if you pay 'em good and keep things simple and clear. And there's a market you wouldn't believe. I'm not talking about the cities. Out in the farm country in the middle of the state. I'm convinced every other person must be using.

The boredom of farmwork, I'm guessing. Hard work and the same boring shit every day."

"Why are you telling me this?" Sam asked.

"Why? You did ask about the business, didn't you? Probably because I'm stalling. You think I'm some kind of psychopath. Fuck, maybe I am. The thing is, once you get started on the path, you have to do the next thing. I get no satisfaction out of it. So start walking. Toward that snag leaning to the left. Water'll be up to your belt. So why did Ronnie Brenchlow try to kill you in that bar?"

"He tried to attack the woman I was interviewing. The volleyball player, the one Brenchlow wanted you to get rid of. I knocked him down."

Sam's heart continued to race. He was going to be shot here, and McCord was going to walk back and have his car put on a trailer and taken somewhere to disappear. Fear sensitized him to the sounds and smells and spectrum of greens that surrounded him. He was sure McCord was telling the truth about the five bodies because he could feel the restless presence of their spirits hovering in the dampness under the canopy of branches. He felt a momentary urge to plead for his life. He would promise anything, to scrap the story, lie, just don't shoot him in the back of the head like the Polish officers. But he didn't open his mouth. His father's quiet stubbornness in his DNA. They had the recording. Leah would figure out where he had gone. Candy Brenchlow would know and talk to someone. He would be the one victim too many for McCord. He was sure now that McCord had killed the girl. They would get the son of a bitch.

"Ronnie Brenchlow was a stupid failure," said McCord. "Can I ask one thing? You know who killed Gary?"

"He raped a woman. She defended herself."

"You don't mean Zoey?"

"No."

McCord looked at him, then nodded once. "The dumb shit."

Silence, except for the chorus of birds. A flutter of wings here and there in the periphery of a person's vision.

"Okay," said McCord. "Sorry, man. You shouldn't have come here."

Sam held himself as steady as he could. Then, to his astonishment, he heard a girl's voice sing out.

"You're the one trying to kill Zoey, aren't you?"

Sam and McCord turned to the sound. The figure of a girl stood at the edge of the forest, looking at McCord along the shaft of an arrow drawn back to her ear. McCord raised the pistol in his hand, but he was not quick enough.

The arrow that had killed his son, blades sharp as a surgeon's scalpel, sailed a flat and silent trajectory across the bog and pierced his chest.

Sam stood in the water, staring at the girl. She held the bow in front of her, frozen in the shooting position, watching as McCord's knees folded. The policeman slid into the water faceup, the arrow pointing to the sky. Sam had braced himself for the impact. His core was drawn so taut the muscles needed a moment to loosen before he could speak. When the muscles released, he expelled the breath he had been holding with a gasp.

"She said you were a hunter," was all he could articulate.

"We need to go," the girl called out. Her voice snapped him out of his trance. He waded the few steps between himself and McCord, who was floating on the water's surface, and grasped the arrow. In the heart. Amazing. Who was this girl who could do this?

The body was unstable in the water. He had to stand with McCord's head between his legs to get a straight pull on the shaft. There was enough strength in his uninjured arm, and he was able to extract the arrow from the body.

How was it possible, he wondered, to have a sequence of events that led to him pulling an arrow out of a man's chest for the second time in a month?

"There's cameras," she said. "Stay behind me."

I have a team after all, he thought.

CHAPTER FIFTY-SEVEN

The girl waved for Sam to follow her, and he did. He would probably do anything she directed him to do. Once back out of the bog and onto firm ground, they pressed into the heavy brush. His legs became shaky and unsteady. The reality of how close he had come to being shot began to register. First his legs, then his arms and torso shook, and his vision blurred. Panic after the fact. There was no path, but the girl didn't hesitate. She pushed ahead as if she remembered her exact route through the brush. Once, she stopped and pointed to the side. He saw it, a camera aimed away from them. It was work, forcing his way through the dense net of vine maples and bushes that slapped across his face and tried to snag his ankles. Vines seemed to wrap around the soaked pants, clinging to his calves as if they didn't want to let him leave. He struggled to keep up with the girl, who slipped without visible effort through the branches. He fell stupidly once but jumped up and drove himself forward, pushed by an irrational fear she would leave him behind. He squeezed his fists as hard as he could for a couple hundred feet, hoping that would calm the shaking. After a long march, more than a mile, he thought, they came to the fence and the road.

The effort had gradually calmed his shakes. She showed him a concealed depression deep enough to let them crawl under the fence. When they were outside, she retrieved the black bow case she had covered with brush. He tried to orient himself.

The familiarity of his car, when he got in and tried to start the engine, began bringing him back from the surreal experience in the woods to the continuity, ragged but present, of his life.

"How'd you know to come here?" he asked.

"Your map," she said.

"And you got here . . . ?"

"Leah drove."

He was having trouble with the ignition, still trembling enough he needed a couple of tries before he could fit the key in the slot. He was sweating heavily from the strenuous hike through the undergrowth, but more than that. He was probably in a state of shock. He needed to sit and take some deep breaths. Letting his heartrate catch up with itself. But thank God not the panic that would have rendered him helpless.

"What do we do now?" he asked.

"Leah's in Shelton."

"That's where we go then."

He tried to look at her without turning his head. She sat rigid, as if frozen, staring straight ahead. After several minutes she spoke with a voice that trembled with stress.

"If I didn't do it, she was going to. I could never let her do anything like that."

"You had to do it because he was going to kill me."

As they approached the town, he saw Alison texting with her phone.

"She's at the Pine Tree on First."

When they found the café and pulled into a parking space, Leah rushed out through the door to Alison and hugged her. Then she turned to Sam and gave him a hug. Not a social-greeting hug, a strong squeeze she held for a moment.

"What happened?"

"We can talk about it later. I think it's okay."

Sam and Alison followed Leah to her seat in the café.

"Did I do the right thing, bringing her here?" Leah asked.

"It's a good thing you did. If she hadn't gone in there, I wouldn't have got out."

"What did she do?"

Sam sucked in a deep breath. "Don't think I can talk about it yet."

Alison got up from her seat in the booth and asked the waitress where the restroom was.

"The bow. Was that it?"

Sam hesitated, then nodded.

"Oh my God. What are we going to do, Sam?"

"She saved my life. We're going to have to think about it."

He knew she was thinking the same thing he was. A sixteen-year-old girl who had killed two men. Even if there were no legal consequences, what would happen to her? What would she become?

Leah picked up a binder from the table and held it out to Sam.

"You have to read this," she said. "It's amazing. That's the only word for it."

"What?"

"She's written a story. It's a short novel, really. It's a version of what's happened to her. But it's really good. I mean, she can write. The grammar needs work, but … it's just really good."

"About being attacked by that asshole?"

"Yes, except it's not just a simple first-person narrative. This girl, Cloey, learns about a friend who's being abused. She learns to use a bow and saves the friend. But there's an abusive family, a mother with no clue what's happening, and a lot of observation. It's overwhelming, all the things she's aware of. I thought I wanted to write a novel once. But I don't have half her talent."

"I remember what she said in the group," said Sam. "About the Frankl book you guys read. How writing about a bad experience could make it survivable."

"You're right." She nodded. "She's made herself a character. Gives herself perspective."

"Any way she's going back to her family, her mom ...?

"No. For the girl in the story, the mom's place isn't safe. Really not even a roof over her head."

A waitress came to the table and looked at Leah.

"The young lady with you, she's in the restroom. You better go in there."

Leah stared at Sam for a second, then jumped up and hurried to the restroom.

"She's crying pretty hard," the waitress said to Sam.

"Thanks," said Sam.

"Refill?"

"Please."

Sam nursed the coffee and waited. The bog, the ghosts he knew were there, the astonishing shout of the girl, he could see and feel it all again as if it had just happened.

Fifteen minutes later Leah and Alison, Leah with an arm around the girl, came back from the restroom. Both had eyes red from crying.

"She's exhausted," said Leah. "Can we get a motel?"

Sam paid the check. He had to drive only a few blocks before he found a motel with the vacancy sign lit. Leah and Alison followed him in Leah's car. Sam waited in one of the plastic stacking chairs lining the walkway in front of the room while Leah got Alison into bed. After a while she came out and closed the door quietly behind her. She took the chair next to Sam, closed her eyes, and took a long breath.

"She admires you," she said.

"Christ! I admire her. She's a little unbelievable. I'm scared to death for her. Did she say anything about what happened?"

"Not really. Mostly she cried. Not many words."

Sam thought. "The people in that place won't want anybody coming out there. I don't think they're going to say anything about what happened."

"This policeman, McCord, is he going to come after her?"

"No."

She looked at him. "You're sure?"

"I'm sure."

"Someday you'll tell me what happened."

Sam nodded.

They sat for a while in silence. The clouds over Shelton had completely dispersed. The afternoon had become warm and pleasant. Cars passed on the street in front of the motel, no one in a particular hurry. Tourists in motorhomes or Subarus with mountain bikes on roof racks, heading for the coast, or locals going shopping for groceries, AA batteries, washers to fix the leaky faucet.

"They let Scott go," she said.

"What'll he do?"

"Try to find an anchor spot, somewhere small market."

"Probably means relocating."

"For sure, there's nothing around here."

"That's too bad. You have a good situation here, teaching, the book group."

"I don't want to relocate."

"That's a hard choice."

"I've made it."

He wanted to know, he badly wanted to know, but he didn't think this was the time to ask.

"What'll happen with her, for now?" he said after they had sat for a few minutes.

"She's staying with Zoey. Too bad you couldn't be a foster dad."

"I'd do it."

"Never be allowed. But I know you'll keep an eye on her."

"If she lets me."

"She will. She's very alert to who she can depend on and who not. You're in her story, you know."

"I am?"

"The helper. A little older than you actually are. But it's you."

Sam gave half a grin. "I probably am a little older."

An hour later Alison came out of the bedroom. Her eyes were puffy, the color drained from her face.

"Are you okay?" Leah asked.

She nodded.

"Should we go back?"

She nodded again.

"You can stay with Zoey?"

"Yes."

The girl's voice was dry and raspy, as if she had been yelling for the home team at a football game until her voice was shredded.

The bow case was on the floor of Sam's car. Alison took a careful look around the motel parking area and opened the case. She took an arrow out of the case, shielding what she was doing with her body, and held it in her hand. She touched the tip with a finger. Sam thought he saw a tremor pass through her.

"Could you help me with something?" she said to him.

"Absolutely."

"Could you get rid of it? Not in the garbage. Smash it up or something."

"Think I understand," said Sam. He put the bow in its case on the floor of the passenger seat of the Toyota and stood looking at the car with the bow resting against the seatback. An idea came to him.

"Tell me when it's done," she said.

"You want to meet me in town in a couple days?"

"Okay."

"Text," he said. "I'll text."

EPILOGUE

Several days later Sam drove the MR-2 to the office at the Peninsula Salvage Company. Alison sat beside him, bow case between her knees. At the office Sam went inside and wrote a check. Then he drove the way he had walked a few weeks ago, to the car compactor. When he got out, Jules recognized him and gave him a wave.

"That's it?" said Jules. "Looks like it's got some miles left."

"Its time has come," said Sam.

"Your call," said Jules. "You paid to get to the front of the line. Let's get it drained. Can't usually drive 'em onto the rack."

He got in Sam's car and drove up the ramp over the drain tray, opened the various drain plugs under the car, then spent three minutes removing the converter.

"Fifteen minutes," he said. "Go talk to Tanya if she isn't busy."

Tanya wasn't busy, though she couldn't leave the phone. She used a dummy coin to get a couple of Sprites out of the dispenser for Alison and Sam.

Fifteen minutes later they returned to the compactor. Jules was centering Sam's car in the box with a forklift.

"Something in the seat there. Want me to get it out?"

"No," said Sam. "It goes too."

He and Alison stood side by side as the steel top of the compactor once again began its descent. The car snapped and screeched until it was a wrinkled package of painted and bare metal twenty inches high, recognizable as a car but not as a Toyota or anything else specific. Hydraulic forces raised the steel plate back up its track to where it began. Jules climbed onto the big forklift, hoisted a sedan from the line of cars awaiting their destruction, and placed it in the cage on top of what had been Sam's Toyota. Down came the crusher again, and the sedan folded like a beer can stepped on before being tossed into the recycling bin. Sam's car and the sedan were now an indistinguishable mass of metal scrap. Jules lifted the package with the forklift and moved it to the top of a stack of crushed cars, maybe fifteen feet off the ground. Sam waved to Jules and began walking toward the exit.

"I didn't even think if there's a bus stop around here," he said.

"Your car drove okay," she said. "Why'd you do that?"

"Getting rid of the bow made me think."

Sam walked beside the girl for several steps before continuing.

"The car's kind of a symbol. My old life and that. Symbol of when I fucked up. Can't fix the mistake. But the car's gone. Now I need to go see somebody and apologize."

Sam stared off in the distance, then drew a long breath.

"Putting our shit on that stack, I see it as a way to put something in the past and leave it there. You see it that way?"

She looked at him in her unwavering manner and nodded.

"People we love are gone. We just have to keep going, right?"

"Who'd you love that's gone?" she asked.

"My daughter. You remind me of her."

She looked at him with the familiar evaluative expression.

"You seem like a father. I'm sorry she's gone."

Someone who's like a father? Was he really? What an astonishing thing for someone to say to him, a girl. He was heartened by the words.

"Think I'll go buy a Hyundai Elantra," he said. "Used, can't afford new. So you ever been fishing?"

She shook her head.

"Want to learn?"

"Maybe," she said.

"Cool," he said with a nod.

CPSIA information can be obtained
at www.ICGtesting.com
Printed in the USA
BVHW04s1219180418
513571BV00003BA/6/P